JOE HALDEMAN

"ONE OF THE BEST PROPHETIC WRITERS
OF OUR TIMES."

David Brin

"ARTISTIC INTEGRITY HAS BEEN
A HALDEMAN TRADEMARK"

Los Angeles Times Book Review

"JOE HALDEMAN ALWAYS
DELIVERS THE GOODS."

Roger Zelazny

NONE SO BLIND

"EXCELLENT . . .
GRABS THE READER BY HIS LAPELS
ANF DRAGS HIM ALONG FOR A RIDE."

St. Petersburg Times

"COMPELLING . . . DISTURBING . . .
AT ONCE TRANSCENDENT AND HORRIFYING . . .
THE VARIETY OF SHORT FICTION IS IMPRESSIVE,
FROM HORROR TO ALIEN-CONTACT-
MULTIUNIVERSE-AND-TIME-TRAVEL STORIES
TO SHORT WHIMSIES ABOUT THE DEATH
OF ALL THE STARS IN THE COSMOS."

Science Fiction Age

"HALDEMAN IS AT HIS BEST."

us Reviews

Other AvoNova Books by
Joe Haldeman

THE FOREVER WAR

Joe Haldeman

NONE SO BLIND

AVON BOOKS · NEW YORK

Copyright notices for each story appear on page v, which serves as an extension of this copyright page.

These stories are works of fiction. Names, characters, places, and incidents either are the product of the author's imagination or are used fictitiously. Any resemblance to actual events, locales, organizations, or persons, living or dead, is entirely coincidental and beyond the intent of either the author or the publisher.

AVON BOOKS
A division of
The Hearst Corporation
1350 Avenue of the Americas
New York, New York 10019

Copyright © 1996 by Joe Haldeman
Cover art by Eric Peterson
Published by arrangement with the author
Visit our website at http://AvonBooks.com
Library of Congress Catalog Card Number: 95-4497
ISBN: 0-380-70802-7

First AvoNova Printing: March 1997
First Morrow/AvoNova Printing: May 1996

AVONOVA TRADEMARK REG. U.S. PAT. OFF. AND IN OTHER COUNTRIES, MARCA REGISTRADA, HECHO EN U.S.A.

Printed in the U.S.A.

RA 10 9 8 7 6 5 4 3 2 1

For Michael Glicksohn and Susan Manchester—
dear hearts and fellow travelers—
a belated wedding gift

contents

NONE SO BLIND

introduction:
what you don't know
can't hurt you

OUR CULTURE AND other cultures have a romantic image of the writer as a man or woman of experience—Jack London slogging through the snow or fighting the high seas, Hemingway jumping into the ring with bulls or prizefighters, Joan Didion going to El Salvador, Norman Mailer daring to wear a white fur coat in Manhattan—but most of us know that what they actually do with their time is stare at a blank space and try desperately to come up with the next sentence. In action, a writer looks pretty much like a clerk. Romantics would rather think of them as "walking point" for us—going out and living life to the fullest: doing, feeling, thinking, and eventually becoming so full of life that they have to sit down at the writing table to try to make sense of it all, for themselves and for their waiting readers.

Writers don't work very hard to dispel this illusion. Many of us use our profession as an excuse to do things that are dangerous or expensive or morally reprehensible—or all three. Every now and then, if you hang around writers, you come across one or two who you suspect write fiction only because it gives them an excuse to say outrageous things, have sex with a variety of odd people, and drink before lunchtime.

The title of this collection was originally *Feedback*, from the first story, one of my favorites. But "None So Blind" won a bunch of awards, including the Hugo for Best Science Fiction Short Story of the Year, and my editor beseeched me to change the title to that. Not only was it marginally more famous, but it was less abstract, and thus less of a headache for the art director. I was generously allowed to keep this introduction, though, and the organization of the book, which tied into the original title.

Some writerly behavior, and misbehavior, can be seen in terms of feedback. Feedback is what happens when part of the output of a system is fed back into the system to regulate it. The screech you get from a microphone is "positive" feedback; it reinforces the output. Negative feedback is more benign, like the governor on a truck's engine or a pressure cooker's regulator. Writers such as Hemingway and Byron, who feel compelled to model their lives after their made-up heroes, are evincing a kind of positive feedback. I suppose there may be negative-feedback writers, too, who are repelled by the excesses of their characters, and so live quiet, normal lives—but of course we only hear about the other kind!

A justification of the more flamboyant behavior is a corollary to a rule that I think is a pernicious lie: *Write what you know.* Teachers from the fourth grade through graduate school keep telling their students to write what they know, and it's a principle that seems so self-evident that neither students nor teachers question it. (It's also why there are so many novels about college professors committing adultery with their students, or at least fantasizing about it.)

I'm a science-fiction writer, and I would certainly be paralyzed if I were restricted to writing about what I, or anybody else, actually knew from experience. Nobody has ever talked to a Martian, or used mental telepathy to control others, or traveled through time. (There are people, somewhat reality-impaired, who do think they have done these things, and one of the bonuses of being a science-fiction writer is that you get to correspond with them and sometimes even meet them in the flesh.)

Science fiction is an interesting perspective for investigating this writing-and-experience business from two different angles. One is the rejection of experience completely: the value of *imagining* events to write about rather than remembering them. And the other is the creative interplay between imagination and experience: I've never fired a ray gun, but I have fired a pistol. I think in both cases you use both hands to steady the weapon; you spend an extra fraction of a second getting a good sight picture; you squeeze the trigger rather than jerk it, and so forth. Knowing the real world makes your imaginary world more believable.

What's more important than those mechanical details, of course, is how well you can know or imagine the emotional state of the person who's holding that ray gun and about to fire. If you do that honestly, you're inventing truth. You're not being dishonest by making up things that haven't happened to you; by and large that's what a fiction writer *does*— and if you write science fiction, fantasy, or horror most of the things you write about have never happened to anybody.

A couple of hobgoblins can't be ignored, though. You ought to shy away from writing directly about a very commonplace experience that you have never experienced. I'd either be a fool or have to consider myself a genius, for instance, to write about how it feels to go through pregnancy and have a baby. The science fiction writer James Tiptree, Jr., revealed to some readers that she was actually female when she tried to write a description of male masturbation in zero gravity.

But it's worth thinking about what actually constitutes universal experience. I see an awful lot of tiresome nonsense written about combat, which rings false to me because I did experience a half year of combat in Vietnam. But most of a writer's audience nowadays wouldn't have experienced combat, either; it's a fairly rare experience even among men of my generation. So very few readers are going to catch you, for instance, if you write about a M-16 rifle firing twenty rounds at a clip. (Reference books will tell you the weapon held twenty rounds; they probably won't tell you that if you loaded more than eighteen, you risked the thing jamming.)

There's a famous example of just making it all up: According to most critics, the best novel about the American Civil War is *The Red Badge of Courage*, written by Stephen Crane many years after the war. Crane was born six years after the conflict ended and had not had any experience of combat anywhere. He interviewed a lot of veterans for specific information, but the main thing is that he could describe very well the interior of his own heart, and he had one hell of an imagination. (An old soldier who reviewed the book in London admired its accuracy but wondered how the writer managed to get the *sound* of the bullets wrong.)

All experience is, of course, memory by the time you sit down to write about it, unless all you write about is typing. So another thing that writers ought to be aware of is that the barrier between memory and imagination can be a very thin membrane indeed. All of us constantly rewrite our own pasts, not just to make ourselves look better, but to try to make sense out of our lives and out of capital L Life in general.

An exercise I give to my writing students at MIT is to have everybody write for five or ten minutes about the earliest childhood memory they can recall. I ask them to try to remember an actual incident rather than just a "sense of place," which is what most people come up with. There must be some reason they remember this incident rather than some other one, something important to them in later life, so it's a logical springboard for a story. But it's also part of a demonstration about the value of experience in writing fiction.

After I collect their papers, I tell them this anecdote about "first memories": The great child psychologist Jean Piaget thought for years that his earliest memory was the dramatic one of having been kidnapped from his stroller. He even remembered that his nurse chased after the man and caught him; her face was scratched up in the struggle. Years later, though, the nurse came back to visit the family and confessed that she had made the whole thing up—she'd gotten the scratches making love with her boyfriend in the bushes! Piaget had heard the story so many times that the details had impressed themselves upon his memory as true data, remembered.

This is not irrelevant to fiction: the actual truth or falsity of that incident was immaterial to its effect on Piaget's personality as he grew from child to adult. The "memory" of the nurse's selfless behavior must have given him a higher opinion of human nature than he otherwise would have had. The incident might even have had some effect on his choice of career.

When we read a piece of fiction, unless it's an obvious roman à clef like *The Sun Also Rises* or *Unanswered Prayers*, we don't have any idea whether the author ever experienced anything like the incidents in the story. It shouldn't make a particle of difference, either—but of course it does. We wonder about the literal authority of the author. We are also snoops and voyeurs.

One reason writers' biographies are interesting is the opportunity to search through them for sources of the fictions. It occurred to me that that would be a useful way to tie together the stories in this book, using hindsight to recall, or try to figure out, which parts of each story are made up and which parts came from so-called real life. I put in those mullings as afterwords, in a different typeface, so that those who just want to read fiction can easily skip over them. But those people aren't reading this either....

Joe Haldeman
Isle of Jersey
April 1993 to October 1995

feedback

THIS GAME WAS easier before I was famous, or infamous, and before the damned process was so efficient. When I could still pretend it was my own art, or at least about my art. Nowadays, once you're doped up and squeezed into the skinsuit, it's hard to tell whose eye is measuring the model. Whose hand is holding the brush.

It was more satisfying back then, twenty years ago, even though it was physically painful, with actual electrodes and blood samplers to effect the transfer. Now I just take the buffer drug and let them roll the skinsuit over me after I fall asleep. When I wake up I'm in the customer's body. The collaborator's.

It works best when I can interview the collaborator beforehand and find out whether he or she has any artistic training or talent. Some of the most interesting work I produce in collaboration comes from the totally inexperienced, their unfamiliarity with the tools and techniques resulting in happy accidents, spontaneity. It's best to know about that ahead of time, so I can use the meditative period before the drug kicks in, to prepare myself for a tighter or looser approach. But I can work cold if I have to; if the millionaire can't spare the time for an interview before the session.

I'll work in any painting or drawing medium the customer wants, within reason, but through most of my career people naturally chose my own specialty, transparent watercolor. Since I became famous, though, with the Manhattan Monster thing, people want to trowel on thick acrylics in primary colors. Boring. But they take the painting home and hang it up and ask their friends, Isn't that just as scary as shit? Because of the stylistic association, usually, rather than the subject matter. Most people's nightmares stay safely hidden when they pick up a brush. Good thing, too. After the Monster a lot of right-thinking citizens wanted to make my profession illegal, claiming it could bring out "the beast" hidden in Everyman. The fact that it had never happened before didn't make a dent in their righteousness. The Supreme Court did.

All an art facilitator does is loan his or her mechanical skills and esthetic sensibilities to the customer. If the customer is a nutcase, the collaboration may be truly disturbing—and perhaps revealing. A lot of us find employment in mental institutions. Some of us find residence in them. Occupational hazard.

At least I make enough per assignment now, thanks to notoriety from the Monster case, that I can take off half the year, to travel and paint for myself. This year I was leaving the first of February, start off the vacation sailing in the Caribbean. One week to go, I could already feel the sun, taste the rum. I'd sublet the apartment and studio and already had all my clothes and gear packed into two small bags. Watercolors don't take up much space, and you don't need a lot of clothes where I was headed.

I was tempted to preempt my itinerary and go on to the islands early. It would have cost extra and confused my friends, who know me to be methodical and punctual. But I should have done it. God, I should have done it.

We had one of those fast hard snows that make Manhattan

beautiful for a while. I walked to and from lunch the long way, through Central Park, willing to trade the slight extra danger for the beauty. Besides, my walking stick supposedly holds enough electricity to stun a horse.

The man waiting for me in the lobby didn't look like trouble, though you never know. Short, balding, old-fashioned John Lennon-style spectacles.

He introduced himself while I was fumbling with overcoat and boots. Juan Carlos Segura, investment counselor.

"Have you ever painted before?" I asked him. "Drawn or sculpted or anything?"

"No. My talents lie elsewhere." I think I was supposed to be able to tell how wealthy he was by upper-class lodge signals—the cut of his conservative blue pinstripe, the heavy gold mechanical watch—but my own talents lie elsewhere. So I asked him directly. "You understand how expensive my services are."

"Exactly. One hundred thousand dollars a day."

"And you know you must accept the work as produced. No money-back guarantee."

"I understand."

"We're in business, then." I buzzed my assistant Allison to start tea while we waited for the ancient elevator.

People who aren't impressed by my studio, with its original Picasso, Monet, Dali, and Turner, are often fascinated by Allison. She is beautiful but very large, six-foot-three but perfectly proportioned, as if some magic device had enlarged her by twenty percent. Mr. Segura didn't blink at her, didn't notice the paintings on the walls. He accepted his tea and thanked her politely.

I blew on my tea and studied him over the cup. He looked serious, studious, calm. So had the Manhattan Monster.

The direct approach sometimes costs me a commission. "There's half a page of facilitators in the phone book," I said. "Every single one of them charges less than I do."

He nodded, studying me back.

"Some people want me just because I *am* the most expensive. Some few want me because they know my work, my own work, and it's very good. Most want a painting by the man who released the Monster from Claude Avery."

"Is it important for you to know?"

"The more I know about you, the better picture you'll get."

He nodded and paused. "Then accept this. Maybe fifty percent of my motivation is because you are the most costly. That is sometimes an index of value. Of your artistic abilities, or anybody else's, I am totally ignorant."

"So fifty percent is the Monster?"

"Not exactly. In the first place, I don't care to pay that much for something that other people have. Two of my acquaintances own paintings they did with you in that disturbing mode.

"Looking at their paintings, it occurred to me that something more subtle was possible. You. Your own anger at being used in this way."

"I've expressed that in my own paintings."

"I am sure that you have. What I want, I suppose, is to express my own anger at my customers, through yours."

That was a new wrinkle. "You're angry at your customers?"

"Not all of them. Most. People give me large amounts of money to invest for them. Once each quarter, I extract a percentage of the profit." He set down the cup and put his hands on his knees. "But most of them want some input. It is their money, after all."

"And you would prefer to follow a single strategy," I said. "The more capital you have behind your investment pattern, the less actual risk—since I assume that you don't have to pay *back* a percentage, if an investment fails."

"For an artist, you know a lot about money."

I shrugged. "I'm a *rich* artist."

"People are emotionally connected to their money, and they want to do things with it, other than make more money. My largest client last year was a bug about space exploitation."

"Oh, no."

"And when the lunar colony collapsed, so did his fortune. I got the blame."

"But you didn't advise him to—"

"No. I tried to talk him out of it, and did manage to convince him to diversify slightly, into related energy and defense issues. Of course, they were depressed too, or nosedived along with the space stocks. Naturally it was my fault for not choosing the *right* collateral investments. He had to sell two of his cars and his ivory collection."

"Poor thing."

"He is only the most obvious, the most amusing. Most of my clients are at least mildly resentful if I don't make them a fortune every quarter. Even though I explain that it's my business to protect their money first; increase it second. A conservative strategy takes real work. Anybody can gamble."

"Interesting. And you see a connection with my work?"

"I saw it when I read the profile in *Forbes* a couple of years ago."

"And you waited for my price to come down?"

"I waited until I could afford the luxury. Your price actually has come down nine percent, because of inflation, since the article. You'll be raising it soon."

"Good timing. I like round numbers, but I'm going up to one-twenty when I return from vacation in August." I picked up a stylus and touchpad and began drawing close parallel lines. It helps me think. "The connection, the analogy, is good. I know that many of my clients must be dissatisfied with the abstract smearings that cost them six figures. But they get exactly what they paid for. I explain it to them beforehand, and if they choose not to hear me, that's their problem."

"You said as much in the article. But I don't want abstract smearings. I want your customary medium, when you work seriously. Old-fashioned hyperrealism."

"You want me to do a Boston School watercolor?"

"Exactly. I know the subject, the setting—"

"That's three weeks' work, minimum. More than two million dollars."

"I can afford it."

"Can you afford to leave your own work for three weeks?" I was drawing very fast lines. This would really screw up my vacation schedule. But it would be half a year's income in three weeks.

"I'm not only going to leave for three weeks ... I'm going exactly where you are. The Cayman Islands. George Town."

I just looked at him.

"They say the beach is wonderful."

I never asked him how he'd found out about my vacation plans. Through my credit card company, I supposed. That he would take the trouble before our initial interview was revealing. He was a man who left nothing to chance.

He wanted a photo-realist painting of a nude woman sitting in a conference room, alone, studying papers. Horn-rimmed glasses. The conference room elegant, old-fashioned.

The room would be no problem, given money, since George Town has as many banks and insurance buildings as bikinis. The model was another matter. Most of the models in George Town would be black, which would complicate the text of the painting, or would be gorgeous beach bums, with tan lines and silicone breasts. I told him I thought we wanted an ordinary woman, trim but severe-looking; someone whose posture would radiate dignity without clothing. (I showed him *Maja Desnuda* and some Delacroix, and a few of Wyeth's Helgas that had that quality.) She also would have to be a damned good model, to do three weeks of sittings in the same position. I suggested we hire someone in New York and fly her down with us. He agreed.

Allison had been watching through the ceiling bug, part of her job. She came in and poured herself a cup of tea. "Nutcase," she said.

"Interesting nutcase, though. Rich."

"If you ever took on a charity nutcase, I wasn't watching." She stirred a spoonful of marmalade into her tea, Russian style. She only does that to watch me cringe. "So I should get tickets to the Caymans for me and M & M?"

"Yeah, Friday."

"First class?"

"What's it worth to you?"

"I don't know. You want a cup of tea in your lap?"

"First class."

Finding the right model was difficult. I knew two or three women who would fill the bill in terms of physical appearance and sitting ability, but they were friends. That would interfere with the client's wishes, since he obviously wanted a cold, clinical approach. I spent an afternoon going through agency files, and another afternoon interviewing people, until I found the right one. Rhonda Speck, thirty, slender enough to show ribs. I disliked her on sight and liked her even less when she took her clothes off, for the way she looked at me—her expression a prim gash of disapproval. Even if I were heterosexual, I wouldn't be ogling her unprofessionally. That edge of resentment might help the painting, I thought. I didn't know the half of it.

I told Rhonda the job involved a free trip to the Cayman Islands and she showed as much enthusiasm as if I had said Long Island. She did brighten a little when I described the setting. She was working on her law degree, and could study while she sat. That also helped to distance me from her, since I am not a great admirer of that profession. I dealt with a lot of lawyers during the years of litigation following the Manhattan Monster, and I liked perhaps one out of five. (One that I liked was a prosecutor, the only one who had the grace not to bring up my sexual orientation, which was irrelevant. I knew that Claude Avery was gay, and I knew he was troubled by it—a facilitator does almost literally get under his client's skin—but there was no way I could tell that he was going to work out his problems by dismembering, or at least de-membering, male prostitutes.)

I called my banker in George Town and described the

office I needed. She knew of a small law firm that was closing
for a February vacation, and would inquire.

It had been a few years since I'd painted nudes, and had
done only two photo-realist ones. I didn't want to work with
Rhonda any more than I had to, or pay her more than I had
to, so I had a friend with a similar figure come over and sit.
For two days I did sketches and photographs, experimenting
with postures and lightings. I took them to Segura and we
agreed on the pose, the woman looking up coldly from her
papers, as if interrupted, strong light from the desk lamp
putting half of her face in shadow. Making the desk lamp
the only source of light also isolated the figure from the
details of the office, which would be rendered in photo-
realist detail, but darkly, making for a sinister background.

Then I spent three days doing a careful portrait of the
model, head and upper body, solving some technical problems about rendering the glossy hair and the small breasts.
I wanted them to look hard, unfeminine, yet realistic.

I took the portrait up to Segura's office and he approved.
His only reservations were about himself. "You're sure I'll be
able to produce something with this kind of control? I literally can't draw a face that looks like a face."

"No problem. Your hands will be stiff, from using undeveloped muscles, but while you're in the skinsuit your move-
ments will be precisely the same as mine.

"Have I told you about the time I hired a facilitator myself?" He said no. "I was curious about how it felt on the
other end. I hired a guitarist-composer, and we spent two
days writing a short fugue in the style of Bach. We started
with the four letters of my last name—which coincidentally
form an A-minor-seventh chord—and made up a marvel-
ously complicated little piece that was unequivocally *mine*.
Even though I can't play it."

"You could play it in the skinsuit, though."

"Beautifully. I have a tape of it, the facilitator sitting beside me playing a silent solid-body guitar while I roam
around the frets with brilliant sensitivity." I laughed. "At the

end of each day my hands were so weak I couldn't pick up a fork, let alone a brush. My fingers were stiff for a week.

"Your experience will be less extreme. Using a brush doesn't involve the unnatural stretching that playing a guitar does."

Not completely convinced, Segura was willing to part with an extra hundred grand for a one-day demonstration. A predictable course, given hindsight, knowing him to be a man boxed in by distrust and driven, or at least directed, by what I would call paranoia.

He suggested a self-portrait. I told him it would have to be done from photographs, since the skinsuit distorts your face almost as much as a bank-robber's panty hose disguise. That interested him. He was going to spend three weeks in the skinsuit; why not have a record of what it was like? I pretended that nobody had come up with the idea before and said sure, sounds interesting.

In fact, I'd done it twice, but both times the collaborators produced thick impasto abstractions that didn't resemble anything. Segura would be different.

By law, a doctor has to be present when you begin the facilitation. After it gets under way, any kind of nurse or medic is adequate for standing guard. A few collaborators have blood pressure spikes or panic attacks. The nurse can terminate the process instantly if the biosensors show something happening. He pushes a button that releases a trank into my bloodstream, which breaks the connection. It also puts me into a Valium haze the rest of the day. A good reason to have people pay in advance.

There's a doctor in my building who's always willing to pop up and earn a hundred dollars for five minutes' work. I always use the same nurse, too, a careful and alert man with the unlikely name Marion Marion. He calls himself M & M, since he's brown and round.

I soaked and taped down four half-sheets of heavy D'Arches cold-press, allowing for three disasters, and prepared my standard portrait palette. I set up the session to

begin at 9:30 sharp. M & M came over early, as usual, to
have tea and joke around with Allison and me. He's a natural
comic and, I think, also a natural psychologist. Whatever, he
puts me at ease before facing what is usually a rather trying
experience.

(I should point out here that it's not always bad. If the
collaborator has talent and training and a pleasant disposition, it can be as refreshing as dancing with a skilled partner.
The facilitator has the satisfaction of doing mechanically ef-
fortless work without the anxiety that's always there to some
extent, working alone: is this *really* any good? Am I going to
make a mistake that consigns it to the rubbish bin?)

The others showed up on time and we got down to business. An anteroom off my studio has two parallel examining
tables. Segura and I stripped and lay down and were injected
with six hours' worth of buffer. I was asleep for most of it,
but know what happens: M & M glued the induction electrodes to the proper places on our shaven heads. The doctor
looked at them, signed a piece of paper, and left. Then
M & M, with Allison's assistance, rolled the loose skinsuits
over us, sealed them, and pumped the air out.

Segura and I woke up simultaneously when M & M turned
on the microcurrent that initiated the process. It's like being
puppet and puppeteer simultaneously. I saw through Segura's eyes. His body sat me up and slid me to the floor, and
walked me into the studio. He perched me on a stool in front
of the nearly horizontal easel and the mirror. Then I took
over.

If you were watching us work, you would see two men
sitting side by side, engaged in what looks like a painstak-
ingly overpracticed mime routine. If one of us scratches his
ear, the other one does. But from the inside it is more complicated: we exchange control second by second. This is why
not every good artist can be a good facilitator. You have to
have an instinct for when to assert your own judgment, your
own skills, and let the client be in control otherwise. It is

literally a thousand decisions per hour, for six hours. It's exhausting. I earn my fee.

My initial idea for the portrait was, in compositional terms, similar to what our nude would be—a realistic face in harsh light glowing in front of an indistinct background. There wouldn't be time to paint in background details, of course.

I made a light, precise drawing of the head and shoulders, taking most of an hour. Not quite centered on the paper. Then I took a chisel brush and carefully painted in the outlines of the drawing with frisket, a compound like rubber cement. You can paint over it and, when the paint dries, rub it off with an eraser or your fingertip, exposing the white paper and the drawing underneath.

When the frisket was dry I mopped the whole painting with clear water and then made an inky wash out of burnt umber and French ultramarine. I worked the wash over the whole painting and, while it was still damp, floated in diffuse shapes of umber and ultramarine that would hint at shadowy background. Then I buzzed Allison in to dry it while I/we walked around, loosening up. She came in with a hair dryer and worked over the wet paper carefully, uniformly, while I didn't watch. Sometimes a dramatic background wash just doesn't work when it dries—looks obvious or cheesy or dull—and there is never any way to fix it. (Maybe you could soak the paper overnight, removing most of the pigment. Better to just start over, though.)

I walked Segura across to the bay window, depolarized it, and looked out over the city. The snow that remained on the shaded part of rooftops was gray or black. Traffic crawled in the thin bright light. Pedestrians hurried through the wind and slush.

Segura's body wanted a cigarette and I allowed him to walk me over to his clothes and light one up. The narcotic rush was disorienting. I had to lean us against a wall to keep from staggering. It was not unpleasant, though, once I surrendered control to him. No need for me to dominate motor responses until we had brush in hand.

Allison said the wash was ready and looked good. It did, vague gloomy shapes suggesting a prison or asylum cell. I rolled up a kneaded eraser and carefully rubbed away the frisket. The light pencil drawing floated over the darkness like a disembodied thought.

I had to apply frisket again, this time in a halo around the drawing, and there was a minor setback: I'd neglected to put the frisket brush into solvent, and the bristles had dried into a solid useless block. I surprised myself by throwing it across the room. That was Segura acting.

I found another square brush and carefully worked a thin frisket mask around the head and shoulders, to keep the dark background from bleeding in, but had to stop several times and lift up the brush because my hand was trembling with Segura's suppressed anger at the mistake. Relax, it was a cheap brush. You must be hell on wheels to work for.

First a very dilute yellow wash, New Gamboge, over the whole face. I picked up the hair dryer and used it for six or seven minutes, making sure the wash was bone-dry, meanwhile planning the next couple of stages.

This technique, "glazing," consists of building up a picture with layer upon layer of dilute paint. It takes patience and precision and judgment—sometimes you want the previous layer to be completely dry, and sometimes you want it damp, to diffuse the lines between the two colors. If it's too damp, you risk muddying the colors, which can be irreversible and fatal. But that's one thing that attracts me to the technique, the challenge of gambling everything on the timing of one stroke of the brush.

Segura obviously felt otherwise. Odd, for a man who essentially gambles for a living, albeit with other people's money. He wanted each layer safely dry before proceeding with the next, once he understood what I was doing.

Well, that's a technique, but it's not *my* technique, which is what he was paying for. It would also turn this portrait, distorted as it was, into a clown's mask.

I could have picked up a pencil and written out that argument for him to see through our eyes, but it's a mistake for the facilitator to blatantly take over that way. It *is* the customer's painting, after all. If he wants to screw it up, let him.

That kind of disassociation was easy with the usual thick acrylic messes, but I was reluctant to screw up a watercolor, especially at that level of subtlety. The prospect of spending three weeks producing a profoundly flawed work was not appealing either.

So I pushed back a little, establishing my authority, so to speak. I didn't want this to become a contest of wills. I just wanted control over the hair dryer, actually, not over Juan Carlos Segura.

There was a slight battle, lasting only seconds. It's hard to describe the sensation to someone who hasn't used a facilitator. It's something like being annoyed at yourself for not being able to make up your mind, rather intensified— "being of two minds," literally.

Of course I won the contest, having about ten thousand times more experience at it than Segura. I set down the hair dryer and the next layer, defining the hollows of the face visible through the skinsuit, went on with appropriately soft edges. I checked the mirror and automatically noted the places I would come back to later with the paper dry, to make actual lines, defining the bottom of the goggle ridges, the top of the lip, the forward part of the ear mass.

The portrait was finished in two hours, but the background still needed something. Pursuing a vague memory from a week before, I flipped through a book of Mathew Brady photographs, visions of the Civil War's hell. Our face in the skinsuit resembled those of some corpses, open-mouthed, staring. I found the background I wanted, a ruined tumble of brick wall, and took the book back to the easel. I worked an intimation of the wall into the background, dry-brushing umber and ultramarine with speckles and threads of clotted blood color, alizarin muted with raw umber. Then I dropped the brushes in water and looked away, buzzing M & M. I didn't want to see the painting again until I saw it with my own eyes.

Coming out of the facilitation state takes longer than going in, especially if you don't go the full six hours. The remaining buffer has to be neutralized with a series of timed shots. Otherwise, Segura and I would hardly have been able to walk, expecting the collaboration of another brain that was no longer there.

I was up and around a few minutes before Segura. Allison had set out some cheese and fruit and an ice bucket with a bottle of white burgundy. I was hungry, as always, but only nibbled a bit, waiting for lunch.

Segura attacked the food like a starved animal. "What do you think?" he said between bites. "Is it any good?"

"Always hard to tell while you're working. Let's take a look." I buzzed Allison and she brought the painting in. She'd done a good job, as usual, the painting set off in a double mat of brick red and forest green, inside a black metal frame.

"It does look good," he said, as if surprised.

I nodded and sipped wine, studying it. The painting was technically good, but it would probably hang in a gallery for years, gathering nervous compliments, before anybody bought it. It was profoundly ugly, a portrait of brutality. The skinsuit seemed to be straining to contain a mask of rage. Something truly sick burned behind the eyes.

He propped it up on the couch and walked back and forth, admiring it from various angles. For a moment I hoped he would say "This will do fine; forget about the nude." I could use the two million but didn't look forward to three weeks of his intimate company.

"It captures something," he said, grinning. "I could use it to intimidate clients."

"The style suits you?"

"Yes. Yes, indeed." He looked at me with a sort of squint.

"I vaguely remember fighting over some aspect of it."

"Technical matter. I prevailed, of course—that's what you pay me for."

He nodded slowly. "Well. I'll see you in George Town, then." He offered his hand, dry and hot.

"Friday morning. I'll be at the Hilton." Allison put the painting in a leather portfolio and ushered him out.

She came back in with a color Xerox of it. "Sick puppy."

I examined the picture, nodding. "There's some talent here, though. A lot of artists are sick puppies."

"Present company excluded. Lunch?"

"No, I'm meeting Harry."

"Harry? You'll be with him all winter."

"Yeah, but we didn't plan on three weeks' business first. I'm taking him to Seasons as a peace offering. One last French meal before we descend to goat curry and fish stew."

"Well, have fun. I'm still on rabbit food until we get down there." She was coming on Thursday. Harry and I were leaving that night, for a few days of sunshine and rest before I had to deal with Segura.

I poured another glass of wine and carried it over to the window. The icy wind was audible through the double-pane glass. The people on the sidewalk hurried hunched over against the gale. Tomorrow I'd be lying on snow-white sand, swimming in blood-warm water. I drank the wine and shivered.

In the eighteenth century, George III was sailing in the Gulf of Mexico when a sudden storm, probably a hurricane, smashed his ship to pieces. Fishermen from one of the Caymans braved the storm to go out and pick up survivors. Saved from what he'd thought would be certain death, King George expressed his gratitude by declaring that no resident of the island would ever have to pay taxes to the British crown, for the rest of eternity.

So where other Caribbean islands have craft shops and laid-back bars, George Town has high-rise banks and insur-

ance buildings. A lot of expatriate Brits and Americans live
and work there, doing business by satellite bounce.

I have a bank account in George Town myself, and may
retire there someday. For this time of my life, it's too peace-
ful, except for the odd hurricane. I need Manhattan's garish
excitement, the constant input, the dangerous "edge."

But it's good to get away. Harry and I are both pretty good
sailors. We rented a thirty-two-foot racing sloop; the original
plan had been to hang around George Town for a week,
getting the feel of the boat while skindiving in the wreck-
strewn harbor, with an afternoon or so given over to banking
business. Then lay a course for Jamaica and points east.

The Segura commission set that back almost a month.
Harry was good enough to come down anyhow. He's on a
year's sabbatical from teaching duties, finishing a book
about Athabascan dialects, and he can work anyplace that
has AA batteries and Razor Points.

So we had two days of thawing out on the beach, swimming, imbibing rum drinks full of vegetation, appreciating
the beautiful men and women—and, one must admit, being
appreciated in return. Money can't buy everything, but can
stave off flab and wrinkles, perhaps until you're old enough
for them not to matter.

The beach is an ideal place for quick figure sketches, so
I loosened up for the commission by filling a notebook with
pictures of women as they walked by or played in the sand
and water. Drawing forces you to see, so for the first time I
was aware that the beauty of the native black women was
fundamentally different from that of the tourists, white or
black. It was mainly a matter of posture and expression, dignified and detached. The tourist women were always to some
extent posing, even at their most casual. Which I think was
the nature of the place, rather than some characteristic female vanity. I normally pay much closer attention to men,
and believe me, we corner the market on that small vice.

My staff came down on Thursday. M & M tore off into
town, to find out whether either of his girlfriends had

learned about the other. Allison joined Harry and me on the beach.

Impressive as she is in office clothes, Allison is spectacular out of them. She has never tanned; her skin is like ivory. Thousands of hours in the gym have given her the sharply defined musculature of a classical statue. She wore a black leather string bikini that revealed everything not absolutely necessary for reproduction or lactation, but I don't think most straight men would characterize her as "sexy." She was too formidable. That was all right with Allison, since she almost never was physically attracted to any man shorter or less well built than she. That dismissed all but a tenth of one percent of the male race. She had yet to find an Einstein, or even a Schwarzenegger, among the qualifiers. They usually turned out to be gentle but self-absorbed, predictably, and sometimes more interested in me than her. The couple of times that happened, she was more understanding than Harry.

The two of them got along well, and we had a pleasant day. We rented a small skiff in the afternoon and went reef fishing. Allison and I watched while Harry caught enough for dinner. We'd brought masks and snorkels, but a big gray hammerhead showed up, and we decided that drinking beer was healthier than swimming.

The chef at the Hilton did a good job with Harry's fish, snapper almondine. We resisted the urge to have one last night on the town. I went over after dinner and made sure everything was ready in the office we'd rented, because I knew that otherwise I'd wake up in the middle of the night worrying about some detail.

The message light was on when I got back to the hotel; both Rhonda Speck and Segura had arrived. It wasn't quite ten, but Harry and I agreed it was too late to return their calls, and retired.

I set up the pose and lighting before we went under, explaining to Rhonda exactly what we were after. Segura was silent, watching. I took longer than necessary, messing with the blinds and the rheostats I'd put on the two light sources. I wanted Segura to get used to Rhonda's nudity. He was obviously straight as a plank, and we didn't want the painting to reveal any sexual curiosity or desire. Rhonda was only slightly more sexy than a mackerel, but you could never tell.

For the same reason, I didn't want to start the actual painting the first day. First we'd do a series of charcoal roughs. I explained to Segura about negative spaces and how important it was to establish balance between the light and dark areas. That was something I'd already worked out, of course. I just wanted him to stare at Rhonda long enough to become bored with the idea.

It didn't quite work out that way.

We didn't need a doctor's certification in George Town, so the setting up took a little less time. Artist and client lockstepped into the office where Rhonda waited, studying the pages of notes stacked neatly on her desk.

There were two piano stools with identical newsprint pads and boxes of charcoal sticks. The idea was to sketch her from eight or ten slightly different angles, Segura moving around her in a small arc while I worked just behind him, looking over his shoulder. Theoretically, I could be anywhere, even in another room, since I was seeing her through his eyes. But it seems to work better this way, especially with a model.

The sketches had a lot of energy—so much energy that Segura actually tore through the paper a few times, blocking out the darkness around the seated figure. I actually got excited myself, and not just by feedback from Segura. The "negative-space" exercise is just that, an art school formalism, but Segura didn't know that, and the result came close to being actual art.

I showed him that after we came out of the buffer. The sketches were good strong abstractions. You could turn them upside down or sideways, retaining symmetry while obliterating text, and they still worked well.

I had a nascent artist on my hands. Segura had real native

talent. The combination could have produced a painting of some value, one that I wouldn't have been able to do by myself. If things had worked out.

Harry and I took the boat out after lunch—or rather, Harry took the boat out with me as ballast, baking inertly under a heavy coat of total sunblock. (Allison and I are almost equally pale, and that's not all we have in common; I'm also nearly as well muscled. We met at the weight machines in a Broadway gym.) He sang songs in Athabascan, probably about blizzards and clubbing seals. I watched billowing clouds form abstract patterns in the impossible cobalt sky. The soothing sounds of the boat lulled me to sleep—the keel slipping through warm water, the lines creaking, the ruffle of the sails.

Harry woke me to help bring her back in. He'd tacked out quite a few miles, the high-rises and cruise ships below the horizon, and had expected a quick run back on a following wind. Of course the wind shifted seaward, and we had to fight it back to the island, dark clouds gathering. One person can handle the thirty-two-foot sloop, but it's a lot easier with two, especially tacking into a strong wind. There was a cool mist of rain that became intermittently heavy. A couple of miles from shore we started to see lightning, so we struck sail and revved up the little motor and drove straight in, prudence conquering seamanship.

We dried off at the marina bar and drank hot chocolate laced with rum, watching a squall line roll across land and water, feeling lucky to be inside.

Sometimes I have difficulty talking with Harry. Circumstances of birth and upbringing left me "cultured" but not particularly well educated; Harry is quite the opposite. How can a person earn four degrees and still be unable to learn how to hold a wineglass? But he can talk knowledgeably about anything from astrophysics to Zoroastrianism. He doesn't draw or paint, but he knows art history and criticism, so we usually wind up talking about my work rather than his, cultural linguistics and anthropology—though in a weak

moment I did agree to go up to the Arctic with him one
summer. Paint mud landscapes while he chats with the natives, compiling examples for a cassette that will go with his
book.

Anyhow, I had earlier described to him the morning's surprising successes. He'd given it some thought.

"I don't want to see them yet," he said. "They'll be more
interesting in the context established by the final painting."

"You just don't want to say anything that might rain on
my parade." He shrugged and laughed. "We know each other
too well, Harry. You know you'd have to be honest, and
you're afraid honesty might not be the best policy now."

"Further deponent sayeth not." He smiled and turned his
attention back to the storm. "Wet and wild. Photography
tomorrow?"

"Yeah. And then drawing drawing drawing."

"The part you like best."

"Oh yes." Actually, I halfway do like it, the way an athlete
can enjoy warming up, in expectation of the actual event.

I could have done the photography and drawing without
Segura, but I wanted him involved, so that he would have a
lot of time and concentration invested before we started
painting. It affects your attitude toward both subject and
working surface.

The next morning I set up the cameras before we went
into the skinsuits. The main one was a fairly complex and
delicate piece of equipment, an antique 8×10 view camera
that took hairline-accurate black-and-white negatives. I
could have accomplished the same thing with a modern
large-format camera, but I liked the smooth working of the
gears, the smell of the oak and leather, the sense of contact
with an earlier, less hurried, age. The paradox of combining
the technology of that age with ours.

The other camera was a medium-format Polaroid. Buffered
and suited, I led Segura through the arcane art and science
of tweaking lights, model, f-stop, and exposure to produce a
subtle spectrum of prints: a sequence of ninety-eight slightly

different, and profoundly different, pictures of one woman. We studied the pictures and her and finally decided on the right combination. I set up the antique 8×10 and reproduced the lighting. We focussed it with his somewhat younger eyes and took three slightly different exposures.

Then we took the film into the darkroom that M & M had improvised in the firm's executive washroom. We developed each sheet in Rodinal, fixed and washed them and hung them weighted up to dry.

We left the darkroom and spent a few minutes smoking, studying Rhonda as she studied her law. I told her she was free for three days; show up Thursday morning. She nodded curtly and left, resentful.

Her annoyance was understandable. She'd been sitting there naked for all that time we were playing in the darkroom. I should have dismissed her when we finished shooting.

We lit up another cigarette and I realized that it wasn't me who had kept her waiting. It was Segura. I'd started to tell her to go and then he manufactured a little crisis that led straight to the darkroom. From then on I hadn't thought of the woman except as a reversed ghost appearing in the developer tray.

Under the circumstances, it wasn't a bad thing to have her hostile toward us, if we could capture the hostility on paper. But it goes against my grain to mistreat an employee, even a temporary one.

We examined each of the negatives with lightbox and loupe, then took the best one back into the darkroom for printing. Plain contact prints on finest-grain paper. The third one was perfect: rich and stark, almost scary in its knife-edge sharpness. You could see one bleached hair standing out from her left nipple.

That was enough work for the day; in fact, we'd gone slightly over the six-hour limit, and both of us were starting to get headaches and cramps. Another half hour and it would be double vision and tremors. More than that—though I'd

never experienced it—you wind up mentally confused, the
two minds still linked electrically but no longer cooperating.
Some poor guinea pigs took it as far as convulsions or cat-
atonia, back when the buffer drug was first being developed.

M & M eased us out of it and helped us down to a taxi.
It was only five blocks to the hotel, but neither of us was
feeling particularly athletic. (For some reason the buffer
hangover hits people like me, in very good shape, particularly hard. Segura was somewhat flabby and overweight, but
he had less trouble getting out of the car.)

Harry wasn't in the room, which suited me fine. I pulled
the blackout blinds and collapsed, desperately hungry but
too tired to do anything about it but dream of food.

Allison had set up the paper, one large sheet of handmade
hot-pressed four-hundred-pound rag, soaking it overnight
and then taping it down with plenty of time to dry completely. That sheet of paper, the one Segura would be drawing on, cost more than some gallery paintings. The sheet I'd
be working on was just paper, with a similar tooth. My drawing would be a random scribble, though it would look fine
while I was working on it.

We had set up two drawing tables with their boards at
identical angles, mine a little higher since I have a larger
frame. An opaque projector mounted above Segura shot a
duplicate of yesterday's photo onto the expensive paper. Our
job for the next three days was to execute a meticulously
accurate but ghost-light tracing of the picture, which would
be gently erased after the painting was done.

Some so-called photo-realists bypass this step with a combination of photography and xerography—make a high-
contrast print and then impress a light Xerox of it onto
watercolor paper. That makes their job a high-salaried kind
of paint-by-numbers. Doing the actual underdrawing puts
you well "into" the painting before the first brush is wet.

We sat down and went to work, starting with the uniformly
bound law books on the shelves behind Rhonda. It was an

unchallenging, repetitive subject to occupy us while we got used to doing this kind of labor together.

For a few minutes we worked on a scrap piece of the same kind of paper that was in front of me, until I was absolutely confident of his eye and hand. Then we started on the real thing.

After five grueling hours we had completed about a third of the background, an area half the size of a newspaper page. I was well pleased with that progress; working by myself I would have done little more.

Segura was not so happy. In the taxi, he cradled his right hand and stared at it, the wrist quivering, the thumb frankly twitching. "How can I possibly keep this up?" he said. "I won't even be able to pick up a pencil tomorrow."

I held out my own hand and wrist, steady, muscular. "But *I* will. That's all that counts."

"It could permanently damage my hand."

"Never happened." Of course, I'd never worked with anyone for three weeks. "Go to that masseur, the man whose card I gave you. He'll make your hand good as new. Do you still have the card?"

"Oh, yeah." He shifted uncomfortably. "I don't mean to be personal, or offensive . . . but is this man gay? I would have trouble with that."

"I wouldn't know. We don't have little badges or a secret handshake." He didn't laugh, but he looked less grim. "My relationship with him is professional; I wouldn't know whether he was gay or not." Actually, since our professional relationship included orgasm, if he wasn't gay, he was quite a method actor. But I assumed he would divine Segura's orientation as quickly as I had. A masseur, so to speak, ought to have a feel for his clients.

The next day went a lot better; like myself, Segura was heartened by the sight of the previous day's careful work outline. We worked faster and with equal care, finishing all of the drawing except for the woman and the things on the desk in front of her.

It was on the third day that I had the first inkling of trouble. Working on the image of Rhonda, Segura wanted to bear down too hard. That could be disastrous; if the pencil point actually broke the fibers of paper along a line, it could never be completely erased. You can't have "outlines" in this kind of painting; just sharply defined masses perfectly joining other sharply defined masses. A pencil line might as well be an inkblot.

If I had correctly interpreted the energy behind that pencil point, I might have stopped the project right then. Give Segura his money back, put the model, Allison, and M & M back on the plane to New York and set sail for Jamaica. I say "might." I'm as curious about human nature as the next person, maybe more curious because of the peculiar insights facilitating gives me. If I had known Segura then as well as I came to know him, I might have gone ahead with it anyhow. Just to see the painting.

At the time, though, I put it down to simple muscular fatigue. Segura was not in good physical shape. His normal workday comprised six hours in conference and six hours talking on the phone or dictating correspondence. He took a perverse pride in not even being able to keyboard. He never lifted anything heavier than a cigarette.

People who think art isn't physically demanding ought to try to sit in one position for six hours, brush or pencil in hand, staring at something or someone and trying to transfer its essence to a piece of paper or canvas. Even an athletic person leaves that arena with aches and twinges. A couch potato like Segura can't even walk away without help.

He never complained, though, other than expressing concern that his fatigue might interfere with the project. I reassured him almost every day. In fact, I had once completed a successful piece with a hemiplegic so frail he couldn't sign his name the same way twice. We taught ourselves how to hold the brush in our teeth.

It was a breathtaking moment when we turned off the overhead projector for the last time. The finished drawing floated on the paper, an exquisite ghost of what the painting would become. Through Segura's eyes I stared at it hungrily for fifteen or twenty minutes, mapping out strategies of frisket and mask, in my mind's eye seeing the paper glow through layer after careful layer of glaze. It would be perfect.

Rhonda wasn't in a great mood, coming back to sit after three days on her own, but even she seemed to share our excitement when she saw the underdrawing. It made the project real.

The first step was to paint a careful frisket over her figure, as well as the chair, lamp, and table with its clutter. That took an hour, since the figure was more than a foot high on the paper. I also masked out reflections on a vase and the glass front of a bookcase.

I realized it would be good to start the curtains with a thin wash of Payne's gray, which is not a color I normally keep on my palette, so I gave Rhonda a five-minute break while I rummaged for it. She put on a robe and walked over to the painting and gasped. We heard her across the room.

I looked over and saw what had distressed her. The beautifully detailed picture of her body had been blotted out with gray frisket, and it did look weird. She was a nonbeing, a featureless negative space hovering in the middle of an almost photographic depiction of a room. All three of us laughed at her reaction. I started to explain, but she knew about frisketing; it had just taken her by surprise.

Even the best facilitators have moments of confusion, when their client's emotional reaction to a situation is totally at odds with their own. This was one of those times: my reaction to Rhonda's startled response was a kind of ironic empathy, but Segura's reaction was malicious glee.

I could see that he disliked Rhonda at a very deep level. What I didn't see (although Allison had known from the first day) was that it wasn't just Rhonda. It was women in general.

I've always liked women, even though I've known since thirteen or fourteen that I would never desire them. It's per-

nicious to generalize, but I think that my friendships with
women have usually been deeper and more honest than they
would have been if I were straight. A straight man can simply
like a woman and desire her friendship, but there's always a
molecule or two of testosterone buzzing between them, if
they are both of an age and social situation where sex might
be a possibility, however remote. I have to handle that complication with some men whom I know or suspect are gay,
even when I feel no particular attraction toward them.

The drawing had gone approximately from upper left to
lower right, then back to the middle for the figure, but the
painting would have to proceed in a less straightforward way.
You work all over the painting at once: a layer of rose mad-
der on the spines of one set of books, and on the shady side
of the vase, and on two of the flowers. You need a complete
mental picture of the finished painting so you can predict
the sequence of glazes, sometimes covering up areas with
frisket or, when there were straight lines, with drafting tape.
The paper was dry, though, so it was usually just a matter of
careful brushwork. Pathologically careful: you can't erase
paint.

Of course Rhonda had to sit even though for the first week
her image would be hidden behind frisket. Her skin tones
affected the colors of everything else. Her emotional presence affected the background. And Segura's feeling toward
her "colored" the painting literally.

The work went very smoothly. It was a good thing Segura had suggested the trial painting; we'd been able to talk
over the necessity for occasional boldness and spontaneity,
to keep the painting from becoming an exercise in careful draftsmanship. Especially with this dark, sinister background, we often had to work glazes wet-into-wet. Making
details soft and diffuse at the periphery of a painting can
render it more realistic rather than less. Our own eyes see
the world with precision only in a surprisingly small area
around the thing that has our attention. The rest is blur,
more or less ignored. (The part of the mind that is not ig-

noring the background is the animal part that waits for a sudden movement or noise; a painting can derive tension from that.)

Segura and I worked so well together that it was going to cost me money; the painting would be complete in closer to two weeks than three. When I mentioned this he said not to worry; if the painting was good he'd pay the second million regardless of the amount of time (he'd paid a million down before we left New York), and he was sure the painting would be good.

Of course there was arithmetic involved there, as well as art. *Fortune* had listed his before-tax income last year as $98 million. He probably wanted to get back to his quarter-million-a-day telephone.

So the total time from photography to finished background was only eleven days, and I was sure we could do the figure and face in a day. We still had a couple of hours' buffer left when we removed the frisket, but I decided to stop at that point. See whether we could finish her completely in one session. We studied her for an hour or so, sketching.

The sketches were accurate, but in a way they were almost caricatures, angular, hostile. As art, they were not bad, though like Segura's initial self-portrait, they were fundamentally, intentionally, ugly. I could feel Manet's careful brush and sardonic eye here: how can a well-shaped breast or the lush curve of a hip be both beautiful and ugly? Cover the dark, dagger-staring face of *Olympia* and drink in the lovely body. Then uncover the face.

That quality would be submerged in the final painting. It would be a beautiful picture, dramatic but exquisitely balanced. The hatred of women there but concealed, like an underpainting.

It was a great physical relief to be nearing the end. I'd never facilitated for more than five days in a row, and the skinsuit was becoming physically repulsive to me. I was earning my long vacation.

That night I drank too much, Harry and I finishing more

than a liter of rum, watching two bad movies on television while a serious storm rattled the windows.

The morning was brilliant but I was not. M & M injected me with a cocktail of vitamins and speed that burned away the hangover. I knew I'd come back down hard by nightfall, but the painting would be done long before then.

Segura was jittery, snappish, as we prepared for the last day. Maybe M & M gave him a little something along with the buffer, to calm him down. Maybe it wasn't a good idea.

Rhonda was weird that morning, too, with good reason. She was finally the focus of our attention and she played her part well. Her concentration on us was ferocious, her contempt palpable.

I dabbed frisket on a few highlights—collarbone, breast, eye, and that glossy raven hair—and then put in a pale flesh-colored wash over everything, cadmium yellow light with a speck of rose. While it dried, we smoked a cigarette and stared at her. Rhonda had made it clear that she didn't like smoke, and we normally went into another room or at least stood by an open window. Not today, though.

I had a little difficulty controlling Segura: he was mesmerized by her face and kept wanting to go back to it. But it doesn't work that way; the glazes go on in a particular order, one color at various places on the body all at once. If you finished the face and then worked your way down, the skin tones wouldn't quite match. And there was actual loathing behind his obsession with her face, the force that compels you to keep looking back at a hideous photograph.

He also had the amateurish desire to speed up; find out what the picture was going to look like. In retrospect, I wonder whether there might have been something sinister about that, as well.

It was obvious that the face and figure would take longer than I had planned, maybe half again as long, with so much attention going into hauling on the reins. His impatience would cost us an extra day in the skinsuits, which made me angry, and further slowed us down.

Here I have to admit to a lack of empathy, which for a facilitator is tantamount to a truck driver admitting falling asleep at the wheel. My own revulsion at having to spend another day confined in plastic masked what Segura was feeling about his own confinement. I was not alert. I had lost some of my professional control. I didn't see where his disgust was leading him, leading us.

This is hindsight again: one of the talents that Segura translated into millions of dollars was an ability to hide his emotions, to make people misread him. This was not something that was usually under his conscious control; he did it automatically, the way a pathological liar will lie even when there's nothing at stake. The misogyny that seemed to flood his attitude toward the painting—and Rhonda—was only a small fraction of what he must have actually felt, emotions amplified by the buffer drug and empath circuitry. Some woman must have hurt him profoundly, repeatedly, when he was a child. Maybe that's just amateur psychology. I don't think so. If it were an antipathy that developed after puberty, as I had encountered in other clients, it would have felt quite different; there would have been a sexual component. His hate was more primitive, inchoate.

Most people reveal themselves during facilitation, but a few tighten up. I knew Segura was that kind, which was a relief; they're easier to work with. Doubly a relief with Segura, since from the beginning I had a feeling I didn't want to know him all that well.

I might have prevented it by quitting early. But I wanted to do all the light passages and then start the next day with a fresh palette, loaded with dark. Perhaps I also wanted to punish Segura, or push him.

The actions were simple, if the motivations were not. We had gone twenty minutes past the six-hour mark, and had perhaps another half hour to go. I had an annoying headache, not bad enough to make me quit. I assumed Segura felt the same.

Every now and then we approached Rhonda to adjust her

pose. Only a mannequin could retain exactly the same posture all day. Her chin had fallen slightly. Segura got up and
walked toward her.

I don't remember feeling his hand slip out and pick up
the large wash brush, one we hadn't used since the first day.
Its handle is a stick of hardwood almost an inch in diameter,
ending in a sharp bevel. I never thought of it as a weapon.

He touched her chin with his left forefinger and she tilted
her head up, closing her eyes. Then with all his strength he
drove the sharp stick into her chest.

The blast of rage hit me without warning. I fell backward
off the stool and struck my head. It didn't knock me out, but
I was stunned, disoriented. I heard Rhonda's scream, which
became a horrible series of liquid coughs, and heard paper
and desk accessories scattering as (we later reconstructed)
she lurched forward and Segura pushed her face down onto
the desk. Then there were three meaty sounds as he punched
her repeatedly in the back with the brush handle.

About this time M & M and Allison came rushing through
the door. I don't know what Allison did, other than not
scream. M & M pulled Segura off Rhonda's body, powerful
forearm scissored across his throat, cutting off his wind.

I couldn't breathe either, of course. I started flopping
around, gagging, and M & M yelled for Allison to unhook
me. She turned me over and ripped off the top part of the
skinsuit and jerked the electrodes free.

Then I could breathe, but little else. I heard the quiet
struggle between M & M and Segura, the one-sided execu-
tion.

Allison carried me into the prep room and completed the
procedure that M & M normally did, stripping off the skinsuit and giving me the shot. In about ten minutes I was able
to dress myself and go back into the office.

M & M had laid out Rhonda's body on a painter's drop-
sheet, facedown in a shockingly large pool of blood. He had
cleaned the blood off the desk and was waxing it. The lemon

varnish smell didn't mask the smell of freshly butchered meat.

Segura lay where he had been dropped, his limbs at odd angles, his face bluish behind the skinsuit mask.

Allison sat on the couch, motionless, prim, impossibly pale. "What now?" she said softly. M & M looked up and raised his eyebrows.

I thought. "One thing we have to agree on before we leave this room," I said, "is whether we go to the police or . . . take care of it ourselves."

"The publicity would be terrible," Allison said.

"They also might hang us," M & M said, "if they do that here."

"Let's not find out," I said, and outlined my plan to them.

It took a certain amount of money—a good thing I had the million in advance—and there was the added complication of having to work around Harry. But we did it: we staged a tragic accident, transferring both of their bodies to a small boat whose inboard motor leaked gasoline. They were less than a mile from shore when thousands saw the huge blossom of flame light up the night, and before rescuers could reach the hulk, the fire had consumed it nearly to the waterline. Burned almost beyond recognition, the "artist" and his model lay in a final embrace.

I finished the face of the picture myself. A look of pleasant surprise, mischievousness. The posture that was to have communicated hardness was transformed into that of a woman galvanized by surprise, perhaps expectation.

We gave it to Segura's family, along with the story we'd given to the press: crusty financier falls in love with young law student/model. It was an unlikely story to anyone who knew Segura well, but the people who knew him well were busy scrambling after his fortune. His sister put the picture up for auction in two weeks, and since its notoriety hadn't faded, it brought her $2.2 million.

There's nothing like a good love story that ends in tragedy.

Harry didn't buy it, since he knew too much about Segura and Rhonda—and human nature, for that matter. We did sail to Jamaica, and that trip was a story in itself: a day becalmed followed by a day where ten-foot waves marched at right angles to twenty-foot swells. A pod of whales that inexplicably followed us for days. Crystalline nights where the Milky Way seemed as bright as the full moon.

But it was a voyage full of silences. Harry wanted me to tell him what had really happened. If I had been the only one involved, I would have told him everything, but I had to protect M & M. So we drifted together for a month and then, as they say, we drifted apart.

Back in New York, I looked at my overall situation and decided I could afford to quit. I gave Allison and M & M generous severance pay, and what I got for the studio paid for even nicer places in Maine and Key West.

I sold the facilitating equipment and have since devoted myself to pure watercolors and photography. People understood. This latest tragedy on top of the grotesque experience with the Monster.

But I downplayed that angle. I wanted to do my own work. I was tired of collaboration, and especially tired of the skin-suit.

You never know whose hand is picking up the brush.

○ ○ ○ *About the only parts of "Feedback" that derive from personal experience are the painting business and the settings—I've been to New York in the winter and George Town in its endless summer. I do have a brush with a wicked beveled handle like the one that was used as a murder weapon, but I've never stabbed anybody with it, or with anything else. (I did learn how to do that as part of "commando training" prior to going to Vietnam. The first rule of knife fighting, according to my instructor, is "Run like hell!")*

This is the only story I've written with a gay protagonist. None of that is from direct experience, except from having observed over the years that the gay and straight couples I've known exhibit about the same ranges of love and stability and mutual help or destruction. Harry and the unnamed protagonist aren't modeled on anyone in particular, but it seems obvious to me that they could be a man and a woman without their relationship materially changing. The main character's homosexuality is there to give him a sardonic distance from the prim model and the homophobic customer; I didn't "know" he was gay when I started the story. (His name, incidentally, is Cage, as you may have figured out from the musical clue.)

Though I'm obviously familiar with watercolor, I'm strictly minor league; I couldn't come remotely close to executing a picture like the one described. Like a lot of dilettantes, I read about art when I should be doing it. Writers come across similar hobbyists, who can talk learnedly about characterization, plot, point of view—but never seem to get any stories finished. I met a man like that once, charming and brilliant, who was the head of a university's writing department. He had a steamer trunk full of false starts, undeveloped ideas, and half-finished stories, but it had been years since he'd been able to complete one without a collaborator.

Literary collaboration might have been the unconscious source of the skinsuit, though I don't recall having thought of it at the time. I've collaborated on one short story and one novel, and I'm not eager to do it again. If the skinsuit existed, I doubt that I would be a customer.

passages

LIFE BEGINS IN a bloody mess and sometimes it ends the same way, and only odd people seek out blood between those times, maybe crazy people. I feel that way now. But the first half of my life ran with blood, most times animal blood, sometimes human. I was a certain kind of hunter's guide.

In those days I didn't have an office on any planet. Not in the sense of a physical place to meet clients. The character of the place where a client asked to meet, his home or otherwise, helped me decide whether to take him on. And the way he dressed, spoke, held himself. It's a special sense, a gestalt. If you took on every darf who had the money, you'd wind up dead, and him too.

It almost always is a "he." There are more women than men with money, but to want to hunt, you need that instinct to point at something and squirt it.

Raj Benhaden III had picked a good meeting place, a milk bar where the young servingwomen wore face veils but nothing substantial from collarbone to ankle, and where wine was available for infidels like me. But he didn't otherwise make a good first impression. He surged through the beaded door curtain, a large muscular man with a looking-for-trouble expression, scanned the room imperiously, nodded at a signal from one of the women, and then stomped over to my table with the chunky gracelessness of the overtrained athlete. His first two words:

"You're white."

"So was my mother."

He nodded at that revelation and sank into a chair. "You don't look like a hunting guide."

"You don't look like a prince."

"Really. What do I look like?"

Time enough for tact later, if I decided to take the job. "You look like a midclass man who was on the team in school. Say, fifteen, twenty years ago. Now you spend a lot of time in the gymnasium. Trying to turn the clock back."

He nodded again, staring. "Slow it down, anyhow."

A beautiful houri floated over with a glass of mint tea. He took it without appearing to notice her. "A cousin of mine from Earth engaged you last year. He recommended you, so I looked up your listing in Registrar Selva. You've worked a lot of places."

The only Earthie I'd guided in a year had almost been the end of me. Crazy man. "M'suya was your cousin?"

"M'suya." He smiled slightly. "Don't worry. The rest of the family is almost normal."

"I've never been hired by a normal person. Normal people don't seek out the company of dangerous animals."

"A point. Selva says your specialty is trailbreaking, taking hunters and collectors to new places."

"Which is why your cousin hired me." We'd gone to a planet called PZ1439, too new even to have a name. "But I prefer to know at least something about the place, the kind of creatures we'll be up against."

"This place is not completely unexplored. The creature has been observed a few times." He paused. "The planet Obelobel. I want the skin of a balaseli."

"I don't know the animal. Think the planet's closed, though."

"The animal is worth the trip. And I can take care of the quarantine. What do you say?"

It sounded okay. "I'll have to do a little research—"

"No. Decide now."

His eyes were actually glittering with excitement. "Sure. Leave soon as you put the fix through."

He stood up. "Tomorrow." I watched his large back sail away.

Rich people always leave you with the check. His mint tea was still steaming, untouched. I tasted it; too sweet. Sipped the wine slowly, appreciating the women, thinking it would be a while before I saw another. If only that had been correct. The next woman I met would turn out to be less pleasant to deal with.

As expected, two drinks' tariff would have bought a good meal on Selva; a banquet on Earth. Raj would pay it back a hundredfold.

I liked working from Qadar, though your daily expenses are the size of some countries' budget deficits. They pay you twice as much as elsewhere, with no argument. And they have a good library. I went back to the Hilton to punch it up, find out what was known about Obelobelians and the balaseli.

Obelobelians are weird, which is no distinction among alien races, and the balaseli is about a hundred kilograms of bloody murder that leaps out of the night. I began to have qualms.

It's a twelve-legged, eyeless (sonar-ranging) creature about twice the size of a human, which is to say about three times the size of an Obelobelian. The six legs on either side are joined with leathery membrane, like the wings of a terran bat. On the inner surface of the wings are tens of thousands of stiff, curved cilia: tiny hooks. It kills by enveloping the prey and ripping its skin off in one swift jerk.

It doesn't have a true mouth. While the prey is still twitching, a slit opens up along half the length of its thorax, ventrally, from the base of the tail to the middle of the chest, and its stomach everts, rippling up over the hooks (which all point outward) to enclose and seal off the dying, flayed animal. Strong acids and enzymes digest the meal in about fifteen minutes, during which time the balaseli is theoretically helpless. It leaves behind a compact husk of undigested hair, bones, and nails, and perhaps corroded jewelry.

You could think of worse ways to die, but it would be a short and disgusting list.

The Obelobelians have a rite of passage, which had been seen only once by humans at the time, that involves going into a cave and offering yourself as food. The balaseli evidently knows what eyes are; it only attacks from behind. You evidently have to sense its approach, turn quickly, and impale it. A test of the hunter's, or soldier's, sixth sense—which I hoped was highly developed in the ruling class of Qadar.

The caves where the beasts live typically form clusters of interconnected hemispheres, each the size of a large sports stadium. During the day, the balaselis cling to stalactites at the tops of the domes. They usually have to go outside to hunt, at night, since few large creatures are stupid enough to wander into their lairs. Their normal prey are young and old strays from the herds of saurian egg-producers that accompany the Obelobelians on their seemingly random migrations around the planet's one continent.

The Obelobelians use the rite as part of a ruthless simple form of population control, sensible on such a barren planet. No one goes through the rite of passage until someone has died. The next night, a young native goes into the cave; he or she comes out sexually mature, and immediately mates with a predetermined partner. A female mates only once in her life, but always has multiple births. The number of offspring she will have, they say, depends on how many die in the rite of passage before one makes it through.

The balaseli kill about half of the youngsters who go into

the caves, but don't bother the natives otherwise, though they sleep unprotected, not having invented the roof. The balaseli haven't bothered the humans yet, either; a few dozen xenologists who perforce also sleep under the stars, though perhaps not as deeply as the Obelobelians.

The three-week trip was uneventful. Raj Benhaden III was unusually reticent for a Qadarem. Their planet doesn't have much commerce beyond the exchange of knowledge, and that exchange is normally quite vigorous. I spent a couple of months on Qadar once, helping set up a xoo there, and you couldn't say one plus one equals two without getting some discussion. A world full of theologians and philosophers.

But Raj was a throwback; he admitted as much in a rare spate of conversation. Most Qadarem are vegetarians, and hunting (as opposed to live collecting) is almost unheard of on the planet. He offered no explanation for his aberration. No, his father didn't hunt. No, he had no philosophical justification for it. No, given a choice in the matter, he didn't eat meat. Yes, he had killed men, in war.

(This we had in common: we had both spent a year of our youth playing at mercenary, on the planet Hell. He did not elaborate, but I got the impression that he hadn't enjoyed the experience much more than I had.)

I couldn't get him to argue about anything, so I pretty much retreated to my books, and he to his body. He had a training chair loaded with weights and springs and pulleys that he could use to isolate any particular muscle and torture it into prominence. A harmless enough compulsion under normal circumstances, but with an ominous aspect here: physical strength was probably going to be irrelevant, since the Obelobelians who went through the rite of passage were as weak as ten-year-old humans. With every bulging muscle, Raj was building up false self-confidence.

When I pointed this out to him, he just nodded amiably and went on sweating.

We came out of orbit to a cloudy spring day, indistinguishable from a cloudy summer-fall-winter day. The planet has a circular orbit and no axial tilt, so no seasons, and the sky is always a uniform thin mist, so no weather. Unless you count heavy dew every night as weather. A gray moldy planet in its large temperate zones, with a lot of caves and a breathable, but unpleasantly musty, atmosphere. The ground was a tangle of presumably inedible mushrooms. Our floater homed in on the silvery dome of the Confederación's research headquarters, slid through the force field, and landed.

I hadn't expected trouble with the local bureaucracy, since the planet had no humans other than the xenologists. As luck would have it, the woman in charge recognized my name.

"'Gregorio Fuentes,'" she read off the first page of the grant. She dropped it on the small folding table and stood up. She looked like she wanted to pace, but the tent wasn't really big enough. So she contented herself with adjusting the heat under the teapot. With her back to us, she said one word: "Poacher."

"Come on, now," I said, "You can't poach where there's nothing to hunt."

"Oh, just in spirit." She turned and looked at us tiredly. "I assume you're interested in the balaselis."

I tapped the folder. "It's all in here."

"Marvelous creature," Raj said.

"Any xoo would pay a fortune for one," she said, her expression not changing. "But you can't have one."

"Nothing could be further from our minds."

"I'm sure." She poured three plastic cups of bitterroot and served us. "I mean you really, physically, *can't*. You're ten or twelve years too early. No individual can be culled until we have a population estimate. And there's no way in hell you can sneak one up to orbit; they're just too big."

Bitterroot is a special taste I have never acquired. I sipped the nasty stuff and tried to keep my voice pleasant. "The grant is quite clear on that. I'll be collecting some common smaller species that may eventually wind up on display. No balaselis."

"We merely wish to observe them *in situ*," Raj said quietly.

She stared at him and then at me. "I see. Thrillseekers."

"Not at all." I picked up the folder and offered it to her. "Our credentials are in order."

She ignored it. "I'm sure they always are. There's never any shortage of hungry universities. Or bored rich people."

Raj smiled at her. "I have never been bored in my life."

"Then you've never been a scientist forced to push government papers around." She snatched the grant and riffled through it. "I'll go over this in detail tonight. If you've dotted all the t's and crossed all the i's, you can leave the dome in the morning. You understand the quarantine procedure?"

"Of course."

"We'll be watching you every moment. No human artifacts. You go out there completely naked. One wristwatch, one *pencil*, and I'll have you confined until the next Confederación inspection team arrives. That will be a long time. Understand?"

"Yeah. But why not cooperate with us?" I said. "The sooner we ... complete our research goals, the sooner we'll be a memory."

"Your *research* could be a disaster," she said, her voice starting to shake. "The Obelobelians are the most primitive alien culture we've ever encountered. Perhaps the most primitive that ever *will* be encountered. We have to proceed with extreme caution. Just the fact that we have to communicate with the Obelobelians contaminates the very data we seek. And we are highly trained, dedicated, and *careful* researchers. Anyone else who comes in contact with them is a wild card."

"We won't try to sell them any trinkets," I said.

"If they had money, I suspect you would." She stood up. "I'll contact you in the morning."

* * *

I thought the quarantine restrictions were ridiculously tough and also hypocritical: the Confederación's presence was marked by a shimmering silver force dome over a hundred meters in diameter, with floaters almost daily dropping out of orbit and returning. The natives might notice.

Dr. Avedon was not happy with our knives, but couldn't confiscate them. They were both genuine Obelobelian artifacts, razor-keen chipped crystal, "on loan" from Selva's Museo Arqueológico. I needed mine to make cages. Raj needed his to make a spear.

I was going into the cave with him, but not as a combatant. The balaselis supposedly would ignore you if you keep your back to the wall, and that was exactly what I intended to do. Unless Raj got into trouble. Then I would help him— if it looked like it would do any good—but my fee would be quadrupled. Raj agreed to this with the easy confidence of a man who lacks the imagination to picture his own death, or who simply holds death in contempt. I never got to know him well enough to figure out which.

Even after we were allowed out of the dome, we had to spend a day in preparation. I had to weave the equivalent of rucksack and canteen out of local materials. A xenologist on Selva had showed me how—but it's one thing to duplicate a primitive craft under controlled conditions, with the help of an experienced tutor, and quite another to go outside and hack down the materials and try to do it from memory. The first half dozen canteens I wove would have made decent colanders.

I gave up trying to work outdoors. The cold didn't bother Raj—Qadar is no tropical paradise—but it made my fingers numb and clumsy. Finally I pieced together two rucksacks and four liter-sized canteens. We rested and set out at first light.

The map I'd memorized didn't do much good. No compass and no sun, just uniform dull gray from horizon to horizon. Fortunately, it was easy to follow the trail the scientists had made, a conspicuous path of crushed fungi.

It was certainly the most depressing world I'd ever seen. The scenery was like the magnified surface of a diseased organ. The dominant form of fungus was a sort of mushroom with an inverted cap, like a bowl, always full of scummy evil-smelling water. Pasty white with streaks of brown and gray. The only green in the landscape was an occasional stand of bamboolike grass, which had provided the material for my weaving and Raj's spear shaft. It was a sickly mottled chartreuse of a green.

Also slightly green was the fungus that began to grow on us after about an hour, a slick powdery fungus that crawled out of armpits and navels and the moist crease between scrotum and thigh. It looked bad enough on my olive skin, but on Raj, whose skin was so black as to be almost blue, it was spectacularly ugly.

(It's very strange for an alien life form to find humans amenable as hosts, or food. Because of divergent evolutionary patterns, we're usually incompatible at the level of DNA. We'd discussed the possibility that the balaselis would turn up their noses, if they had noses, at Raj. In that unhappy case, I would get a "no-kill fee," equal to one-third of the standard guide's fee.)

I'd made my rucksack twice as large as Raj's; it was actually a double-compartmented cage with carrying straps. We both kept our eyes sharp for specimens, and we couldn't have missed much. Anything that twitched on that moldy mausoleum of a landscape would have stood out like a live bug in a plate of cold spaghetti. We went all day without seeing anything, though, which was boring but not surprising. Most of the loathsome creatures who crabbed or slithered through the toadstools were nocturnal. I was sure there would be plenty of them around when we were trying to sleep.

We didn't talk much during the trek. I tried to start conversation a few times, but Raj damped it with monosyllables. So I was sort of relieved, looking for some human contact, when we came over a small rise and saw the archeologists' encampment. It was a well-tramped circle a couple of hundred meters from an Obelobelian "village," which was just a scatter of belongings and shared fires. About a dozen of the skinny, pale horse-sized dinosaurs that the Obelobelians followed around, the tytistu, grazed mushrooms or slept standing up. A thin man with a white beard walked up the path to meet us.

He didn't look happy. Before I could introduce us, he said, "You're the adventurers. Fuentes and Benhaden."

"You're in touch with Dr. Avedon?" I said.

He opened his mouth and pointed to a molar. "Radio. She says your accreditation is in order and we are not to hinder you. Nor cooperate, you might as well know."

"Which is stupid," I said, regretting it but forging on: "Your own project's funding can only benefit from our visit here. There will be publicity."

"Publicity to bring more thrillseekers. We're trying to do *science* here, Fuentes; it's not a freak show." He turned and walked away. That was the last word we heard from any scientist, until they came up the hill to help me with Raj.

We made our "camp"—putting down our rucksacks and kicking away enough of the disgusting undergrowth to make sitting space—just downstream from the scientists' and Obelobelians' camps. The river, wide and shallow, barely moved. The water was gray and smelled like stale cheese. We followed the xenologists' lead and gathered our water upstream from the Obelobelians. We weren't likely to catch any disease from alien pollution, but it did sometimes happen, usually with fatal results.

Raj settled in to make a few backup spears while I went off in search of a good cave. I didn't want to antagonize the scientists by spending too much time talking to the Obelobelians, contaminating their precious data, so rather than ask directions I just followed a conspicuous path that led toward likely-looking hills.

The hills were rocky, inhospitable to the mushrooms; the only vegetation was lichen of muted earth hues. I did find animal life, though, kicking over rocks. Small invertebrates that resembled Terran millipedes, mainly. Not worth collecting and possibly biters.

There were plenty of caves, but it was some time before I found one large enough. All of them probably led to the balaseli domes, but I wanted to be able to exit standing up and moving fast.

When I found a large enough entrance, I shed the rucksack and went in with just the knife. Like Raj's, my knife was a slight violation of technological quarantine. It truly did come from Obelobel, but had made a couple of stops on the way back. I gave the handle a sharp twist and the end of it popped open, exposing a small powerful flashlight.

The balaselis supposedly slept during the day, but my experience with large dangerous animals had led me not to put too much trust in established behavior patterns. Besides, the cave could harbor smaller perils. Its Terran counterparts might be havens during the daytime for rattlesnakes or scorpions or vampire bats. So I entered very tentatively, literally one step at a time, my eyes fixed on the darkness, knife ready and light beaming forward. It was easy to visualize what I must look like to any cave dweller: a dangerous hulking silhouette with one gleaming eye. Most animals confronted with the unknown will either run away, seek refuge in shelter or camouflage, or attack. I wanted to give everybody plenty of time to exercise the first two options.

The cave entrance took a sharp turn to the left and began angling down. I waited at the corner, light off, for several minutes while my eyes became better adapted to the dark. There was a constant tattoo of dripping condensation echoing from the chamber ahead, and the downhill path I stood on was dangerously slick. The fungus odor of the air outside was mixed now with a surprising earthlike cave smell of wet rock, along with an acrid metallic tang I couldn't place. It was cold.

I turned on the light, careful not to look directly at it. The downward path continued on for some fifty meters, widening all the way, ending in a ragged square of blackness that I assumed was the entrance to one of the domes.

I have never liked cave work, but Raj was paying well for me to overcome my aversion. Keeping my naked back pressed cold against the wall, I worked slowly down toward the deeper darkness.

The domed cavern was too large for my light to reach to the other side. In the center was a black lake, evidently shallow, since ghostly fingers of stalagmites broke the surface here and there. The surface was constantly in motion with the widening, intersecting circles of ripples from the water that dripped from above. I suppose it was pretty.

Using the trick of averted vision, I could just make out some details of the cave ceiling. What I saw turned my blood colder than my freezing skin. Nestled among a matrix of stalactites of various sizes were dozens of black shrouds, balaselis in repose. They shifted and flapped languidly in their sleep, perhaps reacting to the intruder below. An imperative buried deep in my reptile brain was trying to persuade me to evacuate my bowels and run. I forced myself to study the scene for a minute or so, trying to visualize Raj standing there with his torch and spears. It looked very bad. If several of them took an interest in you, it was hard to see how you could survive. But every native did go through this, and enough lived to perpetuate the species.

I backed out very slowly, my own fear-smell sharp in my nostrils. I doubted that any animal on this planet would interpret the odor correctly; it might even signal to them that I was poison or at least not food. Raj might have that in his favor, if he was human enough to sweat fear.

I was still somewhat shaken by the time I returned to camp. I almost tried to talk Raj out of it, even though the no-kill fee wouldn't cover my time and expenses.

"They are only animals," Raj said. "We were given dominion over them."

"Don't feed me religion. We're animals too—animals with

sharp sticks, granted—but there are dozens of them, and only two of us."

"One of us. I don't expect you to interfere." He nodded toward the Obelobelian camp. "What they can do, I can do."

"We don't know that. Maybe they have some magic word that turns the beasts into obedient puppies."

"That may be." He laughed politely and returned to his chores, spearmaking and fire-maintaining. He had borrowed, or taken, some fire from the Obelobelians, and was feeding it the way they did. A circle of uprooted fungi surrounded the flame; once dry, it burned about as well as dried animal manure, but smelled worse. Fires were started with kumali, a morel-shaped fungus that was a staple of the native diet. They were so saturated with vegetable oil that, skewered, they could be used as torches. He had collected several.

He was making backup spears out of the bamboo-like stalks. Sharpen the green wood and then blacken it in the fire; anneal it by quenching it in the wet ground; resharpen and start over. After a few iterations you had a black splinter that might spit a balaseli. Or might just annoy it, if you didn't hit it just right.

"Plan to aim for the heart?" He grunted uninformatively. "Or the brain—the brain would be good, if it's not behind too much—"

"Enough subtlety. I understand."

"Well, just how do you plan to kill a large animal with a spear, not knowing where any vital organs are?"

"I don't have just *a* spear." He hefted his heaviest spear, the one with his knife lashed on the end. "This should stun the creature no matter where I hit it. Long enough for me to pierce it with several others."

"And hope one of them—"

"Yes, hope."

"And hope none of the other beasts—"

"Yes, *hope!*" He turned his back to me and resumed work. I watched him for a couple of silent minutes.

"I feel as if I've been hired to preside over an elaborate suicide ritual."

"The first part, you have right. You *have* been hired." He turned around and looked at me, scowling. "And you don't say that to a Qadarem. A man may give his life. But not take it."

I knew that. "It is suicide. If I have any instinct about animals."

"That may be your problem, Fuentes. Too much instinct about animals, and not enough about humans." He stood up and gathered a few spears. "But you are a good guide. Please guide me now to see these monsters."

Since I didn't have to search for the place, we got there in a brisk twenty minutes. I led the way inside. Raj followed my instructions, making slow progress for dark adaptation as well as caution, but his impatience was palpable.

When we got to the dome we both stood against the wall for several silent minutes, studying. With the extra flashlight, I could see that my estimate of a few dozen creatures was far too small. Hundreds of them crowded the high ceiling. With the extra light I could also make out considerable variation in size and color. Most of the large ones had glossy black shrouds, but the smaller ones—some small as a human infant—were mottled or even striped in what seemed to be subtle shades of red and brown. Of course colors are elusive at low light levels.

"Still want to go through with it?" I whispered. "There's enough up there to take care of that whole tribe and go away hungry."

"They must not eat often," he said, "for this barren area to support so many."

"Maybe that's why it's so barren. They killed everything bigger than a mouse."

He snorted. "You don't believe that. There must be ecological balance."

"Not in the short run, there doesn't. Not even in the long run, if we're witnessing a basic evolutionary—"

"I know what it is. Burst metabolism. Large reptiles on my planet have that. They lie dormant for days, or even weeks, until something large enough to be worth eating comes close enough to catch. Then they move with great speed, for a few seconds."

"That's not unreasonable," I had to admit. "I suppose you've hunted them."

"Oh yes." He was smiling, staring upward, white teeth and eyes glowing almost disembodied in the darkness. "Barehanded." Abruptly, he stepped away from the wall, going about halfway to the water's edge.

"Raj!"

"Shouldn't be anything to worry about," he said, far too loudly for my comfort—and then he *shouted* several words in Arabic. When the echoes stopped chasing around the dome, there was another noise: the beasts' wings rustling in reaction.

"Christ—you're waking them up!"

"Maybe one or two." He threw a spear straight up and stepped back to the wall. "I'd like to see them fly."

The stick slowed and began to tumble, and barely brushed one of the large ones. It stretched its wings, dead white inside, and let go of the stalactite. The stone column thrummed a deep bass note. The creature fell slowly, parachuting, and about halfway down beat its wings hard several times, hovering and then climbing back up to its perch. It grabbed the stalactite and folded itself around it.

"Not too fast," Raj said.

"Not awake yet." I was impressed by its grace and evident strength. "Let's get out of here."

"All right. And come back tonight, with torches."

"Unless you have an attack of sanity." If I hadn't been there, I suspected Raj would have just turned his back on them and walked straight out of the cave. But he obediently mooched crabwise along behind me.

Waiting at the cave entrance was a group of four Obelobelians, perhaps a family. Mature male and female, a tall host, and a child who didn't yet have any visible sex. All of the adults wore short black cloaks, made of hide from the bal-aseli's wings.

I greeted the host—the other genders never spoke with humans—and it returned the formal politeness but moved to block our way.

"Not night," it said.

I agreed: "Not night."

"Balaseli sleep?"

"Yes."

"Balaseli growing ritual, you?"

I put my hand on Raj's shoulder. "Him, tonight."

"Not young, him."

I thought for a second. "On his world, young."

It considered that in silence and slowly stepped aside. "Tonight."

They let us get about fifty meters down the trail and then followed in silence. We stopped at our fire and they walked on by as if in a trance. Of course, they were probably gossiping, joking, philosophizing like mad—telepathically.

At that time, the scientists were still looking at the Obelobelians as innocent flea-picking primitives, barely social, preagricultural and so forth. Language limited to a few hundred words, mostly nouns and adjectives. As we later learned, only the hosts use spoken language, and before humans came, they only used it in ritual. One spoken word drowns out real conversation for minutes, echoing in their minds. Active verbs are the "loudest," so they avoid them.

I spitted a few mushrooms and roasted them over the smoldering lumps. The four days' food we'd brought cost more than the expensive knives. It took some delicate bioengineering to make mushrooms that looked like the vile things the Obelobelians ate but were nutritious to humans, and at the same time not poisonous to Obelobelians, just in case they took a bite. You couldn't ask for flavor on top of that. Filet of sock.

Raj seemed to enjoy them; he ate his three and then

roasted another pair. Being vegetarian might have helped. Looking forward to the evening, rather than dreading it, certainly did.

One last try. "There's no way we're getting off this planet with a balaseli skin," I said.

"Leave that to me."

"What, you think you can bribe Dr. Avedon?"

"No. Though I'm sure she has her price." He picked threads of flesh off the outside, saving the best for last. "If she's still the only person in the dome, it's simple. She has to sleep. I leave the hide outside the dome until she does."

"Word of the kill may precede us."

He shrugged. "At worst, they throw us off the planet, I pay a fine, I don't get to keep the skin. That's all right."

"And I pay a fine, too, and lose my license."

"As we discussed. I'll compensate you."

"If you're alive."

"Even if I'm not." True enough; on Qadar, his family would assume responsibility for his debts. "Well. Look at this."

I turned around and saw a group of Obelobelians approaching. A tall host with a cloak, maybe the one we'd encountered at the cave, and eleven females armed with spears.

I spread my hands and spoke to the host. "*¿Padafat oté tekanen?*" I asked; what's up?

It spread its hands the same way, but with two more fingers. "He cannot . . . *do!*"

"But he is young. He desires passage."

The host pointed at Raj's plumbing. "He is, he *has* passage."

"No," I said. "On his world, like mine, even young boys have that. Males are born like that." An Obelobelian's genitalia stay hidden until the rite of passage. Apparently the shock triggers a basic anatomical change—sort of like getting the stuffing scared out of you. (If you could believe what the Obelobelians told the scientists, that is. They wouldn't be the first autochthons to hide a sly sense of humor.)

The host turned its back on me and sat down. Two of the

females sat down facing it. The other nine stared at us, rigid with discipline or fear or boredom.

"Do you think—" Raj began.

"Hush." He nodded. Probably not a good idea to interfere with the ritual.

After a few minutes the host stood and turned back around. The expression on its face would have been chagrin on a human's. He pointed at Raj. "You are die."

Raj was holding one of the fire-annealed spears. I saw his grip tighten. The host slouched and walked back down the path, along with the two it had been sitting with.

The other nine guards stayed, unblinking. Then they stepped forward three steps in unison, toward Raj, ignoring me. The one closest to Raj made an unmistakable gesture, pointing at his spear and then holding her hand out, palm up.

Raj's tone was pleasant and he smiled. "There is no way in seven hells I will give you this spear." She repeated the gesture.

"Better hand it over," I said. "Nine against two is no odds."

He looked at me. "Nine against one. You do what you will."

The guard very slowly wrapped her many fingers around the weapon's shaft. Raj watched the action in a calculating way. He would certainly win any contest of strength. With her other hand, though, she offered Raj her own spear.

"I'll be damned," I said. "She wants to trade."

Raj studied the heavy flint tip, the careful binding that fastened it to the wood. "Not much of a trade." He relinquished his and took the shorter, stronger weapon. "Thank you."

She put her palms together in an all-purpose social gesture, and I told Raj to copy it. Then the nine of them ambled back toward their camp. The one who had made the exchange tossed Raj's spear aside.

"I would regard that as an omen of good fortune," Raj said.

"Acceptance, anyhow."

In retrospect, it seems odd that we didn't realize they were using telepathy. It had not at that time been demonstrated, although a form of it had been suspected for years in the case of the S'kang, of the carbon star Ember. But these creatures seemed so feckless and primitive.

For the next couple of hours we each rounded up bundles of the kumali torches and I improvised holders out of the soft dome tops of the largest fungi—that way we could have several of them burning in the cave and still keep both hands free, for spears.

"What are you going to do if they ignore you?" I asked.

"What do you mean?"

I shrugged. "Suppose the balaseli need some sort of olfactory clue to attack. Or suppose there's some gestural stimulus that young Obelobelians do instinctively."

"In that case, I suppose we'll have to wait until some native goes in for the ritual. If we follow along, we should be attacked as well."

"That could be a long time. What do you propose we eat, waiting for one of them to die?"

"Accidents happen."

That was too much. "I won't be an accessory to murder."

"I didn't say murder." He looked up at the slate sky. "Getting dark."

He was right, and I felt a sudden easing. I hate the waiting around before going into action. What's going to happen will happen, and worrying about it never helps. "Let's go."

I bundled up all of the small kumali torches and the improvised bases, and carried them under one arm, with a lit one in the other hand awkwardly gripped along with the knife, and a canteen hanging from a vine around my neck, bumping with every step. I think humans invented clothes so they could have belts and pockets.

Raj looked slightly more dignified, only slightly, with a bundle of fire-hardened sticks under one arm and the two flint-tipped spears in the other hand. We didn't look like any match for a cross between a manta ray and a vampire bat.

The Obelobelians were waiting for us: the old host, the female guards, and a couple of males, unarmed and smaller than the females.

"Came to wish us luck," Raj said.

"Sure." I approached the elder and laid down my bundle. Before I could deliver the standard greeting, it pointed at Raj again. "He is die," it said.

Well, it hadn't turned out to be a threat last time. A curse? A prediction? "And me?" I asked. "Am I die?"

The host stared at me for more than a minute, with a weird hunched intensity. (Now, of course, I know that it was trying to break through the static in my mind so we could really communicate.) It took a step forward and rolled its shoulders like an exotic dancer, *very* exotic, which I supposed was an Obelobelian shrug. "Not maybe, die maybe. It is . . . self. You must be . . . self." Always good advice. Go forty light-years and find Polonius.

"Why are you here?" I asked.

The shrug again. "Always be for a passage here, there. Where passage be."

"You may be right," I said to Raj. "Just a cheering section." Or pallbearers, I thought and didn't say.

No one tried to interfere as we walked into the cave, and no one followed us, at least not immediately. Best not to use the flashlights, in case. Raj hadn't wanted to, anyhow—trying to duplicate as nearly as possible the native experience—but that was a quirk I would not let interfere with my survival, or even his.

Raj followed the game plan all the way down to the main cavern. We hugged the side of the cave, moving as quietly as possible. With every tiny click of a pebble, though, I felt exposed. Hard to sneak up on a blind monster that feeds by sonar.

As we squeezed into the last cavern we startled something big and white and shiny, like a maggot the size of a horse, that slid into the water and squirmed away. Wings rustled overhead.

After a moment of paralysis I mastered my fear enough to begin lighting torches. Raj took two and sidled ahead of me, both of us keeping our backs pressed against the gritty wall. We worked backward and forward and soon had a staggered line of sixteen greasy big candles guttering in the still air.

There was enough light to see each other clearly, and I didn't care for what I saw. Raj was grinning so hard I could see both rows of white teeth in his black face, and if he was feeling anything except pure ecstasy, he was hiding it real well.

I've seen it before, of course, men getting an almost-sexual thrill from the prospect of facing a dangerous animal. It's sort of amusing when you're protected by laser rifles and body armor. Not so amusing when you're naked as babies and armed with sticks and rocks. Sort of insane, actually, and I had to admit considering for the first time in a long career abandoning a client for fear he was determined to get me killed. I stayed, of course, and shouldn't have been surprised at what happened next.

I didn't actually see Raj make his move, since all my attention was concentrated on the cave ceiling, searching the murk for the humped forms of the balaseli. I couldn't see them yet, though, my eyes still dazzled from lighting and placing the candles. I wonder even now whether Raj could see more than I, or didn't care, or was tired of waiting—or did feel the same fear I did, and dealt with it in his own way.

Whatever it was, I heard a sudden shout, almost a bark, and was appalled to see Raj halfway to the water's edge, a spear in each hand, bellowing a challenge into the gloom. He was answered: a silent wisp of dark umber against the cave's blackness, suddenly behind him, drifting in at eye level—I started to shout but he had sensed it, spun around, hurled the right-hand spear with perfect accuracy. The spear struck the beast dead center with a meaty smack, and it suddenly reared back, tripling in size as its huge wings unfurled, beating the air. The teeth inside the wings glittered like thousands of diamond points. Then the other spear hit even harder, not ten centimeters from the first.

The balaseli made a strange high-pitched sound, unlike any pain cry I know, but rather like the mating challenge of a ba'albeast on Selva or the chittering of a Terran dolphin. Suddenly it seemed to contract in every dimension and then spring back to normal size, as if flexing a huge muscle. Raj stood transfixed as the beast did this three times, meanwhile beating its wings to stay aloft. I shouted for him to come back. He ignored me, reaching down to pick up a pair of the fire-hardened sticks.

The fourth time the creature flexed, both of the spears came loose and clattered on the ground. A dark green fluid pulsed out of it as it reared back, hovering now a few meters from Raj, who had both lances braced against his sides, pointed at the beast. Then a second one dropped from the ceiling and enveloped him from behind.

It was hideous. He roared and struggled; twice, lance tips pierced through from inside. Green ichor and red blood sprayed in every direction. Then it slumped away.

For one terrible year, age nineteen, I hired out on Hell as a mercenary soldier. I saw too much but nothing I saw in that year was as bad as the sight of Raj, face intact but skin flayed off from shoulders to knees, heart and lungs exposed and guts spilling out, uncoiling; beyond mortal help but not beyond realizing what had happened. He faced me and said four clear words—one of them was "Allah" but that exhausts my Arabic—then made a strangling sound and fell over, probably dead, certainly doomed. The creature that had attacked him was writhing soundlessly on the ground. The one he had speared fell flapping, splashing, into the water.

Some basic human, or humane, instinct almost killed me then. I took a couple of steps toward him. A balaseli whispered down between me and the cave wall and enfolded me.

I must not have been in its embrace for more than a second, but that second resonates through my life like a huge bell struck once. I think it resonated backward, weeks, as well as forward, to now and however much longer I have. That's why I had been so jumpy.

Mine must have been larger than the one that killed Raj. It covered me face and all. It was like being smothered by a woolen blanket soaked in animal blood.

I froze. Thousands of tiny teeth pressed gently into my flesh, like the grains of coarse sandpaper but alive. Knife pinned uselessly between my own wrist and abdomen.

Maybe Buddha defeated Allah in this contest. I hadn't been to kiack in twenty years, but the Way lies deep, and in what I thought was my last act as a living being, I tried to compose myself for death. The teeth pressed harder and I surrendered....

And was suddenly spilled out onto the cold wet rock, unharmed.

I rolled back to the safety of the wall, burning my calf on one of the kumalis but heedless of the pain. Calming somewhat, I was surprised to see that the creature seemed not to have harmed me beyond leaving mild abrasions all over, such as you might give yourself by scratching an itch too vigorously.

The one that had attacked me was flopping around as Raj's was; in less than a minute both were limp, dead. Alien protein, of course. There was no way they could sense our toxicity without tasting; evidently one taste was plenty. I supposed the simple creatures mistook us for Obelobelians, which triggered the aggressive behavior. The truth turned out to be somewhat stranger.

I hadn't asked Raj what was to be done with his remains, should the hunter become the quarry, but assumed he was conventionally Moslem in that regard. On Qadar the ceremony goes on for days, and a lot of the ritual involves the physical corpse.

It was an interesting problem. I'm conventionally tolerant of other people's notions, and there was the added incentive that Raj's relatives might not honor his debts with only my word that he had died. But there was no way in hell I was going to saunter out there and drag him away. Just have to wait until daylight, when the balaseli were dormant again. He would be a pretty sight in ten hours.

Something touched me on the shoulder and I almost jumped out of my aching skin. It was the old host. "I watch," it said. "He is die; you are passage."

"Guess so," I said. I did kill a balaseli, though the weapon I used was not especially heroic. Sweat.

The host solved part of my problem. It had a long looped cord that ended in a wooden hook. On the third toss, it snagged Raj behind the knee; together we were able to haul him to the wall. Carrying him out was not something I would ever care to try again. It took a long time. The host would not touch him—probably wise—and his dead weight nearly defeated me. I collapsed twice on the passage out and again as we staggered from the cave entrance. Several of the xenologists were waiting with a pair of improvised stretchers. One of them, an older woman I hadn't seen, touched my arm and I felt a slight pinprick. All the pain washed away and I fell asleep.

I carried Raj back to Qadar frozen solid in a specimen bag. His family paid my fee in gold and had me thrown out of the house, the castle. I decided it would be prudent to leave Qadar immediately.

Odd how things sometimes come together. I had done a lot of soul-searching on the way back, and decided that I had been a hunter for far too long. The fee for this one would allow me to live prudently for several years on Selva or Thelugi, both of which had good universities for xoology and animal behavior. I could finish the degrees I started twenty years ago and stop killing the things that I liked the most.

When I got back to the spaceport there was a Hartford courier waiting for me with a bright red Confederación envelope. It was a message from Dr. Avedon, the xenologist who had been so happy to see me and Raj when we showed up with our phony papers. She said that the Obelobelian tribe they were observing had refused to cooperate with anyone but me, since I was the only human who had undergone the rite of passage. Would I consider coming out to assist them for a regular consultant's fee? She wasn't enthusiastic about having any of her people go into those caves at night, for certification.

I could just see her teeth grinding as she wrote a letter of supplication to Gregorio Fuentes, heartless poacher. She probably knew that the maximum pay she could offer was less than a tenth of my normal fee. I would refuse contemptuously and they would be stuck.

Of course I did go back. I stayed on Obelobel for twenty-two years, and still return every three years for a tribal purification ceremony, which will kill me if I live long enough. That honestly is something that bothers me not at all. Not because I'm old or tired of life.

We've learned a lot from the Obelobelians, including humility. The second surprise was telepathy, which we learned through my own initiation as a host-surrogate. The first surprise was from their biochemistry, a discovery that had been in the making when Raj and I arrived there: the Obelobelians came from another planet. Their body chemistry was as alien to Obelobel as ours was—and the balaseli found them just as poisonous. The ones who survived their rite of passage did exactly as I had. The creature's flaying reflex is triggered by its prey's struggling. If you remain motionless long enough for it to reject you, you may live.

It seems cruel, by human standards, to subject the young to such an awful test. But to their way of thinking a male or female is not born until he or she comes back out of the cave; a child killed by the balaseli is a late miscarriage. To be allowed to reproduce you have to show absolute fearlessness. You have to show that you are grown.

So where did they come from, and how, and why? They are not willing to answer such questions. Able, but not willing, and anyone with a grain of objectivity about human nature would have to agree with them.

We thought it was a case of an advanced civilization dealing with childish savages who could think and communicate only at the most basic level. We were right.

O O O *This story is almost completely a work of the imagination. I've never hunted anything that couldn't shoot back.*

It started with two unrelated events: a typographical error and a dream. The typo came while I was writing the first draft of a novel: instead of "fireworks" I typed "fireworms." The word intrigued me, so I copied it onto a slip of paper and stuck it up on the bulletin board behind my typewriter, where I glanced at it now and then for several years.

The dream came when my wife and I were staying in the old Algonquin Hotel in New York. They had just switched to the new plastic card keys, and we had trouble making them work. That translated into a dream where I was locked inside the room during a fire. Firemen broke down the door with an axe and came in with their thick hose. When they turned it on, it dripped viscous blood. The firemen had ghastly corpse faces, memories of Vietnam.

A Freudian could probably write a whole book about that dream. I wrote an opening paragraph.

I started the story about the professional hunter and the balaseli, and the fireworms that were a sinister symbiote to the batlike carnivores. The story froze up after five or six pages, so I put it away. I took it out every now and then for several years, but just couldn't get it going again.

Finally it occurred to me to get rid of the damned fireworms. Then the story took off and wrote itself.

job security

THE FIRST ONE was like four years ago, four and a half, I remember because that's when I was fifteen years into this job, sweeping up these old observatory domes, halfway to full pension.

They lost a star, big deal, one out of a zillion, you couldn't even see it from here. It was a big one, though, Alfalfa something. Maybe it was in Spanish, three of the guys went down to South America to look at it, look at where it wasn't anymore.

Couple years later they lose another one and all hell breaks loose, even though you couldn't even see it without the telescope. Then another couple years and they lose another, even dimmer, but by this time they know where to look. The next one was gonna be in like six months but in the daytime, so old man Merton and a couple others get to go to Paris where it's dark. Tough job.

This Sirius one got to me, though, like for years and years I seen it all winter. Winter is a bitch on the mountain, have to use the four-wheel in the snow and they can't heat up the domes, one of the guys tried to explain why, but I don't get science.

They knew to the minute when it was gonna go, so I bundled up and went outside and looked. Brightest star in the sky, can't miss it. Then pow, nothing. I mean it didn't blow up or nothing, it just went out.

Maybe it was because I just lost a tooth, the first one, that makes you feel old, kind of, makes you think about things. I watched that Sirius go out and it hit me. No wonder these guys are so worried. What if they all go out? They've got no jobs. And if they got no jobs, I got no job.

I know better than to bother anybody while he's working, but it did keep me awake half the night thinking about it. I mean a guy who can push a broom can always get a job, some kind of job, but starting over at forty-two in some new place didn't sound good.

Anyhow about six I went down to the small dome because I knew Dr. Jake would be getting off, he's a professor too but we get along. He was staying on till noon, he said, but had a cup of coffee with me and I asked him if he was worried. He didn't get it at first. I mean he really was worried, but not about that. They were worried because they couldn't figure it out, why it was happening.

But as to losing all the stars to look at, Dr. Jake said that was no problem, we wouldn't lose more than a couple dozen you could see as long as he or I was going to live, if they had it figured out right with the distances and all. I never got that speed of light stuff.

But he said that even if every one of them did go out, we'd all stay on at the domes, trying to see what was left. Then he said I looked tired and was I losing sleep over this problem, and I admitted that I did, most the night. So he said screw the morning shift, they'd all be working anyhow and didn't need anybody else around, go back to the cabin and catch some Z's.

It's that kind of a job, you know, loose. I slept like a rock.

O O O The only actual "experience" involved in this bit of silliness is that I have been a janitor, and lost teeth. The story came in one complete vision during dinner, while I was reading something totally unrelated.

Some reference in an article about Ursula K. Le Guin made me think of Arthur C. Clarke's science-fantasy classic "The Nine Billion Names of God," with its shocker ending, were the scientist looks up and, one by one, the stars are going out.

Well, I thought, what would happen if all the stars (except the Sun) did go out simultaneously? Nothing. In 4.3 years, Alpha Centauri, the nearest star, would blink out. Then 1.7 years later, the next closest, Barnard's Star, would disappear. And so forth—after ten years, we would only have lost twelve stars, though if they went out in the right order, it would be easy to infer what was happening.

Anyhow, I jumped up from the dinner table, startling my wife, and went into the study and scrawled a note "Stars go out!" and left it on the keyboard. I wrote the story in a couple of hours the next morning.

the Hemingway hoax

1. The Torrents of Spring

OUR STORY BEGINS in a run-down bar in Key West, not so many years from now. The bar is not the one Hemingway drank at, nor yet the one that claims to be the one he drank at, because they are both too expensive and full of tourists. This bar, in a more interesting part of town, is a Cuban place. It is neither clean nor well-lighted, but has cold beer and good strong Cuban coffee. Its cheap prices and rascally charm are what bring together the scholar and the rogue.

Their first meeting would be of little significance to either at the time, though the scholar, John Baird, would never forget it. John Baird was not capable of forgetting anything.

Key West is lousy with writers, mostly poor writers, in one sense of that word or the other. Poor people did not interest our rogue, Sylvester Castlemaine, so at first he didn't take any special note of the man sitting in the corner scribbling on a yellow pad. Just another would-be writer, come down to see whether some of Papa's magic would rub off. Not worth the energy of a con.

But Castle's professional powers of observation caught at a detail or two and focused his attention. The man was wearing jeans and a faded flannel shirt, but his shoes were expensive Italian loafers. His beard had been trimmed by a barber. He was drinking Heineken. The pen he was scribbling with was a fat Mont Blanc Diplomat, two hundred bucks on the hoof, discounted. Castle got his cup of coffee and sat at a table two away from the writer.

He waited until the man paused, set the pen down, took a drink. "Writing a story?" Castle said.

The man blinked at him. "No . . . just an article." He put the cap on the pen with a crisp snap. "An article about stories. I'm a college professor."

"Publish or perish," Castle said.

The man relaxed a bit. "Too true." He riffled through the yellow pad. "This won't help much. It's not going anywhere."

"Tell you what . . . bet you a beer it's Hemingway or Tennessee Williams."

"Too easy." He signaled the bartender. "Dos cervezas. Hemingway, the early stories. You know his work?"

"Just a little. We had to read him in school—*The Old Man and the Fish?* And then I read a couple after I got down here." He moved over to the man's table. "Name's Castle."

"John Baird." Open, honest expression; not too promising. You can't con somebody unless he thinks he's conning you. "Teach up at Boston."

"I'm mostly fishing. Shrimp nowadays." Of course Castle didn't normally fish, not for things in the sea, but the shrimp part was true. He'd been reduced to heading shrimp on the Catalina for five dollars a bucket. "So what about these early stories?"

The bartender set down the two beers and gave Castle a weary look.

"Well . . . they don't exist." John Baird carefully poured the beer down the side of his glass. "They were stolen. Never published."

"So what can you write about them?"

"Indeed. That's what I've been asking myself." He took a sip of the beer and settled back. "Seventy-four years ago they were stolen. December 1922. That's really what got me working on them; thought I would do a paper, a monograph, for the seventy-fifth anniversary of the occasion."

It sounded less and less promising, but this was the first imported beer Castle had had in months. He slowly savored the bite of it.

"He and his first wife, Hadley, were living in Paris. You know about Hemingway's early life?"

"Huh uh. Paris?"

"He grew up in Oak Park, Illinois. That was kind of a prissy, self-satisfied suburb of Chicago."

"Yeah, I been there."

"He didn't like it. In his teens he sort of ran away from home, went down to Kansas City to work on a newspaper.

"World War I started, and like a lot of kids, Hemingway couldn't get into the army because of bad eyesight, so he joined the Red Cross and went off to drive ambulances in Italy. Take cigarettes and chocolate to the troops.

"That almost killed him. He was just doing his cigarettes-and-chocolate routine and an artillery round came in, killed the guy next to him, tore up another, riddled Hemingway with shrapnel. He claims then that he picked up the wounded guy and carried him back to the trench, in spite of being hit in the knee by a machine gun bullet."

"What do you mean, 'claims'?"

"You're too young to have been in Vietnam."

"Yeah."

"Good for you. I was hit in the knee by a machine gun bullet myself, and went down on my ass and didn't get up for five weeks. He didn't carry anybody one step."

"That's interesting."

"Well, he was always rewriting his life. We all do it. But it seemed to be a compulsion with him. That's one thing that makes Hemingway scholarship challenging."

Baird poured the rest of the beer into his glass. "Anyhow,

he actually was the first American wounded in Italy, and they made a big deal over him. He went back to Oak Park a war hero. He had a certain amount of success with women."

"Or so he says?"

"Right, God knows. Anyhow, he met Hadley Richardson, an older woman but quite a number, and they had a steamy courtship and got married and said the hell with it, moved to Paris to live a sort of Bohemian life while Hemingway worked on perfecting his art. That part isn't bullshit. He worked diligently and he did become one of the best writers of his era. Which brings us to the lost manuscripts."

"Do tell."

"Hemingway was picking up a little extra money doing journalism. He'd gone to Switzerland to cover a peace conference for a news service. When it was over, he wired Hadley to come join him for some skiing.

"This is where it gets odd. On her own initiative, Hadley packed up all of Ernest's work. All of it. Not just the typescripts, but the handwritten first drafts and the carbons."

"That's like a Xerox?"

"Right. She packed them in an overnight bag, then packed her own suitcase. A porter at the train station, the Gare de Lyon, put them aboard for her. She left the train for a minute to find something to read—and when she came back, they were gone."

"Suitcase and all?"

"No, just the manuscripts. She and the porter searched up and down the train. But that was it. Somebody had seen the overnight bag sitting there and snatched it. Lost forever."

That did hold a glimmer of professional interest. "That's funny. You'd think they'd get a note then, like 'If you ever want to see your stories again, bring a million bucks to the Eiffel Tower' sort of thing."

"A few years later, that might have happened. It didn't take long for Hemingway to become famous. But at the time, only a few of the literary intelligentsia knew about him."

Castle shook his head in commiseration with the long-dead thief. "Guy who stole 'em probably didn't even read English. Dumped 'em in the river."

John Baird shivered visibly. "Undoubtedly. But people have never stopped looking for them. Maybe they'll show up in some attic someday."

"Could happen." Wheels turning.

"It's happened before in literature. Some of Boswell's diaries were recovered because a scholar recognized his handwriting on an old piece of paper a merchant used to wrap a fish. Hemingway's own last book, he put together from notes that had been lost for thirty years. They were in a couple of trunks in the basement of the Ritz, in Paris." He leaned forward, excited. "Then after he died, they found another batch of papers down here, in a back room in Sloppy Joe's. It could still happen."

Castle took a deep breath. "It could be made to happen, too."

"Made to happen?"

"Just speakin', you know, in theory. Like some guy who really knows Hemingway, suppose he makes up some stories that're like those old ones, finds some seventy-five-year-old paper and an old, what do you call them, not a word processor—"

"Typewriter."

"Whatever. Think he could pass 'em off for the real thing?"

"I don't know if he could fool me," Baird said, and tapped the side of his head. "I have a freak memory: eidetic, photographic. I have just about every word Hemingway ever wrote committed to memory." He looked slightly embarrassed. "Of course that doesn't make me an expert in the sense of being able to spot a phony. I just wouldn't have to refer to any texts."

"So take yourself, you know, or somebody else who spent all his life studyin' Hemingway. He puts all he's got into writin' these stories—he knows the people who are gonna be readin' 'em; knows what they're gonna look for. And he hires like an expert forger to make the pages look like they came out of Hemingway's machine. So could it work?"

Baird pursed his lips and for a moment looked professorial. Then he sort of laughed, one syllable through his nose. "Maybe it could. A man did a similar thing when I was a boy, counterfeiting the memoirs of Howard Hughes. He made millions."

"Millions?"

"Back when that was real money. Went to jail when they found out, of course."

"And the money was still there when he got out."

"Never read anything about it. I guess so."

"So the next question is, how much stuff are we talkin' about? How much was in that old overnight bag?"

"That depends on who you believe. There was half a novel and some poetry. The short stories, there might have been as few as eleven or as many as thirty."

"That'd take a long time to write."

"It would take forever. You couldn't just 'do' Hemingway; you'd have to figure out what the stories were about, then reconstruct his early style—do you know how many Hemingway scholars there are in the world?"

"Huh uh. Quite a few."

"Thousands. Maybe ten thousand academics who know enough to spot a careless fake."

Castle nodded, cogitating. "You'd have to be real careful. But then you wouldn't have to do all the short stories and poems, would you? You could say all you found was the part of the novel. Hell, you could sell that as a book."

The odd laugh again. "Sure you could. Be a fortune in it."

"How much? A million bucks?"

"A million . . . maybe. Well, sure. The last new Hemingway made at least that much, allowing for inflation. And he's more popular now."

Castle took a big gulp of beer and set his glass down decisively. "So what the hell are we waiting for?"

Baird's bland smile faded. "You're serious?"

2. IN OUR TIME

Got a ripple in the Hemingway channel.

Twenties again?

No, funny, this one's in the 1990s. See if you can track it down?

Sure. Go down to the armory first and—

Look—no bloodbaths this time. You solve one problem and start ten more.

Couldn't be helped. It's no tea party, twentieth century America.

Just use good judgment. That Ransom guy...

Manson. Right. That was a mistake.

3. A WAY YOU'LL NEVER BE

You can't cheat an honest man, as Sylvester Castlemaine well knew, but then again, it never hurts to find out just how honest a man is. John Baird refused his scheme, with good humor at first, but when Castle persisted, his refusal took on a sarcastic edge, maybe a tinge of outrage. He backed off and changed the subject, talking for a half hour about commercial fishing around Key West, and then said he had to run. He slipped his business card into John's shirt pocket on the way out. (Sylvester Castlemaine, Consultant, it claimed.)

John left the place soon, walking slowly through the afternoon heat. He was glad he hadn't brought the bicycle; it was pleasant to walk in the shade of the big aromatic trees, a slight breeze on his face from the Gulf side.

One could do it. One could. The problem divided itself into three parts: writing the novel fragment, forging the manuscript, and devising a suitable story about how one had uncovered the manuscript.

The writing part would be the hardest. Hemingway is easy

enough to parody—one-fourth of the take-home final he
gave in English 733 was to write a page of Hemingway pastiche, and some of his graduate students did a credible job—
but parody was exactly what one would not want to do.

It had been a crucial period in Hemingway's development,
those three years of apprenticeship the lost manuscripts rep-
resented. Two stories survived, and they were maddeningly
dissimilar. "My Old Man," which had slipped down behind a
drawer, was itself a pastiche, reading like pretty good Sher-
wood Anderson, but with an O. Henry twist at the end—very
unlike the bleak understated quality that would distinguish
the stories that were to make Hemingway's reputation. The
other, "Up in Michigan," had been out in the mail at the
time of the loss. It was a lot closer to Hemingway's ultimate
style, a spare and, by the standards of the time, pornographic
description of a woman's first sexual experience.

John riffled through the notes on the yellow pad, a talis-
manic gesture, since he could have remembered any page
with little effort. But the sight of the words and the feel of
the paper sometimes helped him think.

One would not do it, of course. Except perhaps as a mental
exercise. Not to show to anybody. Certainly not to profit
from.

You wouldn't want to use "My Old Man" as the model,
certainly; no one would care to publish a pastiche of a pastiche of Anderson, now undeservedly obscure. So "Up in
Michigan." And the first story he wrote after the loss, "Out
of Season," would also be handy. That had a lot of the Hemingway strength.

You wouldn't want to tackle the novel fragment, of course,
not just as an exercise, over a hundred pages....

Without thinking about it, John dropped into a familiar
fugue state as he walked through the run-down neighborhood, his freak memory taking over while his body ambled
along on autopilot. This is the way he usually remembered
pages. He transported himself back to the Hemingway collection at the JFK Library in Boston, last November, snow
swirling outside the big picture windows overlooking the

harbor, the room so cold he was wearing coat and gloves and could see his breath. They didn't normally let you wear a coat up there, afraid you might squirrel away a page out of the manuscript collection, but they had to make an exception because the heat pump was down.

He was flipping through the much-thumbed Xerox of Carlos Baker's interview with Hadley, page 52: "Stolen suitcase," Baker asked; "lost novel?"

The typescript of her reply appeared in front of him, more clear than the cracked sidewalk his feet negotiated: "This novel was a knockout, about Nick, up north in Michigan—hunting, fishing, all sorts of experiences—stuff on the order of 'Big Two-Hearted River,' with more action. Girl experiences well done, too." With an enigmatic addition, evidently in Hadley's handwriting, "Girl experiences too well done."

That was interesting. John hadn't thought about that, since he'd been concentrating on the short stories. Too well done? There had been a lot of talk in the eighties about Hemingway's sexual ambiguity—*gender* ambiguity, actually—could Hadley have been upset, sixty years after the fact, remembering some confidence that Hemingway had revealed to the world in that novel; something girls knew that boys were not supposed to know? Playful pillow talk that was filed away for eventual literary exploitation?

He used his life that way. A good writer remembered everything and then forgot it when he sat down to write, and reinvented it so the writing would be more real than the memory. Experience was important, but imagination was more important.

Maybe I would be a better writer, John thought, if I could learn how to forget. For about the tenth time today, like any day, he regretted not having tried to succeed as a writer, while he still had the independent income. Teaching and research had fascinated him when he was younger, a rich boy's all-consuming hobbies, but the end of this fiscal year would be the end of the monthly checks from the trust fund. So the salary from Boston University wouldn't be mad money any more, but rent and groceries in a city suddenly expensive.

Yes, the writing would be the hard part. Then forging the manuscript, that wouldn't be easy. Any scholar would have access to copies of thousands of pages that Hemingway typed before and after the loss. Could one find the typewriter Hemingway had used? Then duplicate his idiosyncratic typing style—a moment's reflection put a sample in front of him, spaces before and after periods and commas....

He snapped out of the reverie as his right foot hit the first step on the back staircase up to their rented flat. He automatically stepped over the fifth step, the rotted one, and was thinking about a nice tall glass of iced tea as he opened the screen door.

"Scorpions!" his wife screamed, two feet from his face.

"What?"

"We have scorpions!" Lena grabbed his arm and hauled him to the kitchen.

"Look!" She pointed at the opaque plastic skylight. Three scorpions, each about six inches long, cast sharp silhouettes on the milky plastic. One was moving.

"My word."

"Your *word!*" She struck a familiar pose, hands on hips, and glared up at the creatures. "What are we going to do about it?"

"We could name them."

"John."

"I don't know." He opened the refrigerator. "Call the bug man."

"The bug man was just here yesterday. He probably flushed them out."

He poured a glass of cold tea and dumped two envelopes of artificial sweetener into it. "I'll talk to Julio about it. But you know they've been there all along. They're not bothering anybody."

"They're bothering the hell out of me!"

He smiled. "Okay. I'll talk to Julio." He looked into the oven. "Thought about dinner?"

"Anything you want to cook, sweetheart. I'll be damned if I'm going to stand there with three ... poisonous ... arthropods staring down at me."

"Poised to jump," John said, and looked up again. There were only two visible now, which made his skin crawl.

"Julio wasn't home when I first saw them. About an hour ago."

"I'll go check." John went downstairs and Julio, the landlord, was indeed home, but was not impressed by the problem. He agreed that it was probably the bug man, and they would probably go back to where they came from in a while, and gave John a flyswatter.

John left the flyswatter with Lena, admonishing her to take no prisoners, and walked a couple of blocks to a Chinese restaurant. He brought back a few boxes of takeout, and they sat in the living room and wielded chopsticks in silence, listening for the pitter-patter of tiny feet.

"Met a real live con man today." He put the business card on the coffee table between them.

"Consultant?" she read.

"He had a loony scheme about counterfeiting the missing stories." Lena knew more about the missing stories than ninety-eight percent of the people who Hemingway'ed for a living. John liked to think out loud.

"Ah, the stories," she said, preparing herself.

"Not a bad idea, actually, if one had a larcenous nature." He concentrated for a moment on the slippery Moo Goo Gai Pan. "Be millions of bucks in it."

He was bent over the box. She stared hard at his bald spot. "What exactly did he have in mind?"

"We didn't bother to think it through in any detail, actually. You go and find ..." He got the slightly walleyed look that she knew meant he was reading a page of a book a thousand miles away. "Yes. A 1921 Corona portable, like the one Hadley gave him before they were married. Find some old paper. Type up the stories. Take them to Sotheby's. Spend money for the rest of your life. That's all there is to it."

"You left out jail."

"A mere detail. Also the writing of the stories. That could take weeks. Maybe you could get arrested first, write the stories in jail, and then sell them when you got out."

"You're weird, John."

"Well. I didn't give him any encouragement."

"Maybe you should've. A few million would come in handy next year."

"We'll get by."

" 'We'll get by.' You keep saying that. How do you know? You've never had to 'get by.' "

"Okay, then. We won't get by." He scraped up the last of the fried rice. "We won't be able to make the rent and they'll throw us out on the street. We'll live in a cardboard box over a heating grate. You'll have to sell your body to keep me in cheap wine. But we'll be happy, dear." He looked up at her, mooning. "Poor but happy."

"Slap-happy." She looked at the card again. "How do you know he's a con man?"

"I don't know. Salesman type. Says he's in commercial fishing now, but he doesn't seem to like it much."

"He didn't say anything about any, you know, criminal stuff he'd done in the past?"

"Huh uh. I just got the impression that he didn't waste a lot of time mulling over ethics and morals." John held up the Mont Blanc pen. "He was staring at this, before he came over and introduced himself. I think he smelled money."

Lena stuck both chopsticks into the half-finished carton of boiled rice and set it down decisively. "Let's ask him over."

"He's a sleaze, Lena. You wouldn't like him."

"I've never met a real con man. It would be fun."

He looked into the darkened kitchen. "Will you cook something?"

She followed his gaze, expecting monsters. "If you stand guard."

4. ROMANCE IS DEAD
SUBTITLE
THE HELL IT IS

"Be a job an' a half," Castle said, mopping up residual spaghetti sauce with a piece of garlic bread. "It's not like your Howard Hughes guy, or Hitler's notebooks."

"You've been doing some research." John's voice was a little slurred. He'd bought a half gallon of Portuguese wine, the bottle wrapped in straw like cheap Chianti, the wine not quite that good. If you could get past the first couple of glasses, it was okay. It had been okay to John for some time now.

"Yeah, down to the library. The guys who did the Hitler notebooks, hell, nobody'd ever seen a real Hitler notebook; they just studied his handwriting in letters and such, then read up on what he did day after day. Same with the Howard Hughes, but that was even easier, because most of the time nobody knew what the hell Howard Hughes was doing anyhow. Just stayed locked up in that room."

"The Hughes forgery nearly worked, as I recall," John said. "If Hughes himself hadn't broken silence . . ."

"Ya gotta know that took balls. 'Scuse me, Lena." She waved a hand and laughed. "Try to get away with that while Hughes was still alive."

"How did the Hitler people screw up?" she asked.

"Funny thing about that one was how many people they fooled. Afterwards everybody said it was a really lousy fake. But you can bet that before the newspapers bid millions of dollars on it, they showed it to the best Hitlerologists they could find, and they all said it was real."

"Because they wanted it to be real," Lena said.

"Yeah. But one of the pages had some chemical in it that

wouldn't be in paper before 1945. That was kinda dumb."

"People would want the Hemingway stories to be real," Lena said quietly, to John.

John's gaze stayed fixed on the center of the table, where a few strands of spaghetti lay cold and drying in a plastic bowl. "Wouldn't be honest."

"That's for sure," Castle said cheerily. "But it ain't exactly armed robbery, either."

"A gross misuse of intellectual . . . intellectual . . ."

"It's past your bedtime, John," Lena said. "We'll clean up." John nodded and pushed himself away from the table and walked heavily into the bedroom.

Lena didn't say anything until she heard the bedsprings creak. "He isn't always like this," she said quietly.

"Yeah. He don't act like no alky."

"It's been a hard year for him." She refilled her glass. "Me, too. Money."

"That's bad."

"Well, we knew it was coming. He tell you about the inheritance?" Castle leaned forward. "Huh uh."

"He was born pretty well off. Family had textile mills up in New Hampshire. John's grandparents died in an auto accident in the forties and the family sold off the mills—good timing, too. They wouldn't be worth much today.

"Then John's father and mother died in the sixties, while he was in college. The executors set up a trust fund that looked like it would keep him in pretty good shape forever. But he wasn't interested in money. He even joined the army, to see what it was like."

"Jesus."

"Afterwards, he carried a picket sign and marched against the war—you know, Vietnam.

"Then he finished his Ph.D. and started teaching. The trust fund must have been fifty times as much as his salary, when he started out. It was still ten times as much, a couple of years ago."

"Boy . . . howdy." Castle was doing mental arithmetic and

algebra with variables like Porsches and fast boats.

"But he let his sisters take care of it. He let them reinvest the capital."

"They weren't too swift?"

"They were idiots! They took good solid blue-chip stocks and tax-free municipals, too 'boring' for them, and threw it all away gambling on commodities." She grimaced. "*Pork* bellies? I finally had John go to Chicago and come back with what was left of his money. There wasn't much."

"You ain't broke, though."

"Damned near. There's enough income to pay for insurance and eventually we'll be able to draw on an IRA. But the cash payments stop in two months. We'll have to live on John's salary. I suppose I'll get a job, too."

"What you ought to get is a typewriter."

Lena laughed and slouched back in her chair. "That would be something."

"You think he could do it? I mean if he would, do you think he could?"

"He's a good writer." She looked thoughtful. "He's had some stories published, you know, in the literary magazines. The ones that pay four or five free copies."

"Big deal."

She shrugged. "Pays off in the long run. Tenure. But I don't know whether being able to write a good literary story means that John could write a good Hemingway imitation."

"He knows enough, right?"

"Maybe he knows too much. He might be paralyzed by his own standards." She shook her head. "In some ways he's an absolute nut about Hemingway. Obsessed, I mean. It's not good for him."

"Maybe writing this stuff would get it out of his system."

She smiled at him. "You've got more angles than a protractor."

"Sorry; I didn't mean to—"

"No." She raised both hands. "Don't be sorry; I like it. I

like you, Castle. John's a good man, but sometimes he's too good."

He poured them both more wine. "Nobody ever accused me of that."

"I suspect not." She paused. "Have you ever been in trouble with the police? Just curious."

"Why?"

"Just curious."

He laughed. "Nickel-and-dime stuff, when I was a kid. You know, jus' to see what you can get away with." He turned serious. "Then I pulled two months' hard time for somethin' I didn't do. Wasn't even in town when it happened."

"What was it?"

"Armed robbery. Then the guy came back an' hit the same goddamned store! I mean, he was one sharp cookie. He confessed to the first one and they let me go."

"Why did they accuse you in the first place?"

"Used to think it was somebody had it in for me. Like the clerk who fingered me." He took a sip of wine. "But hell. It was just dumb luck. And dumb cops. The guy was about my height, same color hair, we both lived in the neighborhood. Cops didn't want to waste a lot of time on it. Jus' chuck me in jail."

"So you do have a police record?"

"Huh uh. Girl from the ACLU made sure they wiped it clean. She wanted me to go after 'em for what? False arrest an' wrongful imprisonment. I just wanted to get out of town."

"It wasn't here?"

"Nah. Dayton, Ohio. Been here eight, nine years."

"That's good."

"Why the third degree?"

She leaned forward and patted the back of his hand. "Call it a job interview, Castle. I have a feeling we may be working together."

"Okay." He gave her a slow smile. "Anything else you want to know?"

5. THE DOCTOR AND THE DOCTOR'S WIFE

John trudged into the kitchen the next morning, ignored the coffeepot, and pulled a green bottle of beer out of the fridge. He looked up at the skylight. Four scorpions, none of them moving. Have to call the bug man today.

Red wine hangover, the worst kind. He was too old for this. Cheap red wine hangover. He eased himself into a soft chair and carefully poured the beer down the side of the glass. Not too much noise, please.

When you drink too much, you ought to take a couple of aspirin, and some vitamins, and all the water you can hold, before retiring. If you drink too much, of course, you don't remember to do that.

The shower turned off with a bass clunk of plumbing. John winced and took a long drink, which helped a little. When he heard the bathroom door open he called for Lena to bring the aspirin when she came out.

After a few minutes she brought it out and handed it to him. "And how is Dr. Baird today?"

"Dr. Baird needs a doctor. Or an undertaker." He shook out two aspirin and washed them down with the last of the beer. "Like your outfit."

She was wearing only a towel around her head. She simpered and struck a dancer's pose and spun daintily around. "Think it'll catch on?"

"Oh my yes." At thirty-five, she still had the trim model's figure that had caught his eye in the classroom, fifteen years before. A safe, light tan was uniform all over her body, thanks to liberal sunblock and the private sunbathing area on top of the house—private except for the helicopter that came low overhead every weekday at 1:15. She always tried to be there in time to wave at it. The pilot had such white teeth. She wondered how many sunbathers were on his route.

She undid the towel and rubbed her long blond hair vigorously. "Thought I'd cool off for a few minutes before I got dressed. Too much wine, eh?"

"Couldn't you tell from my sparkling repartee last night?" He leaned back, eyes closed, and rolled the cool glass back and forth on his forehead.

"Want another beer?"

"Yeah. Coffee'd be smarter, though."

"It's been sitting all night."

"Pay for my sins." He watched her swivel lightly into the kitchen and, more than ever before, felt the difference in their ages. Seventeen years; he was half again as old as she. A young man would say the hell with the hangover, go grab that luscious thing and carry her back to bed. The organ that responded to this meditation was his stomach, though, and it responded very audibly.

"Some toast, too. Or do you want something fancier?"

"Toast would be fine." Why was she being so nice? Usually if he drank too much, he reaped the whirlwind in the morning.

"Ugh." She saw the scorpions. "Five of them now."

"I wonder how many it will hold before it comes crashing down. Scorpions everywhere, stunned. Then angry."

"I'm sure the bug man knows how to get rid of them."

"In Africa they claimed that if you light a ring of fire around them with gasoline or lighter fluid, they go crazy, run amok, stinging themselves to death in their frenzies. Maybe the bug man could do that."

"Castle and I came up with a plan last night. It's kinda screwy, but it might just work."

"Read that in a book called *Jungle Ways*. I was eight years old and believed every word of it."

"We figured out a way that it would be legal. Are you listening?"

"Uh huh. Let me have real sugar and some milk."

She poured some milk in a cup and put it in the microwave to warm. "Maybe we should talk about it later."

"Oh no. Hemingway forgery. You figured out a way to make it legal. Go ahead. I'm all ears."

"See, you tell the publisher first off what it is, that you wrote it and then had it typed up to look authentic."

"Sure, be a big market for that."

"In fact, there could be. You'd have to generate it, but it could happen." The toast sprang up and she brought it and two cups of coffee into the living room on a tray. "See, the bogus manuscript is only one part of a book."

"I don't get it." He tore the toast into strips, to dunk in the strong Cuban coffee.

"The rest of the book is in the nature of an exegesis of your own text."

"If that con man knows what exegesis is, then I can crack a safe."

"That part's my idea. You're really writing a book *about* Hemingway. You use your own text to illustrate various points—'I wrote it this way instead of that way because. . . .' "

"It would be different," he conceded. "Perhaps the second most egotistical piece of Hemingway scholarship in history. A dubious distinction."

"You could write it tongue-in-cheek, though. It could be really amusing, as well as scholarly."

"God, we'd have to get an unlisted number, publishers calling us night and day. Movie producers. Might sell ten copies, if I bought nine."

"You really aren't getting it, John. You don't have a particle of larceny in your heart."

He put a hand on his heart and looked down. "Ventricles, auricles. My undying love for you, a little heartburn. No particles."

"See, you tell the publisher the truth . . . but the publisher doesn't have to tell the truth. Not until publication day."

"Okay. I still don't get it."

She took a delicate nibble of toast. "It goes like this. They print the bogus Hemingway up into a few copies of bogus bound galleys. Top secret."

"My exegesis carefully left off."

"That's the ticket. They send it out to a few selected scholars, along with Xeroxes of a few sample manuscript pages.

All they say, in effect, is 'Does this seem authentic to you? Please keep it under your hat, for obvious reasons.' Then they sit back and collect blurbs."

"I can see the kind of blurbs they'd get from Scott or Mike or Jack, for instance. Some variation of 'What kind of idiot do you think I am?' "

"Those aren't the kind of people you send it to, dope! You send it to people who think they're experts, but aren't. Castle says this is how the Hitler thing almost worked—they knew better than to show it to historians in general. They showed it to a few people and didn't quote the ones who thought it was a fake. Surely you can come up with a list of people who would be easy to fool."

"Any scholar could. Be a different list for each one; I'd be on some of them."

"So they bring it out on April Fool's Day. You get the front page of the *New York Times Book Review*. *Publishers Weekly* does a story. Everybody wants to be in on the joke. Best-seller list, here we come."

"Yeah, sure, but you haven't thought it through." He leaned back, balancing the coffee cup on his slight potbelly. "What about the guys who give us the blurbs, those second-rate scholars? They're going to look pretty bad."

"We did think of that. No way they could sue, not if the letter accompanying the galleys is carefully written. It doesn't have to say—"

"I don't mean getting sued. I mean I don't want to be responsible for hurting other people's careers—maybe wrecking a career, if the person was too extravagant in his endorsement, and had people looking for things to use against him. You know departmental politics. People go down the chute for less serious crimes than making an ass of yourself and your institution in print."

She put her cup down with a clatter. "You're always thinking about other people. Why don't you think about yourself for a change?" She was on the verge of tears. "Think about *us*."

"All right, let's do that. What do you think would happen to my career at BU if I pissed off the wrong people with this exercise? How long do you think it would take me to make full professor? Do you think BU would make a full professor out of a man who uses his specialty to pull vicious practical jokes?"

"Just do me the favor of thinking about it. Cool down and weigh the pluses and minuses. If you did it with the right touch, your department would love it—and God, Harry wants to get rid of the chairmanship so bad he'd give it to an axe murderer. You know you'll make full professor about thirty seconds before Harry hands you the keys to the office and runs."

"True enough." He finished the coffee and stood up in a slow creak. "I'll give it some thought. Horizontally." He turned toward the bedroom.

"Want some company?"

He looked at her for a moment. "Indeed I do."

6. IN OUR TIME

Back already?

Need to find a meta-causal. One guy seems to be generating the danger flag in various timelines. John Baird, who's a scholar in some of them, a soldier in some, and a rich playboy in a few. He's always a Hemingway nut, though. He does something that starts off the ripples in '95,'96,'97; depending on which time line you're in—but I can't seem to get close to it. There's something odd about him, and it doesn't have to do with Hemingway specifically.

But he's definitely causing the eddy?

Has to be him.

All right. Find a meta-causal that all the doom lines have in common, and forget about the others. Then go talk to him.

There'll be resonance—

But who cares? Moot after A.D. 2006.

That's true. I'll hit all the doom lines at once, then: neutralize the meta-causal, then jump ahead and do some spot checks.

Good. And no killing this time.

I understand. But—

You're too close to 2006. Kill the wrong person, and the whole thing could unravel.

Well, there are differences of opinion. We would certainly feel it if the world failed to come to an end in those lines.

As you say, differences of opinion. My opinion is that you better not kill anybody or I'll send you back to patrol the fourteenth century again.

Understood. But I can't guarantee that I can neutralize the meta-causal without eliminating John Baird.

Fourteenth century. Some people love it. Others think it was nasty, brutish, and long.

7. A Clean, Well-Lighted Place

Most of the sleuthing that makes up literary scholarship takes place in settings either neutral or unpleasant. Libraries' old stacks, attics metaphorical and actual; dust and silverfish, yellowed paper and fading ink. Books and letters that appear in card files but not on shelves.

Hemingway researchers have a haven outside of Boston, the Hemingway Collection at the University of Massachusetts's John F. Kennedy Library. It's a triangular room with one wall dominated by a picture window that looks over Boston Harbor to the sea. Comfortable easy chairs surround a coffee table, but John had never seen them in use; worktables under the picture window provided realistic room for computer and clutter. Skins from animals the Hemingways had dispatched in Africa snarled up from the floor, and one wall was dominated by Hemingway memorabilia and photographs. What made the room Nirvana, though, was row upon row of boxes containing tens of thousands of Xerox pages of Hemingway correspondence, manuscripts, clippings—everything from a boyhood shopping list to all extant versions of every short story and poem and novel.

John liked to get there early so he could claim one of the three computers. He snapped it on, inserted a CD, and typed in his code number. Then he keyed in the database index and started searching.

The more commonly requested items would appear on screen if you asked for them—whenever someone requested a physical copy of an item, an electronic copy automatically was sent into the database—but most of the things John needed were obscure, and he had to haul down the letter boxes and physically flip through them, just like some poor scholar inhabiting the first nine-tenths of the twentieth century.

Time disappeared for him as he abandoned his notes and followed lines of instinct, leaping from letter to manuscript to note to interview, doing what was in essence the opposite of the scholar's job: a scholar would normally be trying to find out what these stories had been about. John instead was trying to track down every reference that might restrict what he himself could write about, simulating the stories.

The most confining restriction was the one he'd first remembered, walking away from the bar where he'd met Castle. The one-paragraph answer that Hadley had given to Carlos Baker about the unfinished novel; that it was a Nick Adams story about hunting and fishing up in Michigan. John didn't know anything about hunting, and most of his fishing experience was limited to watching a bobber and hoping it wouldn't go down and break his train of thought.

There was the one story that Hemingway had left unpublished, "Boys and Girls Together," mostly clumsy self-parody. It covered the right period and the right activities, but using it as a source would be sensitive business, tiptoeing through a minefield. Anyone looking for a fake would go straight there. Of course John could go up to the Michigan woods and camp out, see things for himself and try to recreate them in the Hemingway style. Later, though. First order of business was to make sure there was nothing in this huge collection that would torpedo the whole project—some postcard where Hemingway said "You're going to like this novel because it has a big scene about cleaning fish."

The short stories would be less restricted in subject matter. According to Hemingway, they'd been about growing up in Oak Park and Michigan and the battlefields of Italy.

That made him stop and think. The one dramatic experience he shared with Hemingway was combat—fifty years later, to be sure, in Vietnam, but the basic situations couldn't have changed that much. Terror, heroism, cowardice. The guns and grenades were a little more streamlined, but they did the same things to people. Maybe do a World War I story as a finger exercise, see whether it would be realistic to try a longer growing-up-in-Michigan pastiche.

He made a note to himself about that on the computer, oblique enough not to be damning, and continued the eye-straining job of searching through Hadley's correspondence, trying to find some further reference to the lost novel—damn!

Writing to Ernest's mother, Hadley noted that "the taxi driver broke his typewriter" on the way to the Constantinople conference—did he get it fixed, or just chuck it? A quick check showed that the typeface of his manuscripts did indeed change after July 1924. So they'd never be able to find it. There were typewriters in Hemingway shrines in Key West, Billings, Schruns; the initial plan had been to find which was the old Corona, then locate an identical one and have Castle arrange a swap.

So they would fall back on Plan B. Castle had claimed to be good with mechanical things, and thought if they could find a 1921 Corona, he could tweak the keys around so they would produce a convincing manuscript—lowercase "s" a hair low, "e" a hair high, and so forth.

How he could be so sure of success without ever having

seen the inside of a manual typewriter, John did not know. Nor did he have much confidence.

But it wouldn't have to be a perfect simulation, since they weren't out to fool the whole world, but just a few reviewers who would only see two or three Xeroxed pages. He could probably do a close enough job. John put it out of his mind and moved on to the next letter.

But it was an odd coincidence for him to think about Castle at that instant, since Castle was thinking about him. Or at least asking.

8. The Coming Man

"How was he when he was younger?"

"He never was younger." She laughed and rolled around inside the compass of his arms to face him. "Than you, I mean. He was in his mid-thirties when we met. You can't be much over twenty-five."

He kissed the end of her nose. "Thirty this year. But I still get carded sometimes."

"I'm a year older than you are. So you have to do anything I say."

"So far so good." He'd checked her wallet when she'd gone into the bathroom to insert the diaphragm, and knew she was thirty-five. "Break out the whips and chains now?"

"Not till next week. Work up to it slowly." She pulled away from him and mopped her front with the sheet. "You're good at being slow."

"I like being asked to come back."

"How 'bout tonight and tomorrow morning?"

"If you feed me lots of vitamins. How long you think he'll be up in Boston?"

"He's got a train ticket for Wednesday. But he said he might stay longer if he got onto something."

Castle laughed. "Or into something. Think he might have a girl up there? Some student like you used to be?"

"That would be funny. I guess it's not impossible." She covered her eyes with the back of her hand. "The wife is always the last to know."

They both laughed. "But I don't think so. He's a sweet guy but he's just not real sexy. I think his students see him as kind of a favorite uncle."

"You fell for him once."

"Uh huh. He had all of his current virtues plus a full head of hair, no potbelly—and, hm, what am I forgetting?"

"He was hung like an elephant?"

"No, I guess it was the millions of dollars. That can be pretty sexy."

9. Wanderings

It was a good thing John liked to nose around obscure neighborhoods shopping; you couldn't walk into any old K mart and pick up a 1921 Corona portable. In fact, you couldn't walk into any typewriter shop in Boston and find one, not any. Nowadays they all sold self-contained word processors, with a few dusty electrics in the back room. A few had fancy manual typewriters from Italy or Switzerland; it had been almost thirty years since the American manufacturers had made a machine that wrote without electronic help.

He had a little better luck with pawnshops. Lots of Smith-Coronas, a few L. C. Smiths, and two actual Coronas that might have been old enough. One had too large a typeface and the other, although the typeface was the same as Hemingway's, was missing a couple of letters: Th quick b own fox jump d ov th lazy dog. The challenge of writing a convincing Hemingway novel without using the letters "e" and "r" seemed daunting. He bought the machine anyhow, thinking they might ultimately have two or several broken ones that could be concatenated into one reliable machine.

The old pawnbroker rang up his purchase and made

change and slammed the cash drawer shut. "Now you don't look to me like the kind of man who would hold it against a man who..." He shrugged. "Well, who sold you something and then suddenly remembered that there was a place with lots of those somethings?"

"Of course not. Business is business."

"I don't know the name of the guy or his shop; I think he calls it a museum. Up in Brunswick, Maine. He's got a thousand old typewriters. He buys, sells, trades. That's the only place I know of you might find one with the missing whatever-you-call-ems."

"Fonts." He put the antique typewriter under his arm—the handle was missing—and shook the old man's hand. "Thanks a lot. This might save me weeks."

With some difficulty John got together packing materials and shipped the machine to Key West, along with Xeroxes of a few dozen pages of Hemingway's typed copy and a note suggesting Castle see what he could do. Then he went to the library and found a Brunswick telephone directory. Under "Office Machines & Supplies" was listed Crazy Tom's Typewriter Museum and Sales Emporium. John rented a car and headed north.

The small town had rolled up its sidewalks by the time he got there. He drove past Crazy Tom's and pulled into the first motel. It had a neon VACANCY sign but the innkeeper had to be roused from a deep sleep. He took John's credit card number and directed him to Room 14 and pointedly turned on the NO sign. There were only two other cars in the motel lot.

John slept late and treated himself to a full "trucker's" breakfast at the local diner: two pork chops and eggs and hash browns. Then he worked off ten calories by walking to the shop.

Crazy Tom was younger than John had expected, thirtyish with an unruly shock of black hair. A manual typewriter lay upside down on an immaculate worktable, but most of the place was definitely maculate. Thousands of peanut shells

littered the floor. Crazy Tom was eating them compulsively
from a large wooden bowl. When he saw John standing in
the doorway, he offered some. "Unsalted," he said. "Good for
you."

John crunched his way over the peanut-shell carpet. The
only light in the place was the bare bulb suspended over the
worktable, though two unlit high-intensity lamps were
clamped on either side of it. The walls were floor-to-ceiling
gloomy shelves holding hundreds of typewriters, mostly
black.

"Let me guess," the man said as John scooped up a hand-
ful of peanuts. "You're here about a typewriter."

"A specific one. A 1921 Corona portable."

"Ah." He closed his eyes in thought. "Hemingway. His first.
Or I guess the first after he started writing. A '27 Corona,
now, that'd be Faulkner."

"You get a lot of calls for them?"

"Couple times a year. People hear about this place and
see if they can find one like the master used, whoever the
master is to them. Sympathetic magic and all that. But you
aren't a writer."

"I've had some stories published."

"Yeah, but you look too comfortable. You do something
else. Teach school." He looked around in the gloom. "Corona
Corona." Then he sang the six syllables to the tune of "Corina, Corina." He walked a few steps into the darkness and
returned with a small machine and set it on the table.
"Newer than 1920 because of the way it says 'Corona' here.
Older than 1927 because of the tab setup." He found a
piece of paper and a chair. "Go on, try it."

John typed out a few quick foxes and aids to one's party.
The typeface was identical to the one on the machine Hadley
had given Hemingway before they'd been married. The up-
and-down displacements of the letters were different, of
course, but Castle should be able to fix that once he'd practiced with the backup machine.

John cracked a peanut. "How much?"

"What you need it for?"

"Why is that important?"

"It's the only one I got. Rather rent it than sell it." He didn't look like he was lying, trying to push the price up. "A thousand to buy, a hundred a month to rent."

"Tell you what, then. I buy it, and if it doesn't bring me luck, you agree to buy it back at a pro ratum. My one thousand dollars minus ten percent per month."

Crazy Tom stuck out his hand. "Let's have a beer on it."

"Isn't it a little early for that?"

"Not if you eat peanuts all morning." He took two long-necked Budweisers from a cooler and set them on paper towels on the table. "So what kind of stuff you write?"

"Short stories and some poetry." The beer was good after the heavy greasy breakfast. "Nothing you would've seen unless you read magazines like *Iowa Review* and *Triquarterly*."

"Oh yeah. Foldouts of Gertrude Stein and H.D. I might've read your stuff."

"John Baird."

He shook his head. "Maybe. I'm no good with names."

"If you recognized my name from *The Iowa Review* you'd be the first person who ever had."

"I was right about the Hemingway connection?"

"Of course."

"But you don't write like Hemingway for no *Iowa Review*. Short declarative sentences, truly this truly that."

"No, you were right about the teaching, too. I teach Hemingway up at Boston University."

"So that's why the typewriter? Play show-and-tell with your students?"

"That, too. Mainly I want to write some on it and see how it feels."

From the back of the shop, a third person listened to the conversation with great interest. He, it, wasn't really a "person," though he could look like one: he had never been born and he would never die. But then he didn't really exist, not

in the down-home pinch-yourself-ouch! way that you and I
do.

In another way, he did *more* than exist, since he could slip
back and forth between places you and I don't even have
words for.

He was carrying a wand that could be calibrated for heart
attack, stroke, or metastasized cancer on one end; the other
end induced a kind of aphasia. He couldn't use it unless he
materialized. He walked toward the two men, making no
crunching sounds on the peanut shells because he weighed
less than a thought. He studied John Baird's face from about
a foot away.

"I guess it's a mystical thing, though I'm uncomfortable
with that word. See whether I can get into his frame of
mind."

"Funny thing," Crazy Tom said; "I never thought of him
typing out his stories. He was always sitting in some café
writing in notebooks, piling up saucers."

"You've read a lot about him?" That would be another
reason not to try the forgery. This guy comes out of the
woodwork and says "I sold John Baird a 1921 Corona portable."

"Hell, all I do is read. If I get two customers a day, one of
'em's a mistake and the other just wants directions. I've read
all of Hemingway's fiction and most of the journalism and I
think all of the poetry. Not just the *Querschnitt* period; the
more interesting stuff."

The invisible man was puzzled. Quite obviously John Baird
planned some sort of Hemingway forgery. But then he
should be growing worried over this man's dangerous expertise. Instead, he was radiating relief.

What course of action, inaction? He could go back a few
hours in time and steal this typewriter, though he would
have to materialize for that, and it would cause suspicions.
And Baird could find another. He could kill one or both of
them, now or last week or next, but that would mean duty
in the fourteenth century for more than forever—when you

exist out of time, a century of unpleasantness is long enough for planets to form and die.

He wouldn't have been drawn to this meeting if it were not a strong causal nexus. There must be earlier ones, since John Baird did not just stroll down a back street in this little town and decide to change history by buying a typewriter. But the earlier ones must be too weak, or something was masking them.

Maybe it was a good timeplace to get John Baird alone and explain things to him. Then use the wand on him. But no, not until he knew exactly what he was preventing. With considerable effort of will and expenditure of something like energy, he froze time at this instant and traveled to a couple of hundred adjacent realities that were all in this same bundle of doomed timelines.

In most of them, Baird was here in Crazy Tom's Typewriter Museum and Sales Emporium. In some, he was in a similar place in New York. In two, he was back in the Hemingway collection. In one, John Baird didn't exist: the whole planet was a lifeless blasted cinder. He'd known about that timeline; it had been sort of a dry run.

"He did both," John then said in most of the timelines: "Sometimes typing, sometimes fountain pen or pencil. I've seen the rough draft of his first novel. Written out in a stack of seven French schoolkids' copybooks." He looked around, memory working. A red herring wouldn't hurt. He'd never come across a reference to any other specific Hemingway typewriter, but maybe this guy had. "You know what kind of machine he used in Key West or Havana?"

Crazy Tom pulled on his chin. "Nope. Bring me a sample of the typing and I might be able to pin it down, though. And I'll keep an eye out—got a card?"

John took out a business card and his checkbook. "Take a check on a Boston bank?"

"Sure. I'd take one on a Tierra del Fuego bank. Who'd stiff you on a seventy-year-old typewriter?" Sylvester Castlemaine might, John thought. "I've had this business almost twenty years," Tom continued. "Not a single bounced check or bent plastic."

"Yeah," John said. "Why would a crook want an old typewriter?" The invisible man laughed and went away.

10. BANAL STORY

Dear Lena & Castle,

Typing this on the new/old machine to give you an idea about what has to be modified to mimic EH's:

abcdefghijklmnopqrstuvwxyz
ABCDEFGHIJKLMNOPQRSTUVWXYZ234567890,./ "#$%_&'()*?

Other mechanical things to think about—

1. Paper—One thing that made people suspicious about the Hitler forgery is that experts know that old paper <u>smells</u> old. And of course there was that fatal chemical-composition error that clinched it.

As we discussed, my first thought was that one of us would have to go to Paris and nose around in old attics and so forth, trying to find either a stack of 75-year-old paper or an old blank book we could cut pages out of. But in the JFK Library collection I found out that EH actually did bring some American-made paper along with him. A lot of the rough draft of <u>in our time</u>—written in Paris a year or two after our ''discovery''—was typed on the back of 6 × 7" stationery from his parents' vacation place in Windemere, Xerox enclosed. It should be pretty easy to duplicate on a hand press, and of course it will be a lot easier to find 75-year-old American paper. One complication, unfortunately, is that I haven't really seen the paper; only a Xerox of the pages. Have to come up with some pretext to either visit the vault or have a page brought up, so I can check the color of the ink, memorize the weight and deckle of the paper, check to see how the edges are cut . . .

I'm starting to sound like a real forger. In for a

penny, though, in for a pound. One of the critics who's
sent the fragment might want to see the actual document,
and compare it with the existing Windemere pages.

2. Inks. This should not be a problem. Here's a recipe
for typewriter ribbon ink from a 1918 book of commercial
formulas:

8 oz. lampblack

4 oz. gum arabic

1 quart methylated spirits

That last one is wood alcohol. The others ought to be
available in Miami if you can't find them on the Rock.

Aging the ink on the paper gets a little tricky. I
haven't been able to find anything about it in the libraries around here; no FORGERY FOR FUN & PROFIT. May
check in New York before coming back.

(If we don't find anything, I'd suggest baking it for a
few days at a temperature low enough not to greatly affect the paper, and then interleaving it with blank
sheets of the old paper and pressing them together for a
few days, to restore the old smell, and further absorb
the residual ink solvents.)

Toyed with the idea of actually allowing the manuscript
to mildew somewhat, but that might get out of hand and
actually destroy some of it—or for all I know we'd be
employing a species of mildew that doesn't speak French.
Again, thinking like a true forger, which may be a waste
of time and effort, but I have to admit is kind of fun.
Playing cops and robbers at my age.

Well, I'll call tonight. Miss you, Lena.

Your partner in crime,

11. A DIVINE GESTURE

When John returned to his place in Boston, there was a message on his answering machine: "John, this is Nelson Van Nuys. Harry told me you were in town. I left something in your box at the office and I strongly suggest you take it before somebody else does. I'll be out of town for a week, but give me a call if you're here next Friday. You can take me and Doris out to dinner at Panache."

Panache was the most expensive restaurant in Cambridge. Interesting. John checked his watch. He hadn't planned to go to the office, but there was plenty of time to swing by on his way to returning the rental car. The train didn't leave for another four hours.

Van Nuys was a fellow Hemingway scholar and sometimes drinking buddy who taught at Brown. What had he brought ninety miles to deliver in person, rather than mail? He was probably just in town and dropped by. But it was worth checking.

No one but the secretary was in the office, noontime, for which John was obscurely relieved. In his box were three interdepartmental memos, a textbook catalog, and a brown cardboard box that sloshed when he picked it up. He took it all back to his office and closed the door.

The office made him feel a little weary, as usual. He wondered whether they would be shuffling people around again this year. The department liked to keep its professors in shape by having them haul tons of books and files up and down the corridor every couple of years.

He glanced at the memos and pitched them, irrelevant since he wasn't teaching in the summer, and put the catalog in his briefcase. Then he carefully opened the cardboard box.

It was a half-pint Jack Daniel's bottle, but it didn't have bourbon in it. A cloudy greenish liquid. John unscrewed the top and with the sharp Pernod tang the memory came back. He and Van Nuys had wasted half an afternoon in Paris years ago, trying to track down a source of true absinthe. So he had finally found some.

Absinthe. Nectar of the gods, ruination of several generations of French artists, students, workingmen—outlawed in 1915 for its addictive and hallucinogenic qualities. Where had Van Nuys found it?

He screwed the top back on tightly and put it back in the box and put the box in his briefcase. If its effect really was all that powerful, you probably wouldn't want to drive under its influence. In Boston traffic, of course, a little lane weaving and a few mild collisions would go unnoticed.

Once he was safely on the train, he'd try a shot or two of it. It couldn't be all that potent. Child of the sixties, John had taken LSD, psilocybin, ecstasy, and peyote, and remembered with complete accuracy the quality of each drug's hallucinations. The effects of absinthe wouldn't be nearly as extreme as its modern successors. But it was probably just as well to try it first in a place where unconsciousness or Steve Allen imitations or speaking in tongues would go unremarked.

He turned in the rental car and took a cab to South Station rather than juggle suitcase, briefcase, and typewriter through the subway system. Once there, he nursed a beer through an hour of the Yankees murdering the Red Sox, and then rented a cart to roll his burden down to track 3, where a smiling porter installed him aboard the *Silver Meteor*, its range newly extended from Boston to Miami.

He had loved the train since his boyhood in Washington. His mother hated flying and so they often clickety-clacked from place to place in the snug comfort of first-class compartments. Eidetic memory blunted his enjoyment of the modern Amtrak version. This compartment was as large as the ones he had read and done puzzles in, forty years before—amazing and delighting his mother with his proficiency in word games—but the smell of good old leather was gone, replaced by plastic, and the fittings that had been polished brass were chromed steel now. On the middle of the red plastic seat was a Hospitality Pak, a plastic box encased in plastic wrap that contained a wedge of indestructible "cheese food," as if cheese had to eat, a small plastic bottle of cheap California wine, a plastic glass to contain it, and an apple, possibly not plastic.

John hung up his coat and tie in the small closet provided beside where the bed would fold down, and for a few minutes he watched with interest as his fellow passengers and their accompaniment hurried or ambled to their cars. Mostly old people, of course. Enough young ones, John hoped, to keep the trains alive a few decades more.

"Mr. Baird?" John turned to face a black porter, who bowed slightly and favored him with a blinding smile of white and gold. "My name is George, and I will be at your service as far as Atlanta. Is everything satisfactory?"

"Doing fine. But if you could find me a glass made of glass and a couple of ice cubes, I might mention you in my will."

"One minute, sir." In fact, it took less than a minute. That was one aspect, John had to admit, that had improved in recent years: The service on Amtrak in the sixties and seventies had been right up there with Alcatraz and the Hanoi Hilton.

He closed and locked the compartment door and carefully poured about two ounces of the absinthe into the glass. Like Pernod, it turned milky on contact with the ice.

He swirled it around and breathed deeply. It did smell much like Pernod, but with an acrid tang that was probably oil of wormwood. An experimental sip: the wormwood didn't dominate the licorice flavor, but it was there.

"Thanks, Nelson," he whispered, and drank the whole thing in one cold fiery gulp. He set down the glass and the train began to move. For a weird moment that seemed hallucinatory, but it always did, the train starting off so smoothly and silently.

For about ten minutes he felt nothing unusual, as the train did its slow tour of Boston's least attractive backyards. The conductor who checked his ticket seemed like a normal human being, which could have been a hallucination.

John knew that some drugs, like amyl nitrite, hit with a swift slap, while others creep into your mind like careful infiltrators. This was the way of absinthe; all he felt was a slight alcohol buzz, and he was about to take another shot, when it subtly began.

There were *things* just at the periphery of his vision, odd things with substance, but somehow without shape, that of course moved away when he turned his head to look at them. At the same time a whispering began in his ears, just audible over the train noise, but not intelligible, as if in a language he had heard before but not understood. For some reason the effects were pleasant, though of course they could be frightening if a person were not expecting weirdness. He enjoyed the illusions for a few minutes, while the scenery outside mellowed into woodsy suburbs, and the visions and voices stopped rather suddenly.

He poured another ounce and this time diluted it with water. He remembered the sad woman in "Hills Like White Elephants" lamenting that everything new tasted like licorice, and allowed himself to wonder what Hemingway had been drinking when he wrote that curious story.

Chuckling at his own—what? Effrontery?—John took out the 1921 Corona and slipped a sheet of paper into it and balanced it on his knees. He had earlier thought of the first two lines of the WWI pastiche; he typed them down and kept going:

```
The dirt on the sides of the trenches was never com-
pletely dry in the morning. If Nick could find an old
newspaper he would put it between his chest and the dirt
when he went out to lean on the side of the trench and
wait for the light. First light was the best time. You
might have luck and see a muzzle flash. But patience was
better than luck. Wait to see a helmet or a head without
a helmet.
    Nick looked at the enemy line through a rectangular box
```

of wood that went through the trench at about ground
level. The other end of the box was covered by a square
of gauze the color of dirt. A person looking directly at
it might see the muzzle flash when Nick fired through the
box. But with luck, the flash would be the last thing he
saw.

Nick had fired through the gauze six times, perhaps
killing three enemy, and the gauze now had a ragged hole
in the center.

Okay, John thought, he'd be able to see slightly better
through the hole in the center but staring that way would
reduce the effective field of view, so he would deliberately
try to look to one side or the other. How to type that down
in a simple way? Someone cleared his throat.

John looked up from the typewriter. Sitting across from
him was Ernest Hemingway, the weathered, wise Hemingway
of the famous Karsh photograph.

"I'm afraid you must not do that," Hemingway said.

John looked at the half-full glass of absinthe and looked
back. Hemingway was still there. "Jesus Christ," he said.

"It isn't the absinthe." Hemingway's image rippled and he
became the handsome teenager who had gone to war, the
war John was writing about. "I am quite real. In a way, I am
more real than you are." As it spoke it aged: the mustachioed
leading-man-handsome Hemingway of the twenties; the
slightly corpulent, still magnetic media hero of the thirties
and forties; the beard turning white, the features hard and
sad and then twisting with impotence and madness, and then
a sudden loud report and the cranial vault exploding, the
mahogany veneer of the wall splashed with blood and brains
and imbedded chips of skull. There was a strong smell of
cordite and blood. The almost-headless corpse shrugged,
spreading its hands. "I can look like anyone I want." The
mess disappeared and it became the young Hemingway
again.

John slumped and stared.

"This thing you just started must never be finished. This Hemingway pastiche. It will ruin something very important."

"What could it ruin? I'm not even planning to—"

"Your plans are immaterial. If you continue with this project, it will profoundly affect the future."

"You're from the future?"

"I'm from the future and the past and other temporalities that you can't comprehend. But all you need to know is that you must not write this Hemingway story. If you do, I or someone like me will have to kill you."

It gestured and a wand the size of a walking stick, half-black and half-white, appeared in its hand. It tapped John's knee with the white end. There was a slight tingle.

"Now you won't be able to tell anybody about me, or write anything about me down. If you try to talk about me, the memory will disappear—and reappear moments later, along with the knowledge that I will kill you if you don't cooperate." It turned into the bloody corpse again. "Understood?"

"Of course."

"If you behave, you will never have to see me again." It started to fade.

"Wait. What do you really look like?"

"This...." For a few seconds John stared at an ebony presence deeper than black, at once points and edges and surfaces and volume and hints of further dimensions. "You can't really see or know," a voice whispered inside his head. He reached into the blackness and jerked his hand back, rimed with frost and numb. The thing disappeared.

He stuck his hand under his armpit and feeling returned. That last apparition was the unsettling one. He had Hemingway's appearance at every age memorized, and had seen the corpse in his mind's eye often enough. A drug could conceivably have brought them all together and made up this fantastic demand—which might actually be nothing more than a reasonable side of his nature trying to make him stop wasting time on this silly project.

But that thing. His hand was back to normal. Maybe a

drug could do that, too; make your hand feel freezing. LSD did more profound things than that. But not while arguing about a manuscript.

He considered the remaining absinthe. Maybe take another big blast of it and see whether ol' Ernie comes back again. Or no—there was a simpler way to check.

The bar was four rocking and rolling cars away, and bouncing his way from wall to window helped sober John up. When he got there, he had another twinge for the memories of the past. Stained Formica tables. No service; you had to go to a bar at the other end. Acrid with cigarette fumes. He remembered linen tablecloths and endless bottles of Coke with the names of cities from everywhere stamped on the bottom and, when his father came along with them, the rich sultry smoke of his Havanas. The fat Churchills from Punch that emphysema stopped just before Castro could. "A Coke, please." He wondered which depressed him more, the red can or the plastic cup with miniature ice cubes.

The test. It was not in his nature to talk to strangers on public conveyances. But this was necessary. There was a man sitting alone who looked about John's age, a Social Security-bound hippy with wire-rimmed John Lennon glasses, white hair down to his shoulders, bushy grey beard. He nodded when John sat down across from him, but didn't say anything. He sipped beer and looked blankly out at the gathering darkness.

"Excuse me," John said, "but I have a strange thing to ask you."

The man looked at him. "I don't mind strange things. But please don't try to sell me anything illegal."

"I wouldn't. It may have something to do with a drug, but it would be one I took."

"You do look odd. You tripping?"

"Doesn't feel like it. But I may have been ... slipped something." He leaned back and rubbed his eyes. "I just talked to Ernest Hemingway."

"The writer?"

"In my roomette, yeah."

"Wow. He must be pretty old."

"He's dead! More than thirty years."

"Oh wow. Now that is something weird. What he say?"

"You know what a pastiche is?"

"French pastry?"

"No, it's when you copy . . . when you create an imitation of another person's writing. Hemingway's, in this case."

"Is that legal? I mean, with him dead and all."

"Sure it is, as long as you don't try to foist it off as Hemingway's real stuff."

"So what happened? He wanted to help you with it?"

"Actually, no . . . he said I'd better stop."

"Then you better stop. You don't fuck around with ghosts." He pointed at the old brass bracelet on John's wrist. "You in the 'Nam."

"Sixty-eight," John said. "Hue."

"Then you oughta know about ghosts. You don't fuck with ghosts."

"Yeah." What he'd thought was aloofness in the man's eyes, the set of his mouth, was aloneness, something slightly different. "You okay?"

"Oh yeah. Wasn't for a while, then I got my shit together." He looked out the window again, and said something weirdly like Hemingway: "I learned to take it a day at a time. The day you're in's the only day that's real. The past is shit and the future, hell, some day your future's gonna be that you got no future. So fuck it, you know? One day at a time."

John nodded. "What outfit were you in?"

"Like I say, man, the past is shit. No offense?"

"No, that's okay." He poured the rest of his Coke over the ice and stood up to go.

"You better talk to somebody about those ghosts. Some kinda shrink, you know? It's not that they're not real. But just you got to deal with 'em."

"Thanks. I will." John got a little more ice from the barman and negotiated his way down the lurching corridor back to

his compartment, trying not to spill his drink while also jug-
gling fantasy, reality, past, present, memory. . . .

He opened the door and Hemingway was there, drinking
his absinthe. He looked up with weary malice. "Am I going
to have to kill you?"

What John did next would have surprised Castlemaine,
who thought he was a nebbish. He closed the compartment
door and sat down across from the apparition. "Maybe you
can kill me and maybe you can't."

"Don't worry. I can."

"You said I wouldn't be able to talk to anyone about you.
But I just walked down to the bar car and did."

"I know. That's why I came back."

"So if one of your powers doesn't work, maybe another
doesn't. At any rate, if you kill me, you'll never find out what
went wrong."

"That's very cute, but it doesn't work." It finished off the
absinthe and then ran a finger around the rim of the glass,
which refilled out of nowhere.

"You're making assumptions about causality that are necessarily naïve, because you can't perceive even half of the
dimensions that you inhabit."

"Nevertheless, you haven't killed me yet."

"And assumptions about my 'psychology' that are absurd.
I am no more a human being than you are a paramecium."

"I'll accept that. But I would make a deal with a paramecium if I thought I could gain an advantage from it."

"What could you possibly have to deal with, though?"

"I know something about myself that you evidently don't,
that enables me to overcome your don't-talk restriction.
Knowing that might be worth a great deal to you."

"Maybe something."

"What I would like in exchange is, of course, my life, and
an explanation of why I must not do the Hemingway pastiche. Then I wouldn't do it."

"You wouldn't do it if I killed you, either."

John sipped his Coke and waited.

"All right. It goes something like this. There is not just one universe, but actually uncountable zillions of them. They're all roughly the same size and complexity as this one, and they're all going off in a zillion different directions, and it is one hell of a job to keep things straight."

"You do this by yourself? You're God?"

"There's not just one of me. In fact, it would be meaningless to assign a number to us, but I guess you could say that altogether, we are God ... and the Devil, and the Cosmic Puppet Master, and the Grand Unification Theory, the Great Pumpkin and everything else. When we consider ourselves as a group, let me see, I guess a human translation of our name would be the Spatio-Temporal Adjustment Board."

"STAB?"

"I guess that is unfortunate. Anyhow, what STAB does is more the work of a scalpel than a knife." The Hemingway scratched its nose, leaving the absinthe suspended in midair. "Events are supposed to happen in certain ways, in certain sequences. You look at things happening and say cause and effect, or coincidence, or golly, that couldn't have happened in a million years—but you don't even have a clue. Don't even try to think about it. It's like an ant trying to figure out General Relativity."

"It wouldn't have a clue. Wouldn't know where to start."

The apparition gave him a sharp look and continued. "These universes come in bundles. Hundreds of them, thousands, that are pretty much the same. And they affect each other. Resonate with each other. When something goes wrong in one, it resonates and screws up all of them."

"You mean to say that if I write a Hemingway pastiche, hundreds of universes are going to go straight to hell?"

The apparition spread its hands and looked to the ceiling. "Nothing is simple. The only thing that's simple is that nothing is simple.

"I'm a sort of literature specialist. American literature of the nineteenth and twentieth centuries. Usually. Most of my timespace is taken up with guys like Hemingway, Teddy Roosevelt, Heinlein, Bierce. Crane, Spillane, Twain."

"Not William Dean Howells?"

"Not him or James or Carver or Coover or Cheever or any of those guys. If everybody gave me as little trouble as William Dean Howells, I could spend most of my timespace on a planet where the fishing was good."

"Masculine writers?" John said. "But not all hairy-chested macho types."

"I'll give you an A— on that one. They're writers who have an accumulating effect on the masculine side of the American national character. There's no one word for it, though it is a specific thing: individualistic, competence-worshiping, short-term optimism and long-term existentialism. 'There may be nothing after I die but I sure as hell will do the job right while I'm here, even though I'm surrounded by idiots.' You see the pattern?"

"Okay. And I see how Hemingway fits in. But how could writing a pastiche interfere with it?"

"That's a limitation I have. I don't know specifically. I do know that the accelerating revival of interest in Hemingway from the seventies through the nineties is vitally important. In the Soviet Union as well as the United States. For some reason, I can feel your pastiche interfering with it." He stretched out the absinthe glass into a yard-long amber crystal, and it changed into the black-and-white cane. The glass reappeared in the drink holder by the window. "Your turn."

"You won't kill me after you hear what I have to say?"

"No. Go ahead."

"Well . . . I have an absolutely eidetic memory. Everything I've ever seen—or smelled or tasted or heard or touched, or even dreamed—I can instantly recall.

"Every other memory freak I've read about was limited—numbers, dates, calendar tricks, historical details—and most of them were *idiots savants*. I have at least normal intelligence. But from the age of about three, I have never forgotten anything."

The Hemingway smiled congenially. "Thank you. That's exactly it." It fingered the black end of the cane, clicking something. "If you had the choice, would you rather die of a heart attack, stroke, or cancer?"

"That's it?" The Hemingway nodded. "Well, you're human enough to cheat. To lie."

"It's not something you could understand. Stroke?"

"It might not work."

"We're going to find out right now." He lowered the cane.

"Wait! What's death? Is there ... anything I should do, anything you know?"

The rod stopped, poised an inch over John's knee. "I guess you just end. Is that so bad?"

"Compared to not ending, it's bad."

"That shows how little you know. I and the ones like me can never die. If you want something to occupy your last moment, your last thought, you might pity me."

John stared straight into his eyes. "Fuck you."

The cane dropped. A fireball exploded in his head.

12. Marriage Is a Dangerous Game

"We'll blackmail him." Castle and Lena were together in the big antique bathtub, in a sea of pink foam, her back against his chest.

"Sure," she said. " 'If you don't let us pass this manuscript off as the real thing, we'll tell everybody you faked it.' Something wrong with that, but I can't quite put my finger on it."

"Here, I'll put mine on it."

She giggled. "Later. What do you mean, blackmail?"

"Got it all figured out. I've got this friend Pansy, she used to be a call girl. Been out of the game seven, eight years; still looks like a million bucks."

"Sure. We fix John up with this hooker—"

"Call girl isn't a hooker. We're talkin' class."

"In the first place, John wouldn't pay for sex. He did that in Vietnam and it still bothers him."

"Not talkin' about pay. Talkin' about fallin' in love. While she meanwhile fucks his eyeballs out."

"You have such a turn of phrase, Sylvester. Then while his eyeballs are out, you come in with a camera."

"Yeah, but you're about six steps ahead."

"Okay, step two; how do we get them together? Church social?"

"She moves in next door." There was another upstairs apartment, unoccupied. "You and me and Julio are conveniently somewhere else when she shows up with all these boxes and that big flight of stairs."

"Sure, John would help her. But that's his nature; he'd help her if she were an ugly old crone with leprosy. Carry a few boxes, sit down for a cup of coffee, maybe. But not jump into the sack."

"Okay, you know John." His voice dropped to a husky whisper and he cupped her breasts. "But I know men, and I know Pansy . . . and Pansy could give a hard-on to a corpse."

"Sure, and then fuck his eyeballs out. They'd come out easier."

"What?"

"Never mind. Go ahead."

"Well . . . look. Do you know what a call girl does?"

"I suppose you call her up and say you've got this eyeball problem."

"Enough with the eyeballs. What she does, she works for like an escort service. That part of it's legal. Guy comes into town, business or maybe on vacation, he calls up the service and they ask what kind of companion he'd like. If he says, like, give me some broad with a tight ass, can suck the chrome off a bumper hitch—the guy says like 'I'm sorry, sir, but this is not that kind of a service.' But mostly the customers are pretty hip to it, they say, oh, a pretty young blonde who likes to go dancing."

"Meanwhile they're thinking about bumper hitches and eyeballs."

"You got it. So it starts out just like a date, just the guy pays the escort service like twenty bucks for getting them together. Still no law broken.

"Now about one out of three, four times, that's it. The guy knows what's going on but he don't get up the nerve to ask, or he really doesn't know the score, and it's like a real dull date. I don't think that happened much with Pansy."

"In the normal course of things, though, the subject of bumper hitches comes up."

"Uh huh, but not from Pansy. The guy has to pop the question. That way if he's a cop it's, what, entrapment."

"Do you know whether Pansy ever got busted?"

"Naw. Mainly the cops just shake down the hookers, just want a blowjob anyhow. This town, half of 'em want a blowjob from guys.

"So they pop the question and Pansy blushes and says for you, I guess I could. Then, on the way to the motel or wherever she says, you know, I wouldn't ask this if we weren't really good friends, but I got to make a car payment by tomorrow, and I need like two hundred bucks before noon tomorrow?"

"And she takes MasterCard and VISA."

"No, but she sure as hell knows where every bank machine in town is. She even writes up an I.O.U." Castle laughed. "Told me a guy from Toledo's holdin' five grand of I.O.U.s from her."

"All right, but that's not John. She could suck the chrome off his eyeballs and he still wouldn't be interested in her if she didn't know Hemingway from hummingbirds."

Castle licked behind her ear, a weird gesture that made her shiver. "That's the trump card. Pansy reads like a son of a bitch. She's got like a thousand books. So this morning I called her up and asked about Hemingway."

"And?"

"She's read them all."

She nodded slowly. "Not bad, Sylvester. So we promote this love affair and sooner or later you catch them in the act. Threaten to tell me unless John accedes to a life of crime."

"Think it could work? He wouldn't say hell, go ahead and tell her?"

"Not if I do my part... starting tomorrow. I'm the best, sweetest, lovingest wife in this sexy town. Then in a couple of weeks Pansy comes into his life, and there he is, luckiest man alive. Best of both worlds. Until you accidentally catch them *in flagrante delicioso*."

"So to keep both of you, he goes along with me."

"It might just do it. It might just." She slowly levered herself out of the water and smoothed the suds off her various assets.

"Nice."

"Bring me that bumper hitch, Sylvester. Hold on to your eyeballs."

13. IN ANOTHER COUNTRY

John woke up with a hangover of considerable dimension. The diluted glass of absinthe was still in the drink holder by the window. It was just past dawn, and a verdant forest rushed by outside. The rails made a steady hum; the car had a slight rocking that would have been pleasant to a person who felt well.

A porter knocked twice and inquired after Mr. Baird. "Come in," John said. A short white man, smiling, brought in coffee and Danish.

"What happened to George?"

"Pardon me, sir? George who?"

John rubbed his eyes. "Oh, of course. We must be past Atlanta."

"No, sir." The man's smile froze as his brain went into

nutty-passenger mode. "We're at least two hours from Atlanta."

"George . . . is a tall back guy with gold teeth who—"

"Oh, you mean George Mason, sir. He does do this car, but he picks up the train in Atlanta, and works it to Miami and back. He hasn't had the northern leg since last year."

John nodded slowly and didn't ask what year it was. "I understand." He smiled up and read the man's name tag. "I'm sorry, Leonard. Not at my best in the morning." The man withdrew with polite haste.

Suppose that weird dream had not been a dream. The Hemingway creature had killed him—the memory of the stroke was awesomely strong and immediate—but all that death amounted to was slipping into another universe where George Mason was on a different shift. Or perhaps John had gone completely insane.

The second explanation seemed much more reasonable.

On the tray underneath the coffee, juice, and Danish was a copy of *USA Today*, a paper John normally avoided because, although it had its comic aspects, it didn't have any funnies. He checked the date, and it was correct. The news stories were plausible—wars and rumors of war—so at least he hadn't slipped into a dimension where Martians ruled an enslaved Earth or Barry Manilow was president. He turned to the weather map and stopped dead.

Yesterday the country was in the middle of a heat wave that had lasted weeks. It apparently had ended overnight. The entry for Boston, yesterday, was "72/58/sh." But it hadn't rained and the temperature had been in the nineties.

He went back to the front page and began checking news stories. He didn't normally pay much attention to the news, though, and hadn't seen a paper in several days. They'd canceled their *Globe* delivery for the six weeks in Key West and he hadn't been interested enough to go seek out a newsstand.

There was no mention of the garbage collectors' strike in New York; he'd overheard a conversation about that yesterday. A long obituary for a rock star he was sure had died the year before.

An ad for DeSoto automobiles. That company had gone out of business when he was a teenager.

Bundles of universes, different from each other in small ways. Instead of dying, or maybe because of dying, he had slipped into another one. What would be waiting for him in Key West?

Maybe John Baird.

He set the tray down and hugged himself, trembling. Who or what was he in this universe? All of his memories, all of his personality, were from the one he had been born in. What happened to the John Baird that was born in this one? Was he an associate professor in American Literature at Boston University? Was he down in Key West wrestling with a paper to give at Nairobi—or working on a forgery? Or was he a Fitzgerald specialist snooping around the literary attics of St. Paul, Minnesota?

The truth came suddenly. Both John Bairds were in this compartment, in this body. And the body was slightly different.

He opened the door to the small washroom and looked in the mirror. His hair was a little shorter, less grey, beard better trimmed.

He was less paunchy and . . . something felt odd. There was feeling in his thigh. He lowered his pants and there was no scar where the sniper bullet had opened his leg and torn up the nerves there.

That was the touchstone. As he raised his shirt, the parallel memory flooded in. Puckered round scar on the abdomen; in this universe the sniper had hit a foot higher—and instead of the convalescent center in Cam Ranh Bay, the months of physical therapy and then back into the war, it had been peritonitis raging; surgery in Saigon and Tokyo and Walter Reed, and no more army.

But slowly they converged again. Amherst and U. Mass.— perversely using the G.I. Bill in spite of his access to millions—the doctorate on *The Sun Also Rises* and the instructorship at B.U., meeting Lena and virtuously waiting until after the semester to ask her out. Sex on the second date, and the third . . . but there they verged again. This John Baird hadn't gone back into combat to have his midsection sprayed with shrapnel from an American grenade that bounced off a tree; never had dozens of bits of metal cut out of his dick—and in the ensuing twenty-five years had made more use of it. Girlfriends and even one disastrous homosexual encounter with a stranger. As far as he knew, Lena was in the dark about this side of him; thought that he had remained faithful other than one incident seven years after they married. He knew of one affair she had had with a colleague, and suspected more.

The two Johns' personalities and histories merged, separate but one, like two vines from a common root, climbing a single support.

Schizophrenic but not insane.

John looked into the mirror and tried to address his new or his old self—John A, John B. There were no such people. There was suddenly a man who had existed in two separate universes and, in a way, it was no more profound than having lived in two separate houses.

The difference being that nobody else knows there is more than one house.

He moved over to the window and set his coffee in the holder, picked up the absinthe glass and sniffed it, considered pouring it down the drain, but then put it in the other holder, for possible future reference.

Posit this: is it more likely that there are bundles of parallel universes prevailed over by a Hemingway look-alike with a magic cane, or that John Baird was exposed to a drug that he had never experienced before and it had had an unusually disorienting effect?

He looked at the paper. He had not hallucinated two weeks of drought. The rock star had been dead for some time. He had not seen a DeSoto in twenty years, and that was a hard car to miss. Tail fins that had to be registered as lethal weapons.

But maybe if you take a person who remembers every trivial thing, and zap his brain with oil of wormwood, that is exactly the effect: perfectly recalled things that never actually happened.

The coffee tasted repulsive. John put on a fresh shirt and decided not to shave and headed for the bar car. He bought the last imported beer in the cooler and sat down across from the long-haired white-bearded man who had an earring that had escaped his notice before, or hadn't existed in the other universe.

The man was staring out at the forest greening by. "Morning," John said.

"How do." The man looked at him with no sign of recognition.

"Did we talk last night?"

He leaned forward. "What?"

"I mean did we sit in this car last night and talk about Hemingway and Vietnam and ghosts?"

He laughed. "You're on somethin', man. I been on this train since two in the mornin' and ain't said boo to nobody but the bartender."

"You were in Vietnam?"

"Yeah, but that's over; that's shit." He pointed at John's bracelet. "What, you got ghosts from over there?"

"I think maybe I have."

He was suddenly intense. "Take my advice, man; I been there. You got to go talk to somebody. Some shrink. Those ghosts ain't gonna go 'way by themself."

"It's not that bad."

"It ain't the ones you killed." He wasn't listening. "Fuckin' dinks, they come back but they don't, you know, they just stand around." He looked at John and tears came so hard they actually spurted from his eyes. "It's your fuckin' friends, man, they all died and they come back now...." He took a deep breath and wiped his face. "They used to come back every night. That like you?" John shook his head, helpless, trapped by the man's grief. "Every fuckin' night, my old lady, finally she said you go to a shrink or go to hell." He fumbled with the button on his shirt pocket and took out a brown plastic prescription bottle and stared at the label. He shook out a capsule. "Take a swig?" John pushed the beer over to him. He washed the pill down without touching the bottle to his lips.

He sagged back against the window. "I musta not took the pill last night, sometimes I do that. Sorry." He smiled weakly. "One day at a time, you know? You get through the one day. Fuck the rest. Sorry." He leaned forward again suddenly and put his hand on John's wrist. "You come outa nowhere and I lay my fuckin' trip on you. You don' need it."

John covered the hand with his own. "Maybe I do need it. And maybe I didn't come out of nowhere." He stood up. "I will see somebody about the ghosts. Promise."

"You'll feel better. It's no fuckin' cure-all, but you'll feel better."

"Want the beer?"

He shook his head. "Not supposed to."

"Okay." John took the beer and they waved at each other and he started back.

He stopped in the vestibule between cars and stood in the rattling roar of it, looking out the window at the flashing green blur. He put his forehead against the cool glass and hid the blur behind the dark red of his eyelids.

Were there actually a zillion of those guys each going through a slightly different private hell? Something he rarely asked himself was "What would Ernest Hemingway have done in this situation?"

He'd probably have the sense to leave it to Milton.

14. The Dangerous Summer

Castle and Lena met him at the station in Miami and they drove back to Key West in Castle's old pickup. The drone of the air conditioner held conversation to a minimum, but it kept them cool, at least from the knees down.

John didn't say anything about his encounter with the infinite, or transfinite, not wishing to bring back that fellow with the cane just yet. He did note that the two aspects of his personality hadn't quite become equal partners yet, and small details of this world kept surprising him. There was a monorail being built down to Pigeon Key, where Disney was digging an underwater park. Gasoline stations still sold Regular. Castle's car radio picked up TV as well as AM/FM, but sound only.

Lena sat between the two men and rubbed up against John affectionately. That would have been remarkable for John-one and somewhat unusual for John-two. It was a different Lena here, of course; one who had had more of a sex life with John, but there was something more than that, too. She was probably sleeping with Castle, he thought, and the extra attention was a conscious or unconscious compensation, or defense.

Castle seemed a little harder and more serious in this world than the last, not only from his terse moodiness in the pickup, but from recollections of parallel conversations. John wondered how shady he actually was, whether he'd been honest about his police record.

(He hadn't been. In this universe, when Lena had asked him whether he had ever been in trouble with the police, he'd answered a terse "no." In fact, he'd done eight hard years in Ohio for an armed robbery he hadn't committed— the real robber hadn't been so stupid, here—and he'd come out of prison bitter, angry, an actual criminal. Figuring the world owed him one, a week after getting out he stopped for a hitchhiker on a lonely country road, pulled a gun, walked him a few yards off the road into a field of high corn, and shot him point-blank at the base of the skull. It didn't look anything like the movies.)

(He drove off without touching the body, which a farmer's child found two days later. The victim turned out to be a college student who was on probation for dealing—all he'd really done was buy a kilo of green and make his money back by selling bags to his friends, and one enemy—so the papers said DRUG DEALER FOUND SLAIN IN GANGLAND-STYLE KILLING and the police pursued the matter with no enthusiasm. Castle was in Key West well before the farmer's child smelled the body, anyhow.)

As they rode along, whatever Lena had or hadn't done with Castle was less interesting to John than what *he* was planning to do with her. Half of his self had never experienced sex, as an adult, without the sensory handicaps engendered by scar tissue and severed nerves in the genitals, and he was looking forward to the experience with a relish that was obvious, at least to Lena. She encouraged him in not-so-subtle ways, and by the time they crossed the last bridge into Key West, he was ready to tell Castle to pull over at the first bush.

He left the typewriter in Castle's care and declined help with the luggage. By this time Lena was smiling at his obvious impatience; she was giggling by the time they were momentarily stalled by a truculent door key; laughed her delight as he carried her charging across the room to the couch, then clawing off a minimum of clothing and taking her with fierce haste, wordless, and keeping her on a breathless edge he drifted the rest of the clothes off her and carried her into the bedroom, where they made so much noise Julio banged on the ceiling with a broomstick.

They did quiet down eventually, and lay together in a puddle of mingled sweat, panting, watching the fan push the humid air around. "Guess we both get to sleep in the wet spot," John said.

"No complaints." She raised up on one elbow and traced a figure eight on his chest. "You're full of surprises tonight, Dr. Baird."

"Life is full of surprises."

"You should go away more often—or at least come back more often."

"It's all that Hemingway research. Makes a man out of you."

"You didn't learn this in a book," she said, gently taking his penis and pantomiming a certain motion.

"I did, though, an anthropology book." In another universe. "It's what they do in the Solomon Islands."

"Wisdom of Solomon," she said, lying back. After a pause: "They have anthropology books at JFK?"

"Uh, no." He remembered he didn't own that book in this universe. "Browsing at Wordsworth's."

"Hope you bought the book."

"Didn't have to." He gave her a long slow caress. "Memorized the good parts."

On the other side of town, six days later, she was in about the same position on Castle's bed, and even more exhausted.

"Aren't you overdoing the loving little wifey bit? It's been a week."

She exhaled audibly. "What a week."

"Missed you." He nuzzled her and made an unsubtle preparatory gesture.

"No, you don't." She rolled out of bed. "Once is plenty." She went to the mirror and ran a brush through her damp hair. "Besides, it's not me you missed. You missed *it*." She sat at the open window, improving the neighborhood's scenery. "*It's* gonna need a Teflon lining installed."

"Old boy's feelin' his oats?"

"Not feeling *his* anything. God, I don't know what's gotten into him. Four, five times a day; six."

"Screwed, blewed, and tattooed. You asked for it."

"As a matter of fact, I didn't. I haven't had a chance to start my little act. He got off that train with an erection, and he still has it. No woman would be safe around him. Nothing wet and concave would be safe."

"So does that mean it's a good time to bring in Pansy? Or is he so stuck on you he wouldn't even notice her?"

She scowled at the brush, picking hair out of it. "Actually, Castle, I was just about to ask you the same thing. Relying on your well-known expertise in animal behavior."

"Okay." He sat up. "I say we oughta go for it. If he's a walkin' talkin' hard-on like you say . . . Pansy'd pull him like a magnet. You'd have to be a fuckin' monk not to want Pansy."

"Like Rasputin."

"Like who?"

"Never mind." She went back to the brush. "I guess, I guess one problem is that I really am enjoying the attention. I guess I'm not too anxious to hand him over to this champion sexpot."

"Aw, Lena—"

"Really. I do love him in my way, Castle. I don't want to lose him over this scheme."

"You're not gonna lose him. Trust me. You catch him dickin' Pansy, get mad, forgive him. Hell, you'll have him wrapped around your finger."

"I guess. You make the competition sound pretty formidable."

"Don't worry. She's outa there the next day."

"Unless she winds up in love with him. That would be cute."

"He's almost twice her age. Besides, she's a whore. Whores don't fall in love."

"They're women, Castle. Women fall in love."

"Yeah, sure. Just like on TV."

She turned away from him; looked out the window. "You really know how to make a woman feel great, you know?"

"Come on." He crossed over and smoothed her hair. She turned around but didn't look up. "Don't run yourself down, Lena. You're still one hell of a piece of ass."

"Thanks." She smiled into his leer and grabbed him. "If you weren't such a poet, I'd trade you in for a vibrator."

15. In Praise of His Mistress

Pansy was indeed beautiful, even under normal conditions; delicate features, wasp waist combined with generous secondary sexual characteristics. The conditions under which John first saw her were calculated to maximize sexiness and vulnerability. Red nylon running shorts, tight and very short, and a white sleeveless T-shirt from a local bar that was stamped LAST HETEROSEXUAL IN KEY WEST—all clinging to her golden skin with a healthy sweat, the cloth made translucent enough to reveal no possibility of underwear.

John looked out the screen door and saw her at the other door, struggling with a heavy box while trying to make the key work. "Let me help you," he said through the screen, and stepped across the short landing to hold the box while she got the door open.

"You're too kind." John tried not to stare as he handed the box back. Pansy, of course, was relieved at his riveted attention. It had taken days to set up this operation, and would take more days to bring it to its climax, so to speak, and more days to get back to normal. But she did owe Castle a big favor and this guy seemed nice enough. Maybe she'd learn something about Hemingway in the process.

"More to come up?" John asked.

"Oh, I couldn't ask you to help. I can manage."

"It's okay. I was just goofing off for the rest of the day."

It turned out to be quite a job, even though there was only one load from a small rented truck. Most of the load was uniform and heavy boxes of books, carefully labeled LIT A–B, GEN REF, ENCY 1–12, and so forth. Most of her furniture, accordingly, was cinder blocks and boards, the standard student bookshelf arrangement.

John found out that despite a couple of dozen boxes marked LIT, Pansy hadn't majored in literature, but rather Special Education; during the school year, she taught third grade at a school for the retarded in Key Largo. She didn't tell him about the several years she'd spent as a call girl, but if she had, John might have seen a connection that Castle would never have made—that the driving force behind both of the jobs was the same, charity. The more or less easy forty dollars an hour for going on a date and then having sex was a factor, too, but she really did like making lonely men feel special, and had herself felt more like a social worker than a woman of easy virtue. And the hundreds of men who had fallen for her, for love or money, weren't responding only to her cheerleader's body. She had a sunny disposition and a natural, artless way of concentrating on a man that made him for a while the only man in the world.

John would not normally be an easy conquest. Twenty years of facing classrooms full of coeds had given him a certain wariness around attractive young women. He also had an impulse toward faithfulness, Lena having suddenly left town, her father ill. But he was still in the grip of the weird overweening horniness that had animated him since inheriting this new body and double-image personality. If Pansy had said "Let's do it," they would be doing it so soon that she would be wise to unwrap the condom before speaking. But she was being as indirect as her nature and mode of dress would allow.

"Do you and your wife always come down here for the summer?"

"We usually go somewhere. Boston's no fun in the heat."

"It must be wonderful in the fall."

And so forth. It felt odd for Pansy, probably the last time she would ever seduce a man for reasons other than personal interest. She wanted it to be perfect. She wanted John to have enough pleasure in her to compensate for the embarrassment of their "accidental" exposure, and whatever hassle his wife would put him through afterwards.

She was dying to know why Castle wanted him set up. How Castle ever met a quiet, kindly gentleman like John was a mystery, too—she had met some of Castle's friends, and they had other virtues.

Quiet and kindly, but horny. Whenever she contrived, in

the course of their working together, to expose a nipple or a little beaver, he would turn around to adjust himself, and blush. More like a teenager, discovering his sexuality, than a middle-aged married man.

He was a pushover, but she didn't want to make it too easy. After they had finished putting the books up on shelves, she said thanks a million; I gotta go now, spending the night house-sitting up in Islamorada. You and your wife come over for dinner tomorrow? Oh, then come on over yourself. No, that's all right, I'm a big girl. Roast beef okay? See ya.

Driving away in the rented truck, Pansy didn't feel especially proud of herself. She was amused at John's sexiness and looking forward to trying it out. But she could read people pretty well, and sensed a core of deep sadness in John. Maybe it was from Vietnam; he hadn't mentioned it, but she knew what the bracelet meant.

Whatever the problem, maybe she'd have time to help him with it—before she had to turn around and add to it.

Maybe it would work out for the best. Maybe the problem was with his wife, and she'd leave, and he could start over....

Stop kidding yourself. Just lay the trap, catch him, deliver him. Castle was not the kind of man you want to disappoint.

16. Fiesta

She had baked the roast slowly with wine and fruit juice, along with dried apricots and apples plumped in port wine, seasoned with cinnamon and nutmeg and cardamom. Onions and large cubes of acorn squash simmered in the broth. She served new potatoes steamed with parsley and dressed Italian style, with garlicky olive oil and a splash of vinegar. Small Caesar salad and air-light *pan de agua*, the Cuban bread that made you forget every other kind of bread.

The way to a man's heart, her mother had contended, was through his stomach, and although she was accustomed to aiming rather lower, she thought it was probably a good approach for a longtime married man suddenly forced to fend for himself. That was exactly right for John. He was not much of a cook, but he was an accomplished eater.

He pushed the plate away after three helpings. "God, I'm such a pig. But that was irresistible."

"Thank you." She cleared the table slowly, accepting John's offer to help. "My mother's 'company' recipe. So you think Hadley might have just thrown the stories away, and made up the business about the train?"

"People have raised the possibility. There she was, eight years older than this handsome hubby—with half the women on the Left Bank after him, at least in her mind—and he's starting to get published, starting to build a reputation. . . ."

"She was afraid he was going to 'grow away' from her? Or did they have that expression back then?"

"I think she was afraid he would start making money from his writing. She had an inheritance, a trust fund from her grandfather, that paid over two thousand a year. That was plenty to keep the two of them comfortable in Paris. Hemingway talked poor in those days, starving artist, but he lived pretty well."

"He probably resented it, too. Not making the money himself."

"That would be like him. Anyhow, if she chucked the stories to ensure his dependency, it backfired. He was still furious thirty years later—three wives later. He said the stuff had been 'fresh from the mint,' even if the writing wasn't so great, and he was never able to reclaim it."

She opened a cabinet and slid a bottle out of its burlap bag, and selected two small glasses. "Sherry?" He said why not? and they moved into the living room.

The living room was mysteriously devoid of chairs, so they had to sit together on the small couch. "You don't actually think she did it."

"No." John watched her pour the sherry. "From what I've

read about her, she doesn't seem at all calculating. Just a sweet gal from St. Louis who fell in love with a cad."

"Cad. Funny old-fashioned word."

John shrugged. "Actually, he wasn't really a cad. I think he sincerely loved every one of his wives...at least until he married them."

They both laughed. "Of course it could have been something in between," Pansy said, "I mean, she didn't actually throw away the manuscripts, but she did leave them sitting out, begging to be stolen. Why did she leave the compartment?"

"That's one screwy aspect of it. Hadley herself never said, not on paper. Every biographer seems to come up with a different reason: she went to get a newspaper, she saw some people she recognized and stepped out to talk with them, wanted some exercise before the long trip...even Hemingway had two different versions—she went out to get a bottle of Evian water or to buy something to read. That one pissed him off, because she did have an overnight bag full of the best American writing since Mark Twain."

"How would you have felt?"

"Felt?"

"I mean, you say you've written stories, too. What if somebody, your wife, made a mistake and you lost everything?"

He looked thoughtful. "It's not the same. In the first place, it's just hobby with me. And I don't have that much that hasn't been published—when Hemingway lost it, he lost it for good. I could just go to a university library and make new copies of everything."

"So you haven't written much lately?"

"Not stories. Academic stuff."

"I'd love to read some of your stories."

"And I'd love to have you read them. But I don't have any here. I'll mail you some from Boston."

She nodded, staring at him with a curious intensity. "Oh

hell," she said, and turned her back to him. "Would you help me with this?"

"What?"

"The zipper." She was wearing a clingy white summer dress. "Undo the zipper a little bit."

He slowly unzipped it a few inches. She did it the rest of the way, stood up and hooked her thumbs under the shoulder straps and shrugged. The dress slithered to the floor. She wasn't wearing anything else.

"You're blushing." Actually, he was doing a good imitation of a beached fish. She straddled him, sitting back lightly on his knees, legs wide, and started unbuttoning his shirt.

"Uh," he said.

"I just get impatient. You don't mind?"

"Uh . . . no?"

17. ON BEING SHOT AGAIN

John woke up happy but didn't open his eyes for nearly a minute, holding on to the erotic dream of the century. Then he opened one eye and saw it hadn't been a dream: the tousled bed in the strange room, unguents and sex toys on the nightstand, the smell of her hair on the other pillow. A noise from the kitchen; coffee and bacon smells.

He put on pants and went into the living room to pick up the shirt where it had dropped. "Good morning, Pansy."

"Morning, stranger." She was wearing a floppy terry cloth bathrobe with the sleeves rolled up to her elbows. She turned the bacon carefully with a fork. "Scrambled eggs okay?"

"Marvelous." He sat down at the small table and poured himself a cup of coffee. "I don't know what to say."

She smiled at him. "Don't say anything. It was nice."

"More than nice." He watched her precise motions behind the counter. She broke the eggs one-handed, two at a time, added a splash of water to the bowl, plucked some chives from a windowbox and chopped them with a small Chinese cleaver, rocking it in a staccato chatter; scraped them into the bowl, and followed them with a couple of grinds of pepper. She set the bacon out on a paper towel, with another towel to cover. Then she stirred the eggs briskly with the fork and set them aside. She picked up the big cast-iron frying pan and poured off a judicious amount of grease. Then she poured the egg mixture into the pan and studied it with alertness.

"Know what I think?" John said.

"Something profound?"

"Huh uh. I think I'm in a rubber room someplace, hallucinating the whole thing. And I hope they never cure me."

"I think you're a butterfly who's dreaming he's a man. I'm glad I'm in your dream." She slowly stirred and scraped the eggs with a spatula.

"You like older men?"

"One of them." She looked up, serious. "I like men who are considerate . . . and playful." She returned to the scraping. "Last couple of boyfriends I had were all dick and no heart. Kept to myself the last few months."

"Glad to be of service."

"You could rent yourself out as a service." She laughed. "You must have been impossible when you were younger."

"Different." Literally.

She ran hot water into a serving bowl, then returned to her egg stewardship. "I've been thinking."

"Yes?"

"The lost manuscript stuff we were talking about last night, all the different explanations." She divided the egg into four masses and turned each one. "Did you ever read any science fiction?"

"No. Vonnegut."

"The toast." She hurriedly put four pieces of bread in the toaster. "They write about alternate universes. Pretty much like our own, but different in one way or another. Important or trivial."

"What, uh, what silliness."

She laughed and poured the hot water out of the serving bowl, and dried it with a towel. "I guess maybe. But what if . . . what if all of those versions were equally true? In different universes. And for some reason they all came together here." She started to put the eggs into the bowl when there was a knock on the door.

It opened and Ernest Hemingway walked in. Dapper, just twenty, wearing the Italian army cape he'd brought back from the war. He pointed the black-and-white cane at Pansy. "Bingo."

She looked at John and then back at the Hemingway. She dropped the serving bowl; it clattered on the floor without breaking. Her knees buckled and she fainted dead away, executing a half turn as she fell so that the back of her head struck the wooden floor with a loud thump and the bathrobe drifted open from the waist down.

The Hemingway stared down at her frontal aspect. "Sometimes I wish I were human," it said. "Your pleasures are intense. Simple, but intense." It moved toward her with the cane.

John stood up. "If you kill her—"

"Oh?" It cocked an eyebrow at him. "What will you do?"

John took one step toward it and it waved the cane. A waist-high brick wall surmounted by needle-sharp spikes appeared between them. It gestured again and an impossible moat appeared, deep enough to reach down well into Julio's living room. It filled with water and a large crocodile surfaced and rested its chin on the parquet floor, staring at John. It yawned teeth.

The Hemingway held up its cane. "The white end. It doesn't kill, remember?" The wall and moat disappeared and the cane touched Pansy lightly below the navel. She twitched minutely but continued to sleep. "She'll have a headache," it said. "And she'll be somewhat confused by the uncommunicatable memory of having seen me. But that will all fade, compared to the sudden tragedy of having her new lover die here, just sitting waiting for his breakfast."

"Do you enjoy this?"

"I love my work. It's all I have." It walked toward him, footfalls splashing as it crossed where the moat had been. "You have not personally helped, though. Not at all."

It sat down across from him and poured coffee into a mug that said ON THE SIXTH DAY GOD CREATED MAN—SHE MUST HAVE HAD PMS.

"When you kill me this time, do you think it will 'take'?"

"I don't know. It's never failed before." The toaster made a noise. "Toast?"

"Sure." Two pieces appeared on his plate; two on the Hemingway's. "Usually when you kill people they stay dead?"

"I don't kill that many people." It spread margarine on its toast, gestured, and marmalade appeared. "But when I do, yeah. They die all up and down the Omniverse, every time-space. All except you." He pointed toast at John's toast. "Go ahead. It's not poison."

"Not my idea of a last meal."

The Hemingway shrugged. "What would you like?"

"Forget it." He buttered the toast and piled marmalade on it, determined out of some odd impulse to act as if nothing unusual were happening. Breakfast with Hemingway, big deal.

He studied the apparition and noticed that it was somewhat translucent, almost like a traditional TV ghost. He could barely see a line that was the back of the chair, bisecting its chest below shoulder-blade level. Was this something new? There hadn't been too much light in the train; maybe he had just failed to notice it before.

"A penny for your thoughts."

He didn't say anything about seeing through it. "Has it occurred to you that maybe you're not *supposed* to kill me? That's why I came back?"

The Hemingway chuckled and admired its nails. "That's a nearly content-free assertion."

"Oh really." He bit into the toast. The marmalade was strong, pleasantly bitter.

"It presupposes a higher authority, unknown to me, that's watching over my behavior, and correcting me when I do wrong. Doesn't exist, sorry."

"That's the oldest one in the theologian's book." He set down the toast and kneaded his stomach; shouldn't eat something so strong first thing in the morning. "You can only *assert* the nonexistence of something; you can't prove it."

"What you mean is *you* can't." He held up the cane and looked at it. "The simplest explanation is that there's something wrong with the cane. There's no way I can test it; if I kill the wrong person, there's hell to pay up and down the Omniverse. But what I can do is kill you without the cane. See whether you come back again, some timespace."

Sharp, stabbing pains in his stomach now. "Bastard." Heart pounding slow and hard: shirt rustled in time to its spasms.

"Cyanide in the marmalade. Gives it a certain *frisson*, don't you think?"

He couldn't breathe. His heart pounded once, and stopped. Vicious pain in his left arm, then paralysis. From an inch away, he could just see the weave of the white tablecloth. It turned red and then black.

18. The Sun Also Rises

From blackness to brilliance: the morning sun pouring through the window at a flat angle. He screwed up his face and blinked.

Suddenly smothered in terry cloth, between soft breasts. "John, John."

He put his elbow down to support himself, uncomfortable on the parquet floor, and looked up at Pansy. Her face was wet with tears. He cleared his throat. "What happened?"

"You, you started putting on your foot and...you just fell over. I thought..."

John looked down over his body, hard ropy muscle and deep tan under white body hair, the puckered bullet wound a little higher on the abdomen. Left leg ended in a stump just above the ankle.

Trying not to faint. His third past flooding back. Walking down a dirt road near Kontum, the sudden loud bang of the mine and he pitched forward, unbelievable pain, rolled over and saw his bloody boot yards away; grey, jagged shinbone sticking through the bloody smoking rag of his pant leg, bright crimson splashing on the dry dust, loud in the shocked silence; another bloodstain spreading between his legs, the deep mortal pain there—and he started to buck and scream and two men held him while the medic took off his belt and made a tourniquet and popped morphine through the cloth and unbuttoned his fly and slowly worked his pants down: penis torn by shrapnel, scrotum ripped open in a bright red flap of skin, bloody grey-blue egg of a testicle separating, rolling out. He fainted, then and now.

And woke up with her lips against his, her breath sweet in his lungs, his nostrils pinched painfully tight. He made a strangled noise and clutched her breast.

She cradled his head, panting, smiling through tears, and kissed him lightly on the forehead. "Will you stop fainting now?"

"Yeah. Don't worry." Her lips were trembling. He put a finger on them. "Just a longer night than I'm accustomed to. An overdose of happiness."

The happiest night of his life, maybe of three lives. Like coming back from the dead.

"Should I call a doctor?"

"No. I faint every now and then." Usually at the gym, from pushing too hard. He slipped his hand inside the terry cloth and covered her breast. "It's been...do you know how long it's been since I...did it? I mean...three times in one night?"

"About six hours." She smiled. "And you can say 'fuck.' I'm no schoolgirl."

"I'll say." The night had been an escalating progression of intimacies, gymnastics, accessories. "Had to wonder where a sweet girl like you learned all that."

She looked away, lips pursed, thoughtful. With a light fingertip she stroked the length of his penis and smiled when it started to uncurl. "At work."

"What?"

"I was a prostitute. That's where I learned the tricks. Practice makes perfect."

"Prostitute. Wow."

"Are you shocked? Outraged?"

"Just surprised." That was true. He respected the sorority and was grateful to it for having made Vietnam almost tolerable, an hour or so at a time. "But now you've got to do something really mean. I could never love a prostitute with a heart of gold."

"I'll give it some thought." She shifted. "Think you can stand up?"

"Sure." She stood and gave him her hand. He touched it but didn't pull; rose in a smooth practiced motion, then took one hop and sat down at the small table. He started strapping on his foot.

"I've read about those new ones," she said, "the permanent kind."

"Yeah; I've read about them, too. Computer interface, graft your nerves onto sensors." He shuddered. "No, thanks. No more surgery."

"Not worth it for the convenience?"

"Being able to wiggle my toes, have my foot itch? No. Besides, the VA won't pay for it." That startled John as he said it: here, he hadn't grown up rich. His father had spent all the mill money on a photocopy firm six months before Xerox came on the market. "You say you 'were' a prostitute. Not anymore?"

"No, that was the truth about teaching. Let's start this egg thing over." She picked up the bowl she had dropped in the other universe. "I gave up whoring about seven years ago." She picked up an egg, looked at it, set it down. She half turned and stared out the kitchen window. "I can't do this to you."

"You . . . can't do what?"

"Oh, lie. Keep lying." She went to the refrigerator. "Want a beer?"

"Lying? No, no thanks. What lying?"

She opened a beer, still not looking at him. "I like you, John. I really like you. But I didn't just . . . spontaneously fall into your arms." She took a healthy swig and started pouring some of the bottle into a glass.

"I don't understand."

She walked back, concentrating on pouring the beer, then sat down gracelessly. She took a deep breath and let it out, staring at his chest. "Castle put me up to it."

"*Castle?*"

She nodded. "Sylvester Castlemaine, boy wonder."

John sat back stunned. "But you said you don't do that anymore," he said without too much logic. "Do it for money."

"Not for money," she said in a flat, hurt voice.

"I should've known. A woman like you wouldn't want . . ." He made a gesture that dismissed his body from the waist down.

"You do all right. Don't feel sorry for yourself." Her face showed a pinch of regret for that, but she plowed on. "If it were just the obligation, once would have been enough. I wouldn't have had to fuck and suck all night long to win you over."

"No," he said, "that's true. Just the first moment, when you undressed. That was enough."

"I owe Castle a big favor. A friend of mine was going to be prosecuted for involving a minor in prostitution. It was a setup, pure and simple."

"She worked for the same outfit you did?"

"Yeah, but this was freelance. I think it was the escort

service that set her up, sort of delivered her and the man in return for this or that."

She sipped at the beer. "Guy wanted a three-way. My friend had met this girl a couple of days before at the bar where she worked part-time . . . she looked old enough, said she was in the biz."

"She was neither?"

"God knows. Maybe she got caught as a juvie and made a deal. Anyhow, he'd just slipped it to her and suddenly cops comin' in the windows. Threw the book at him. 'Two inches, twenty years,' my friend said. He was a county commissioner somewhere, with enemies. Almost dragged my friend down with him. I'm *sorry*." Her voice was angry.

"Don't be," John said, almost a whisper. "It's understandable. Whatever happens, I've got last night."

She nodded. "So two of the cops who were going to testify got busted for possession, cocaine. The word came down and everybody remembered the woman was somebody else."

"So what did Castle want you to do? With me?"

"Oh, whatever comes natural—or *un*-natural, if that's what you wanted. And later be doing it at a certain time and place, where we'd be caught in the act."

"By Castle?"

"And his trusty little VCR. Then I guess he'd threaten to show it to your wife, or the university."

"I wonder. Lena . . . she knows I've had other women."

"But not lately."

"No. Not for years."

"It might be different now. She might be starting to feel, well, insecure."

"Any woman who looked at you would feel insecure."

She shrugged. "That could be part of it. Could it cost you your job, too?"

"I don't see how. It would be awkward, but it's not as if you were one of my students—and even that happens, without costing the guy his job." He laughed. "Poor old Larry. He had a student kiss and tell, and had to run the Speakers'

Committee for four or five years. Got allergic to wine and cheese. But he made tenure."

"So what is it?" She leaned forward. "Are you an addict or something?"

"Addict?"

"I mean how come you even *know* Castle? He didn't pick your name out of a phone book and have me come seduce you, just to see what would happen."

"No, of course not."

"So? I confess, you confess."

John passed a hand over his face and pressed the other hand against his knee, bearing down to keep the foot from tapping. "You don't want to be involved."

"What do you call last night, Spin the Bottle? I'm in*volved*!"

"Not the way I mean. It's illegal."

"Oh golly. Not really."

"Let me think." John picked up their dishes and limped back to the sink. He set them down there and fiddled with the straps and pad that connected the foot to his stump, then poured himself a cup of coffee and came back, not limping.

He sat down slowly and blew across the coffee. "What it is, is that *Castle* thinks there's a scam going on. He's wrong. I've taken steps to ensure that it couldn't work." His foot tapped twice.

"You think. You hope."

"No. I'm sure. Anyhow, I'm stringing Castle along because I need his expertise in a certain matter."

" 'A certain matter,' yeah. Sounds wholesome."

"Actually, that part's not illegal."

"So tell me about it."

"Nope. Still might backfire."

She snorted. "You know what might *back*fire. Fucking with Castle."

"I can take care of him."

"You don't know. He may be more dangerous than you think he is."

"He talks a lot."

"You men." She took a drink and poured the rest of the bottle into the glass. "Look, I was at a party with him, couple of years ago. He was drunk, got into a little coke, started babbling."

"In vino veritas?"

"Yeah, and Coke is It. But he said he'd killed three people, strangers, just to see what it felt like. He liked it. I more than halfway believe him."

John looked at her silently for a moment, sorting out his new memories of Castle. "Well . . . he's got a mean streak. I don't know about murder. Certainly not over this thing."

"Which is?"

"You'll have to trust me. It's not because of Castle that I can't tell you." He remembered her one universe ago, lying helpless while the Hemingway lowered its cane onto her nakedness. "Trust me?"

She studied the top of the glass, running her finger around it. "Suppose I do. Then what?"

"Business as usual. You didn't tell me anything. Deliver me to Castle and his video camera; I'll try to put on a good show."

"And when he confronts you with it?"

"Depends on what he wants. He knows I don't have much money." John shrugged. "If it's unreasonable, he can go ahead and show the tape to Lena. She can live with it."

"And your department head?"

"He'd give me a medal."

19. IN OUR TIME

So it wasn't the cane. He ate enough cyanide to kill a horse, but evidently only in one universe.

You checked the next day in all the others?

All 119. He's still dead in the one where I killed him on the train—

That's encouraging.

—but there's no causal resonance in the others.

Oh, but there is some resonance. He remembered you in the universe where you poisoned him. Maybe in all of them.

That's impossible.

Once is impossible. Twice is a trend. A hundred and twenty means something is going on that we don't understand.

What I suggest—

No. You can't go back and kill them all one by one.

If the wand had worked the first time, they'd all be dead anyhow. There's no reason to think we'd cause more of an eddy by doing them one at a time.

It's not something to experiment with. As you well know.

I don't know how we're going to solve it otherwise.

Simple. Don't kill him. Talk to him again. He may be getting frightened, if he remembers both times he died.

Here's an idea. What if someone else killed him?

I don't know. If you just hired someone—made him a direct agent of your will—it wouldn't be any different from the cyanide. Maybe as a last resort. Talk to him again first.

All right. I'll try.

20. OF WOUNDS AND OTHER CAUSES

Although John found it difficult to concentrate, trying not to think about Pansy, this was the best time he would have for the foreseeable future to summon the Hemingway demon and try to do something about exorcising it. He didn't want either of the women around if the damned thing went on a killing spree again. They might just do as he did, and slip over into another reality—as unpleasant as that was, it was at least living—but the Hemingway had said otherwise. There was no reason to suspect it was not the truth.

Probably the best way to get the thing's attention was to resume work on the Hemingway pastiche. He decided to rewrite the first page to warm up, typing it out in Hemingway's style:

ALONG WITH YOUTH

1. Mitraigliatrice

The dirt on the side of the trench was never dry in the morning. If Fever could find a dry newspaper he could put it between his chest and the dirt when he went out to lean on the side of the trench and wait for the light .First light was the best time . You might have luck and see a muzzle flash to aim at . But patience was better than luck. Wait to see a helmet or a head without a helmet.

Fever looked at the enemy trench line through a rectangular box of wood that pushed through the trench wall at about ground level. The other end of the box was covered with a square of gauze the color of dirt. A man looking directly at it might see the muzzle flash when Fever fired through the box. But with luck, the flash would be the last thing he saw.

Fever had fired through the gauze six times. He'd potted at least three Austrians. Now the gauze had a ragged hole in the center. One bullet had come in the other way, an accident, and chiseled a deep gouge in the floor of the wooden box. Fever knew that he would be able to see the splinters sticking up before he could see any detail at the enemy trench line.

That would be maybe twenty minutes. Fever wanted a cigarette. There was plenty of time to go down in the bunker and light one. But it would fox his night vision. Better to wait.

Fever heard movement before he heard the voice. He picked up one of the grenades on the plank shelf to his left and his thumb felt the ring on the cotter pin. Someone was crawling in front of his position. Slow crawling but not too quiet. He slid his left forefinger through the ring and waited.

——Help me, came a strained whisper.

Fever felt his shoulders tense. Of course many Austrians could speak Italian.

——I am wounded. Help me. I can go no farther.

——What is your name and unit, Fever whispered through the box.

——Jean-Franco Dante. Four forty-seventh.

That was the unit that had taken such a beating at the evening show.——At first light they will kill me.

——All right. But I'm coming over with a grenade in my hand. If you kill me, you die as well.

——I will commend this logic to your superior officer. Please hurry.

Fever slid his rifle into the wooden box and eased himself to the top of the trench. He took the grenade out of his pocket and carefully worked the pin out, the arming lever held secure. He kept the pin around his finger so he could replace it.

He inched his way down the slope, guided by the man's whispers. After a few minutes his probing hand found the man's shoulder.——Thank God. Make haste, now.

The soldier's feet were both shattered by a mine. He would have to be carried.

——Don't cry out, Fever said. This will hurt.

——No sound, the soldier said. And when Fever raised him up onto his back there was only a breath. But his canteen was loose. It fell on a rock and made a loud hollow sound.

Firecracker pop above them and the night was all glare and bobbing shadow. A big machine gun opened up rong, cararong, rong, rong. Fever headed for the parapet above as fast as he could but knew it was hopeless. He saw dirt spray twice to his right and then felt the thud of the bullet into the Italian, who said ''Jesus'' as if only annoyed, and they almost made it then but on the lip of the trench a hard snowball hit Fever behind the kneecap and they both went down in a tumble. They fell two yards to safety but the Italian was already dead.

Fever had sprained his wrist and hurt his nose falling and they hurt worse than the bullet. But he couldn't move his toes and he knew that must be bad. Then it started to hurt.

A rifleman closed the Italian's eyes and with the help of another clumsy one dragged Fever down the trench to the medical bunker. It hurt awfully and his shoe filled up with blood and he puked. They stopped to watch him puke and then dragged him the rest of the way.

The surgeon placed him between two kerosene lanterns. He removed the puttee and shoe and cut the bloody pants leg with a straight razor. He rolled Fever onto his stomach and had four men hold him down while he probed for the bullet. The pain was great but Fever was insulted enough by the four men not to cry out. He heard the bullet clink into a metal dish. It sounded like the canteen.

"That's a little too pat, don't you think?" John turned around and there was the Hemingway, reading over his shoulder. " 'It sounded like the canteen,' indeed." Khaki army uniform covered with mud and splattered with bright blood. Blood dripped and pooled at its feet.

"So shoot me. Or whatever it's going to be this time. Maybe I'll rewrite the line in the next universe."

"You're going to run out soon. You only exist in eight more universes."

"Sure. And you've never lied to me." John turned back around and stared at the typewriter, tensed.

The Hemingway sighed. "Suppose we talk, instead."

"I'm listening."

The Hemingway walked past him toward the kitchen. "Want a beer?"

"Not while I'm working."

"Suit yourself." It limped into the kitchen, out of sight, and John heard it open the refrigerator and pry the top off of a beer. It came back out as the five-year-old Hemingway, dressed up in girl's clothing, both hands clutching an incongruous beer bottle. It set the bottle on the end table and crawled up onto the couch with childish clumsiness.

"Where's the cane?"

"I knew it wouldn't be necessary this time," it piped. "It occurs to me that there are better ways to deal with a man like you."

"Do tell." John smiled. "What is 'a man like me'? One on whom your cane for some reason doesn't work?"

"Actually, what I was thinking of was curiosity. That is supposedly what motivates scholars. You *are* a real scholar, not just a rich man seeking legitimacy?"

John looked away from the ancient eyes in the boy's face. "I've sometimes wondered myself. Why don't you cut to the chase, as we used to say. A few universes ago."

"I've done spot checks on your life through various universes," the child said. "You're always a Hemingway buff, though you don't always do it for a living."

"What else do I do?"

"It's probably not healthy for you to know. But all of you are drawn to the missing manuscripts at about this time, the seventy-fifth anniversary."

"I wonder why that would be."

The Hemingway waved the beer bottle in a disarmingly mature gesture. "The Omniverse is full of threads of coincidence like that. They have causal meaning in a dimension you can't deal with."

"Try me."

"In a way, that's what I want to propose. You will drop this dangerous project at once, and never resume it. In return, I will take you back in time, back to the Gare de Lyon on December 14, 1921."

"Where I will see what happens to the manuscripts."

Another shrug. "I will put you on Hadley's train, well before she said the manuscripts were stolen. You will be able to observe for an hour or so, without being seen. As you know, some people have theorized that there never was a thief; never was an overnight bag; that Hadley simply threw the writings away. If that's the case, you won't see anything dramatic. But the absence of the overnight bag would be powerful indirect proof."

John looked skeptical. "You've never gone to check it out for yourself?"

"If I had, I wouldn't be able to take you back. I can't exist twice in the same timespace, of course."

"How foolish of me. Of course."

"Is it a deal?"

John studied the apparition. The couch's plaid upholstery showed through its arms and legs. It did appear to become less substantial each time. "I don't know. Let me think about it a couple of days."

The child pulled on the beer bottle and it stretched into a long amber stick. It turned into the black-and-white cane. "We haven't tried cancer yet. That might be the one that works." It slipped off the couch and sidled toward John. "It does take longer and it hurts. It hurts 'awfully.'"

John got out of the chair. "You come near me with that and I'll drop kick you into next Tuesday."

The child shimmered and became Hemingway in his mid-forties, a big-gutted barroom brawler. "Sure you will, Champ." It held out the cane so that the tip was inches from John's chest. "See you around." It disappeared with a barely audible pop, and a slight breeze as air moved to fill its space.

John thought about that as he went to make a fresh cup of coffee. He wished he knew more about science. The thing obviously takes up space, since its disappearance caused a vacuum, but there was no denying that it was fading away.

Well, not fading. Just becoming more transparent. That might not affect its abilities. A glass door is as much of a door as an opaque one, if you try to walk through it.

He sat down on the couch, away from the manuscript so he could think without distraction. On the face of it, this offer by the Hemingway was an admission of defeat. An admission, at least, that it couldn't solve its problem by killing him over and over. That was comforting. He would just as soon not die again, except for the one time.

But maybe he should. That was a chilling thought. If he made the Hemingway kill him another dozen times, another hundred... what kind of strange creature would he become? A hundred overlapping autobiographies, all perfectly remembered? Surely the brain has a finite capacity for storing information; he'd "fill up," as Pansy said. Or maybe it wasn't finite, at least in his case—but that was logically absurd. There are only so many cells in a brain. Of course he might be "wired" in some way to the John Bairds in all the other universes he had inhabited.

And what would happen if he died in some natural way, not dispatched by an interdimensional assassin? Would he still slide into another identity? That was a lovely prospect: sooner or later he would be 130 years old, on his deathbed, dying every fraction of a second for the rest of eternity.

Or maybe the Hemingway wasn't lying, this time, and he had only eight lives left. In context, the possibility was reassuring.

The phone rang; for a change, John was grateful for the interruption. It was Lena, saying her father had come home from the hospital, much better, and she thought she could come on home day after tomorrow. Fine, John said, feeling a little wicked; I'll borrow a car and pick you up at the airport. Don't bother, Lena said; besides, she didn't have a flight number yet.

John didn't press it. If, as he assumed, Lena was in on the plot with Castle, she was probably here in Key West, or somewhere nearby. If she had to buy a ticket to and from Omaha to keep up her end of the ruse, the money would come out of John's pocket.

He hung up and, on impulse, dialed her parents' number. Her father answered. Putting on his professorial tone, he said he was Maxwell Perkins, Blue Cross claims adjuster, and he needed to know the exact date when Mr. Monaghan entered the hospital for this recent confinement. He said you must have the wrong guy; I haven't been inside a hospital in twenty years, knock on wood. Am I not speaking to John Franklin Monaghan? No, this is John *Frederick* Monaghan. Terribly sorry, natural mistake. That's okay; hope the other guy's okay, good-bye, good night, sir.

So tomorrow was going to be the big day with Pansy. To his knowledge, John hadn't been watched during sex for more than twenty years, and never by a disinterested, or at least dispassionate, observer. He hoped that knowing they were being spied upon wouldn't affect his performance. Or knowing that it would be the last time.

A profound helpless sadness settled over him. He knew that the last thing you should do, in a mood like this, was go out and get drunk. It was barely noon, anyhow. He took enough money out of his wallet for five martinis, hid the wallet under a couch cushion, and headed for Duval Street.

21. DYING, WELL OR BADLY

John had just about decided it was too early in the day to get drunk. He had polished off two martinis in Sloppy Joe's and then wandered uptown because the tourists were getting to him and a band was setting up, depressingly young and cheerful. He found a grubby bar he'd never noticed before, dark and smoky and hot. In the other universes it was a yuppie boutique. Three Social Security drunks were arguing politics almost loudly enough to drown out the game show on the television. It seemed to go well with the headache and sour stomach he'd reaped from the martinis and the walk in the sun. He got a beer and some peanuts and a couple of aspirin from the bartender, and sat in the farthest booth with a copy of the local classified ad newspaper. Somebody had obscurely carved FUCK ANARCHY into the tabletop.

Nobody else in this world knows what anarchy *is*, John thought, and the helpless anomie came back, intensified somewhat by drunken sentimentality. What he would give to go back to the first universe and undo this all by just not . . .

Would that be possible? The Hemingway was willing to take him back to 1921; why not back a few weeks? Where the hell was that son of a bitch when you needed him, it, whatever.

The Hemingway appeared in the booth opposite him, an Oak Park teenager smoking a cigarette. "I felt a kind of vibration from you. Ready to make your decision?"

"Can the people at the bar see you?"

"No. And don't worry about appearing to be talking to yourself. A lot of that goes on around here."

"Look. Why can't you just take me back to a couple of weeks before we met on the train, back in the first universe? I'll just . . ." The Hemingway was shaking its head slowly. "You can't."

"No. As I explained, you already exist there—"

"You said that *you* couldn't be in the same place twice. How do you know I can't?"

"How do you know you can't swallow that piano? You just can't."

"You thought I couldn't talk about you, either, you thought your stick would kill me. I'm not like normal people."

"Except in that alcohol does nothing for your judgment."

John ate a peanut thoughtfully. "Try this on for size. At 11:46 on June 3, a man named Sylvester Castlemaine sat down in Dos Hermosas and started talking with me about the lost manuscripts. The forgery would never have occurred to me if I hadn't talked to him. Why don't you go back and keep him from going into that cafe? Or just go back to 11:30 and kill him."

The Hemingway smiled maliciously. "You don't like him much."

"It's more fear than like or dislike." He rubbed his face hard, remembering. "Funny how things shift around. He was kind of likable the first time I met him. Then you killed me on the train and in the subsequent universe, he became colder, more serious. Then you killed me in Pansy's apartment and in this universe, he has turned mean. Dangerously mean, like a couple of men I knew in Vietnam. The ones who really love the killing. Like you, evidently."

It blew a chain of smoke rings before answering. "I don't 'love' killing, or anything else. I have a complex function and I fulfill it, because that is what I do. That sounds circular because of the limitations of human language.

"I can't go killing people right and left just to see what happens. When a person dies at the wrong time it takes forever to clean things up. Not that it wouldn't be worth it in your case. But I can tell you with certainty that killing Castlemaine would not affect the final outcome."

"How can you say that? He's responsible for the whole thing." John finished off most of his beer and the Hemingway touched the mug and it refilled. "Not poison."

"Wouldn't work," it said morosely. "I'd gladly kill Castlemaine any way you want—cancer of the penis is a possibility—if there was even a fighting chance that it would clear things up. The reason I know it wouldn't is that I am not in the least attracted to that meeting. There's no probability nexus associated with it, the way there was with your buying the Corona or starting the story on the train, or writing it down here. You may think that you would never have come up with the idea for the forgery on your own, but you're wrong."

"That's preposterous."

"Nope. There are universes in this bundle where Castle isn't involved. You may find that hard to believe, but your beliefs aren't important."

John nodded noncommittally and got his faraway remembering look. "You know ... reviewing in my mind all the conversations we've had, all five of them, the only substantive reason you've given me not to write this pastiche, and I quote, is that 'I or someone like me will have to kill you.' Since that doesn't seem to be possible, why don't we try some other line of attack?"

It put out the cigarette by squeezing it between thumb and forefinger. There was a smell of burning flesh. "All right, try this: give it up or I'll kill Pansy. Then Lena."

"I've thought of that, and I'm gambling that you won't, or can't. You had a perfect opportunity a few days ago—maximum dramatic effect—and you didn't do it. Now you say it's an awfully complicated matter."

"You're willing to gamble with the lives of the people you love?"

"I'm gambling with a lot. Including them." He leaned forward. "Take me into the future instead of the past. Show me what will happen if I succeed with the Hemingway hoax. If I agree that it's terrible, I'll give it all up and become a plumber."

The old, wise Hemingway shook a shaggy head at him. "You're asking me to please fix it so you can swallow a piano. I can't. Even I can't go straight to the future and look around; I'm pretty much tied to your present and past until this matter is cleared up."

"One of the first things you said to me was that you were from the future. And the past. And 'other temporalities,' whatever the hell that means. You were lying then?"

"Not really." It sighed. "Let me force the analogy. Look at the piano."

John twisted half around. "Okay."

"You can't eat it—but after a fashion, I can." The piano suddenly transformed itself into a piano-shaped mountain of cold capsules, which immediately collapsed and rolled all over the floor. "Each capsule contains a pinch of sawdust or powdered ivory or metal, the whole piano in about a hundred thousand capsules. If I take one with each meal, I will indeed eat the piano, over the course of the next three hundred-some years. That's not a long time for me."

"That doesn't prove anything."

"It's not a *proof*; it's a demonstration." It reached down and picked up a capsule that was rolling by, and popped it into its mouth. "One down, 99,999 to go. So how many ways could I eat this piano?"

"Ways?"

"I mean I could have swallowed any of the hundred thousand first. Next I can choose any of the remaining 99,999. How many ways can—"

"That's easy. One hundred thousand factorial. A huge number."

"Go to the head of the class. It's ten to the godzillionth power. That represents the number of possible paths—the number of futures—leading to this one guaranteed, preordained event: my eating the piano. They are all different, but in terms of whether the piano gets eaten, their differences are trivial.

"On a larger scale, every possible trivial action that you or anybody else in this universe takes puts us into a slightly different future than would have otherwise existed. An overwhelming majority of actions, even seemingly significant ones, make no difference in the long run. All of the futures bend back to one central, unifying event—except for the ones that you're screwing up!"

"So what is this big event?"

"It's impossible for you to know. It's not important, anyhow." Actually, it would take a rather cosmic viewpoint to consider the event unimportant: the end of the world.

Or at least the end of life on Earth. Right now there were two earnest young politicians, in the United States and Russia, who on 11 August 2006 would be President and Premier of their countries. On that day, one would insult the other beyond forgiveness, and a button would be pushed, and then another button, and by the time the sun set on Moscow, or rose on Washington, there would be nothing left alive on the planet at all—from the bottom of the ocean to the top of the atmosphere—not a cockroach, not a paramecium, not a virus, and all because there are some things a man just doesn't have to take, not if he's a real man.

Hemingway wasn't the only writer who felt that way, but

he was the one with the most influence on this generation.
The apparition who wanted John dead or at least not typing
didn't know exactly what effect his pastiche was going to
have on Hemingway's influence, but it was going to be de-
cisive and ultimately negative. It would prevent or at least
delay the end of the world in a whole bundle of universes,
which would put a zillion adjacent realities out of kilter, and
there would be hell to pay all up and down the Omniverse.
Many more people than six billion would die—and it's even
possible that all of Reality would unravel, and collapse back
to the Primordial Hiccup from whence it came.

"If it's not important, then why are you so hell-bent on
keeping me from preventing it? I don't believe you."

"*Don't* believe me, then!" At an imperious gesture, all the
capsules rolled back into the corner and reassembled into a
piano, with a huge crashing chord. None of the barflies
heard it. "I should think you'd cooperate with me just to
prevent the unpleasantness of dying over and over."

John had the expression of a poker player whose opponent
has inadvertently exposed his hole card. "You get used to
it," he said. "And it occurs to me that sooner or later I'll
wind up in a universe that I really like. This one doesn't have
a hell of a lot to recommend it." His foot tapped twice and
then twice again.

"No," the Hemingway said. "It will get worse each time."

"You can't know that. This has never happened before."

"True so far, isn't it?"

John considered it for a moment. "Some ways. Some ways
not."

The Hemingway shrugged and stood up. "Well. Think
about my offer." The cane appeared. "Happy cancer." It
tapped him on the chest and disappeared.

The first sensation was utter tiredness, immobility. When
he strained to move, pain slithered through his muscles and
viscera, and stayed. He could hardly breathe, partly because
his lungs weren't working and partly because there was
something in the way. In the mirror beside the booth he

looked down his throat and saw a large white mass, veined, pulsing. He sank back into the cushion and waited. He remembered the young wounded Hemingway writing his parents from the hospital with ghastly cheerfulness: "If I should have died it would have been very easy for me. Quite the easiest thing I ever did." I don't know, Ernie; maybe it gets harder with practice. He felt something tear open inside and hot stinging fluid trickled through his abdominal cavity. He wiped his face and a patch of necrotic skin came off with a terrible smell. His clothes tightened as his body swelled.

"Hey buddy, you okay?" The bartender came around in front of him and jumped. "Christ, Harry, punch nine-one-one one!"

John gave a slight ineffectual wave. "No rush," he croaked.

The bartender cast his eyes to the ceiling. "Always on my shift?"

22. DEATH IN THE AFTERNOON

John woke up behind a Dumpster in an alley. It was high noon and the smell of fermenting garbage was revolting. He didn't feel too well in any case; as if he'd drunk far too much and passed out behind a Dumpster, which was exactly what had happened in this universe.

In this universe. He stood slowly to a quiet chorus of creaks and pops, brushed himself off, and staggered away from the malefic odor. Staggered, but not limping—he had both feet again, in this present. There was a hand-sized numb spot at the top of his left leg where a .51 caliber machine gun bullet had missed his balls by an inch and ended his career as a soldier.

And started it as a writer. He got to the sidewalk and stopped dead. This was the first universe where he wasn't a college professor. He taught occasionally—sometimes creative writing; sometimes Hemingway—but it was only a hobby now, and a nod toward respectability.

He rubbed his fringe of salt-and-pepper beard. It covered the bullet scar there on his chin. He ran his tongue along the metal teeth the army had installed thirty years ago. Jesus. Maybe it does get worse every time. Which was worse, losing a foot or getting your dick sprayed with shrapnel, numb from severed nerves, plus bullets in the leg and face and arm? If you knew there was a Pansy in your future, you would probably trade a foot for a whole dick. Though she had done wonders with what was left.

Remembering furiously, not watching where he was going, he let his feet guide him back to the oldster's bar where the Hemingway had showed him how to swallow a piano. He pushed through the door and the shock of air-conditioning brought him back to the present.

Ferns. Perfume. Lacy underthings. An epicene sales clerk sashayed toward him, managing to look worried and determined at the same time. His nose was pierced, decorated with a single diamond button. "Si-i-r," he said in a surprisingly deep voice, "may I *help* you?"

Crotchless panties. Marital aids. The bar had become a store called The French Connection. "Guess I took a wrong turn. Sorry." He started to back out.

The clerk smiled. "Don't be shy. Everybody needs *some*-thing here."

The heat was almost pleasant in its heavy familiarity. John stopped at a convenience store for a six-pack of greenies and walked back home.

An interesting universe; much more of a divergence than the other had been. Reagan had survived the Hinckley assassination and actually went on to a second term. Bush was elected rather than succeeding to the presidency, and the country had not gone to war in Nicaragua. The Iran/Contra scandal nipped it in the bud.

The United States was actually cooperating with the Soviet Union in a flight to Mars. There were no DeSotos. Could there be a connection?

And in this universe he had actually met Ernest Hemingway.

Havana, 1952. John was eight years old. His father, a doctor in this universe, had taken a break from the New England winter to treat his family to a week in the tropics. John got a nice sunburn the first day, playing on the beach while his parents tried the casinos. The next day they made him stay indoors, which meant tagging along with his parents, looking at things that didn't fascinate eight-year-olds.

For lunch they went to La Florida, on the off chance that they might meet the famous Ernest Hemingway, who supposedly held court there when he was in Havana.

To John it was a huge dark cavern of a place, full of adult smells. Cigar smoke, rum, beer, stale urine. But Hemingway was indeed there, at the end of the long dark wood bar, laughing heartily with a table full of Cubans.

John was vaguely aware that his mother resembled some movie actress, but he couldn't have guessed that that would change his life. Hemingway glimpsed her and then stood up and was suddenly silent, mouth open. Then he laughed and waved a huge arm. "Come on over here, daughter."

The three of them rather timidly approached the table, John acutely aware of the careful inspection his mother was receiving from the silent Cubans. "Take a look, Mary," he said to the small blond woman knitting at the table. "The Kraut."

The woman nodded, smiling, and agreed that John's mother looked just like Marlene Dietrich ten years before. Hemingway invited them to sit down and have a drink, and they accepted with an air of genuine astonishment. He gravely shook John's hand, and spoke to him as he would to an adult. Then he shouted to the bartender in fast Spanish, and in a couple of minutes his parents had huge daiquiris and he had a Coke with a wedge of lime in it, tropical and grown-up. The waiter also brought a tray of boiled shrimp. Hemingway even ate the heads and tails, crunching loudly, which impressed John more than any Nobel Prize. Hemingway might have agreed, since he hadn't yet received one, and Faulkner had.

For more than an hour, two Cokes, John watched as his parents sat hypnotized in the aura of Hemingway's famous charm. He put them at ease with jokes and stories and questions—for the rest of his life John's father would relate how impressed he was with the sophistication of Hemingway's queries about cardiac medicine—but it was obvious even to a child that they were in awe, electrified by the man's presence.

Later that night John's father asked him what he thought of Mr. Hemingway. Forty-four years later, John of course remembered his exact reply: "He has fun all the time. I never saw a grown-up who plays like that."

Interesting. That meeting was where his eidetic memory started. He could remember a couple of days before it pretty well, because they had still been close to the surface. In other universes, he could remember back well before grade school. It gave him a strange feeling. All of the universes were different, but this was the first one where the differentness was so tightly connected to Hemingway.

He was flabby in this universe, fat over old, tired muscle, like Hemingway at his age, perhaps, and he felt a curious anxiety that he realized was a real *need* to have a drink. Not just desire, not thirst. If he didn't have a drink, something very very bad would happen. He knew that was irrational. Knowing didn't help.

John carefully mounted the stairs up to their apartment, stepping over the fifth one, also rotted in this universe. He put the beer in the refrigerator and took from the freezer a bottle of icy vodka—that was different—and poured himself a double shot and knocked it back, medicine drinking.

That spiked the hangover pretty well. He pried the top off a beer and carried it into the living room, thoughtful as the alcoholic glow radiated through his body. He sat down at the typewriter and picked up the air pistol, a fancy Belgian target model. He cocked it and, with a practiced two-handed grip, aimed at a paper target across the room. The pellet struck less than half an inch low.

All around the room the walls were pocked from where he'd fired at roaches, and once a scorpion. Very Hemingwayish, he thought; in fact, most of the ways he was different from the earlier incarnations of himself were in Hemingway's direction.

He spun a piece of paper into the typewriter and made a list:

```
                    EH & me--

--both had doctor fathers

--both forced into music lessons

--in high school wrote derivative stuff that didn't show
promise

--Our war wounds were evidently similar in severity and
location. Maybe my groin one was worse; army doctor
there said that in Korea (and presumably WWI), without
helicopter dustoff, I would have been dead on the bat-
tlefield. (Having been wounded in the kneecap and foot
myself, I know that H's story about carrying the wounded
guy on his back is unlikely. It was a month before I could
put any stress on the knee.) He mentioned genital
wounds, possibly similar to mine, in a letter to Bernard
Baruch, but there's nothing in the Red Cross report
about them.
  But in both cases, being wounded and surviving was the
central experience of our youth. Touching death.

--We each wrote the first draft of our first novel in six
weeks (but his was better and more ambitious).

--Both had unusual critical success from the beginning.

--Both shy as youngsters and gregarious as adults.
```

--Always loved fishing and hiking and guns; I loved the
bullfight from my first corrida, but may have been influ-
enced by H's books.

--Spain in general

--have better women than we deserve

--drink too much

--hypochondria

--accident proneness

--a tendency toward morbidity

--One difference. I will never stick a shotgun in my
mouth and pull the trigger. Leaves too much of a mess.

He looked up at the sound of the cane tapping. The Hemingway was in the Karsh wise-old-man mode, but was nearly
transparent in the bright light that streamed from the open
door. "What do I have to do to get your attention?" it said.
"Give you cancer again?"

"That was pretty unpleasant."

"Maybe it will be the last." It half sat on the arm of the
couch and spun the cane around twice. "Today is a big day.
Are we going to Paris?"

"What do you mean?"

"Something big happens today. In every universe where
you're alive, this day glows with importance. I assume that
means you've decided to go along with me. Stop writing this
thing in exchange for the truth about the manuscripts."

As a matter of fact, he had been thinking just that. Life
was confusing enough already, torn between his erotic love
for Pansy and the more domestic, but still deep, feeling for
Lena . . . writing the pastiche was kind of fun, but he did have
his own fish to fry. Besides, he'd come to truly dislike Castle,
even before Pansy had told him about the setup. It would be
fun to disappoint him.

"You're right. Let's go."

"First destroy the novel." In this universe, he'd completed seventy pages of the Up-in-Michigan novel.

"Sure." John picked up the stack of paper and threw it into the tiny fireplace. He lit it several places with a long barbecue match, and watched a month's work go up in smoke. It was only a symbolic gesture, anyhow; he could re-type the thing from memory if he wanted to.

"So what do I do? Click my heels together three times and say 'There's no place like the Gare de Lyon'?"

"Just come closer."

John took three steps toward the Hemingway and suddenly fell up down sideways—

It was worse than dying. He was torn apart and scattered throughout space and time, being nowhere and everywhere, everywhen, being a screaming vacuum forever—

Grit crunched underfoot and coalsmoke was choking thick in the air. It was cold. Grey Paris skies glowered through the long skylights, through the complicated geometry of the black steel trusses that held up the high roof. Bustling crowds chattering French. A woman walked through John from behind. He pressed himself with his hands and felt real.

"They can't see us," the Hemingway said. "Not unless I will it."

"That was awful."

"I hoped you would hate it. That's how I spend most of my timespace. Come on." They walked past vendors selling paper packets of roasted chestnuts, bottles of wine, stacks of baguettes and cheeses. There were strange resonances as John remembered the various times he'd been here more than a half century in the future. It hadn't changed much.

"There she is." The Hemingway pointed. Hadley looked worn, tired, dowdy. She stumbled, trying to keep up with the porter who strode along with her two bags. John recalled that she was just recovering from a bad case of the grippe. She'd probably still be home in bed if Hemingway hadn't sent the telegram urging her to come to Lausanne because the skiing was so good, at Chamby.

"Are there universes where Hadley doesn't lose the manuscripts?"

"Plenty of them," the Hemingway said. "In some of them he doesn't sell 'My Old Man' next year, or anything else, and he throws all the stories away himself. He gives up fiction and becomes a staff writer for the Toronto *Star*. Until the Spanish Civil War; he joins the Abraham Lincoln Battalion and is killed driving an ambulance. His only effect on American literature is one paragraph in *The Autobiography of Alice B. Toklas*."

"But in some, the stories actually do see print?"

"Sure, including the novel, which is usually called *Along With Youth*. There." Hadley was mounting the steps up into a passenger car. There was a microsecond of agonizing emptiness, and they materialized in the passageway in front of Hadley's compartment. She and the porter walked through them.

"*Merci*," she said, and handed the man a few sou. He made a face behind her back.

"*Along With Youth*?" John said.

"It's a pretty good book, sort of prefiguring *A Farewell To Arms*, but he does a lot better in universes where it's not published. *The Sun Also Rises* gets more attention."

Hadley stowed both the suitcase and the overnight bag under the seat. Then she frowned slightly, checked her wristwatch, and left the compartment, closing the door behind her.

"Interesting," the Hemingway said. "So she didn't leave it out in plain sight, begging to be stolen."

"Makes you wonder," John said. "This novel. Was it about World War I?"

"The trenches in Italy," the Hemingway said.

A young man stepped out of the shadows of the vestibule, looking in the direction Hadley took. Then he turned around and faced the two travelers from the future.

It was Ernest Hemingway. He smiled. "Close your mouth, John. You'll catch flies." He opened the door to the compartment, picked up the overnight bag, and carried it into the next car.

John recovered enough to chase after him. He had disappeared.

The Hemingway followed. "What *is* this?" John said. "I thought you couldn't be in two timespaces at once."

"That wasn't me."

"It sure as hell wasn't the real Hemingway. He's in Lausanne with Lincoln Steffens."

"Maybe he is and maybe he isn't."

"He knew my *name!*"

"That he did." The Hemingway was getting fainter as John watched.

"Was he another one of you? Another STAB agent?"

"No. Not possible." It peered at John. "What's happening to you?"

Hadley burst into the car and ran right through them, shouting in French for the conductor. She was carrying a bottle of Evian water.

"Well," John said, "that's what—"

The Hemingway was gone. John just had time to think *Marooned in 1922?* when the railroad car and the Gare de Lyon dissolved in an inbursting cascade of black sparks and it was no easier to handle the second time, spread impossibly thin across all those light years and millennia, wondering whether it was going to last forever this time, realizing that it did anyhow, and coalescing with an impossibly painful *snap*:

Looking at the list in the typewriter. He reached for the Heineken; it was still cold. He set it back down. "God," he whispered. "I hope that's that."

The situation called for higher octane. He went to the freezer and took out the vodka. He sipped the gelid syrup straight from the bottle, and almost dropped it when out of the corner of his eye he saw the overnight bag.

He set the open bottle on the counter and sleepwalked over to the dining room table. It was the same bag, slightly beat-up, monogrammed EHR, Elizabeth Hadley Richardson. He opened it and inside was a thick stack of manila envelopes.

He took out the top one and took it and the vodka bottle back to his chair. His hands were shaking. He opened the folder and stared at the familiar typing.

ERNEST M. HEMINGWAY

ONE-EYE FOR MINE

Fever stood up. In the moon light he could xx see blood starting on his hands. His pants were torn at the knee and he knew it would be bleeding there too. He watched the lights of the caboose disppear in the trees where the track curved.

That lousy crut of a brakeman. He would get him xxxday some day.

Fever scuffed xxxxxxx off the end of a tie and sat down to pick the cinders out of his hands and knee. He could use some water. The brakeman had his canteen.

He could smell a campfire. He wondered if it would be smart to go find it. He knew about the wolves, the human kind that lived along the rails and the disgusting things they liked. He wasn't afraid of them but you didn't look for trouble.

You don't have to look for trouble, his father would say. Trouble will find you. His father didn't tell him about wolves, though, or about women.

There was a noise in the brush. Fever stood up and slipped his hand around the horn grip of the fat Buck clasp knife in his pocket.

The screen door creaked open and he looked up to see Pansy walk in with a strange expression on her face. Lena followed, looking even stranger. Her left eye was swollen shut and most of that side of her face was bruised blue and brown.

He stood up, shaking with the sudden collision of emotions. "What the hell—"

"Castle," Pansy said. "He got outta hand."

"Real talent for understatement." Lena's voice was tightly controlled but distorted.

"He went nuts. Slappin' Lena around. Then he started to rummage around in a closet, rave about a shotgun, and we split."

"I'll call the police."

"We've already been there," Lena said. "It's all over."

"Of course. We can't work with—"

"No, I mean he's a *criminal*. He's wanted in Mississippi for second-degree murder. They went to arrest him, hold him for extradition. So no more Hemingway hoax."

"What Hemingway?" Pansy said.

"We'll tell you all about it," Lena said, and pointed at the bottle. "A little early, don't you think? You could at least get us a couple of glasses."

John went into the kitchen, almost floating with vodka buzz and anxious confusion. "What do you want with it?" Pansy said oh-jay and Lena said ice. Then Lena screamed.

He turned around and there was Castle standing in the door, grinning. He had a pistol in his right hand and a sawed-off shotgun in his left.

"You cunts," he said. "You fuckin' cunts. Go to the fuckin' cops."

There was a butcher knife in the drawer next to the refrigerator, but he didn't think Castle would stand idly by and let him rummage for it. Nothing else that might serve as a weapon, except the air pistol. Castle knew that it wouldn't do much damage.

He looked at John. "You three're gonna be my hostages. We're gettin' outta here, lose 'em up in the Everglades. They'll have a make on my pickup, though."

"We don't have a car," John said.

"I *know* that, asshole! There's a Hertz right down on One.
You go rent one and don't try nothin' cute. I so much as
smell a cop, I blow these two cunts away."

He turned back to the women and grinned crookedly,
talking hard-guy through his teeth. "Like I did those two
they sent, the spic and the nigger. They said somethin' about
comin' back with a warrant to look for the shotgun and I
was just bein' as nice as could be, I said hell, come on in,
don't need no warrant. I got nothin' to hide, and when they
come in I take the pistol from the nigger and kill the spic
with it and shoot the nigger in the balls. You shoulda heard
him. Some nigger. Took four more rounds to shut him up."

Wonder if that means the pistol is empty, John thought.
He had Pansy's orange juice in his hand. It was an old-
fashioned Smith & Wesson .357 Magnum six-shot, but from
this angle he couldn't tell whether it had been reloaded. He
could try to blind Castle with the orange juice.

He stepped toward him. "What kind of car do you want?"

"Just a *car*, damn it. Big enough." A siren whooped about
a block away. Castle looked wary. "Bitch. You told 'em where
you'd be."

"No," Lena pleaded. "We didn't tell them anything."

"Don't do anything stupid," John said.

Two more sirens, closer. "I'll show you *stupid!*" He raised
the pistols toward Lena. John dashed the orange juice in his
face.

It wasn't really like slow motion. It was just that John
didn't miss any of it. Castle growled and swung around and
in the cylinder's chambers John saw five copper-jacketed
slugs. He reached for the gun and the first shot shattered
his hand, blowing off two fingers, and struck the right side
of his chest. The explosion was deafening and the shock of
the bullet was like being hit simultaneously in the hand
and chest with baseball bats. He rocked, still on his feet, and
coughed blood spatter on Castle's face. He fired again, and
the second slug hit him on the other side of the chest, this
time spinning him half around. Was somebody screaming?

Hemingway said it felt like an icy snowball, and that was pretty close, except for the inside part, your body saying Well, time to close up shop. There was a terrible familiar radiating pain in the center of his chest, and John realized that he was having a totally superfluous heart attack. He pushed off from the dinette and staggered toward Castle again. He made a grab for the shotgun and Castle emptied both barrels into his abdomen. He dropped to his knees and then fell over on his side. He couldn't feel anything. Things started to go dim and red. Was this going to be the last time?

Castle cracked the shotgun and the two spent shells flew up in an arc over his shoulder. He took two more out of his shirt pocket and dropped one. When he bent over to pick it up, Pansy leaped past him. In a swift motion that was almost graceful—it came to John that he had probably practiced it over and over, acting out fantasies—he slipped both shells into their chambers and closed the gun with a flip of the wrist. The screen door was stuck. Pansy was straining at the knob with both hands. Castle put the muzzles up to the base of her skull and pulled one trigger. Most of her head covered the screen or went through the hole the blast made. The crown of her skull, a bloody bowl, bounced off two walls and went spinning into the kitchen. Her body did a spastic little dance and folded, streaming.

Lena was suddenly on his back, clawing at his face. He spun and slammed her against the wall. She wilted like a rag doll and he hit her hard with the pistol on the way down. She unrolled at his feet, out cold, and with his mouth wide open laughing silently he lowered the shotgun and blasted her point-blank in the crotch. Her body jackknifed and John tried with all his will not to die but blackness crowded in and the last thing he saw was that evil grin as Castle reloaded again, peering out the window, presumably at the police.

It wasn't the terrible sense of being spread infinitesimally thin over an infinity of pain and darkness; things had just gone black, like closing your eyes. If this is death, John thought, there's not much to it.

But it changed. There was a little bit of pale light, some vague figures, and then colors bled into the scene, and after a moment of disorientation he realized he was still in the apartment, but apparently floating up by the ceiling. Lena was conscious again, barely, twitching, staring at the river of blood that pumped from between her legs. Pansy looked unreal, headless but untouched from the neck down, lying in a relaxed, improbable posture like a knocked-over department store dummy, blood still spurting from a neck artery out through the screen door.

His own body was a mess, the abdomen completely excavated by buckshot. Inside the huge wound, behind the torn coils of intestine, the shreds of fat and gristle, the blood, the shit, he could see sharp splintered knuckles of backbone. Maybe it hadn't hurt so much because the spinal cord had been severed in the blast.

He had time to be a little shocked at himself for not feeling more. Of course most of the people he'd known who had died did die this way, in loud spatters of blood and brains. Even after thirty years of the occasional polite heart attack or stroke carrying off friend or acquaintance, most of the dead people he knew had died in the jungle.

He had been a hero there, in this universe. That would have surprised his sergeants in the original one. Congressional Medal of Honor, so-called, which hadn't hurt the sales of his first book. Knocked out the NVA machine gun emplacement with their own satchel charge, then hauled the machine gun around and wiped out their mortar and command squads. He managed it all with bullet wounds in the face and triceps. Of course without the bullet wounds he wouldn't have lost his cool and charged the machine gun emplacement, but that wasn't noted in the citation.

A pity there was no way to trade the medals in—melt them down into one big fat bullet and use it to waste that crazy motherfucker who was ignoring the three people he'd

just killed, laughing like a hyena while he shouted obsceni-
ties at the police gathering down below.

Castle fires a shot through the lower window and then
ducks and a spray of automatic weapon fire shatters the upper window, filling the air with a spray of glass; bullets and
glass fly painlessly through John where he's floating and he
hears them spatter into the ceiling and suddenly everything
is white with plaster dust—it starts to clear and he is much
closer to his body, drawing down closer and closer; he
merges with it and there's an instant of blackness and he's
looking out through human eyes again.

A dull noise and he looked up to see hundreds of shards
of glass leap up from the floor and fly to the window; plaster
dust in billows sucked up into bullet holes in the ceiling,
which then disappeared.

The top windowpane reformed as Castle *un*crouched,
pointed the shotgun, then jerked forward as a blossom of
yellow flame and white smoke rolled back into the barrel.

His hand was whole, the fingers restored. He looked down
and saw rivulets of blood running back into the hole in his
abdomen, then individual drops; then it closed and the
clothing restored itself; then one of the holes in his chest
closed up and then the other.

The clothing was unfamiliar. A tweed jacket in this
weather? His hands had turned old, liver spots forming as
he watched. Slow like a plant growing, slow like the moon
turning, thinking slowly too, he reached up and felt the
beard, and could see out of the corner of his eye that it was
white and long. He was too fat, and a belt buckle bit painfully
into his belly. He sucked in and pried out and looked at the
buckle, yes, it was old brass and said GOTT MIT UNS, the buckle he'd taken from a dead German so long ago. The buckle
Hemingway had taken.

John got to one knee. He watched fascinated as the stream
of blood gushed back into Lena's womb, disappearing as Castle grinning jammed the barrels in between her legs,
flinched, and did a complicated dance in reverse (while Pan-

sy's decapitated body writhed around and jerked upright);
Lena, sliding up off the floor, leaped up between the man's
back and the wall, then fell off and ran backwards as he
flipped the shotgun up to the back of Pansy's neck and seem-
ing gallons of blood and tissue came flying from every direction to assemble themselves into the lovely head and face,
distorted in terror as she jerked awkwardly at the door and
then ran backwards, past Castle as he did a graceful pirou-
ette, unloading the gun and placing one shell on the floor,
which flipped up to his pocket as he stood and put the other
one there.

John stood up and walked through some thick resistance
toward Castle. Was it *time* resisting him? Everything else was
still moving in reverse: Two empty shotgun shells sailed
across the room to snick into the weapon's chambers; Castle
snapped it shut and wheeled to face John—

But John wasn't where he was supposed to be. As the shotgun swung around, John grabbed the barrels—hot!—and
pulled the pistol out of Castle's waistband. He lost his grip
on the shotgun barrels just as he jammed the pistol against
Castle's heart and fired. A spray of blood from all over the
other side of the room converged on Castle's back and John
felt the recoil sting of the Magnum just as the shotgun muzzle cracked hard against his teeth, mouthful of searing heat
then blackness forever, back in the featureless infinite timespace hell that the Hemingway had taken him to, forever,
but in the next instant, a new kind of twitch, a twist . . .

23. THE TIME EXCHANGED

What does that mean, you "lost" him?

We were in the railroad car in the Gare de Lyon, in the
normal observation mode. This entity that looked like Hemingway walked up, greeted us, took the manuscripts, and disappeared.

Just like that.

No. He went into the next car. John Baird ran after him. Maybe that was my mistake. I translated instead of running.

That's when you lost him.

Both of them. Baird disappeared, too. Then Hadley came running in—

Don't confuse me with Hadleys. You checked the adjacent universes.

All of them, yes. I think they're all right.

Think?

Well...I can't quite get to that moment. When I disappeared. It's as if I were still there for several more seconds, so I'm excluded.

And John Baird is still there?

Not by the time I can insert myself. Just Hadley running around—

No Hadleys. No Hadleys. So naturally you went back to 1996.

Of course. But there is a period of several minutes there from which I'm excluded as well. When I can finally insert myself, John Baird is dead.

Ah.

In every doom line, he and Castlemaine have killed each other. John is lying there with his head blown off, Castle next to him with his heart torn out from a point-blank pistol shot, with two very distraught women screaming while police pile in through the door. And this.

The overnight bag with the stories.

I don't think anybody noticed it. With Baird dead, I could spot-check the women's futures; neither of them mentions the bag. So perhaps the mission is accomplished.

Well, Reality is still here. So far. But the connection between Baird and this Hemingway entity is disturbing. That Baird is able to return to 1996 without your help is *very* disturbing. He has obviously taken on some of your characteristics, your abilities, which is why you're excluded from the last several minutes of his life.

I've never heard of that happening before.

It never has. I think that John Baird is no more human than you and I.

Is?

I suspect he's still around somewhen.

24. ISLANDS IN THE STREAM

and the unending lightless desert of pain becomes suddenly one small bright spark and then everything is dark red and a taste, a bitter taste, Hoppe's No. 9 gun oil and the twin barrels of the fine Boss pigeon gun cold and oily on his tongue and biting hard against the roof of his mouth; the dark red is light on the other side of his eyelids, sting of pain before he bumps a tooth and opens his eyes and mouth and lowers the gun and with shaking hands unloads—no, dis-loads—both barrels and walks backwards, shuffling in the slippers, slumping, stopping to stare out into the Idaho morning dark, helpless tears coursing up from the snarled white beard, walking backwards down the stairs with the shotgun heavily cradled in his elbow, backing into the storeroom and replacing it in the rack, then back up the stairs and slowly put the keys there in plain sight on the kitchen windowsill, a bit of mercy from Miss Mary, then sit and stare at the cold bad coffee as it warms back to one acid sip—

A tiny part of the mind saying *wait! I am John Baird it is 1996*

and back to a spiritless shower, numb to the needle spray, and cramped constipation and a sleep of no ease; an evening with Mary and George Brown tiptoeing around the blackest of black-ass worse and worse each day, only one thing to look forward to

got to throw out an anchor

faster now, walking through the Ketchum woods like a jerky cartoon in reverse, fucking FBI and IRS behind every tree, because you sent Ezra that money, felt sorry for him because he was crazy, what a fucking joke, should have finished the *Cantos* and shot himself.

effect preceding cause but I can read or hear scraps of thought somehow speeding to a blur now, driving in reverse hundreds of miles per hour back from Ketchum to Minnesota, the Mayo Clinic, holding the madness in while you talk to the shrink, promise not to hurt myself have to go home and write if I'm going to beat this, figuring what he wants to hear, then the rubber mouthpiece and smell of your own hair and flesh slightly burnt by the electrodes then deep total blackness

sharp stabs of thought sometimes stretching

hospital days blur by in reverse, cold chrome and starch white, a couple of mouthfuls of claret a day to wash down the pills that seem to make it worse and worse

what will happen to me when he's born?

When they came back from Spain was when he agreed to the Mayo Clinic, still all beat-up from the plane crashes six years before in Africa, liver and spleen shot to hell, brain, too, nerves, can't write or can't stop: all day on one damned sentence for the Kennedy book but a hundred thousand fast words, pure shit, for the bullfight article. Paris book okay but stuck. Great to find the trunks in the Ritz but none of the stuff Hadley lost.

Here it stops. A frozen tableau:

Afternoon light slanting in through the tall cloudy windows of the Cambon bar, where he had liberated, would liberate, the hotel in August 1944. A good large American-style martini gulped too fast in the excitement. The two small trunks unpacked and laid out item by item. Hundreds of pages of notes that would become the Paris book. But nothing before '23, of course. *the manuscripts* The novel and the stories and the poems still gone. One moment nailed down with the juniper sting of the martini and then time crawling rolling flying backwards again—

no control?

Months blurring by, Madrid Riviera Venice feeling sick and busted up, the plane wrecks like a quick one-two punch

brain and body, blurry sick even before them at the Finca
Vigia, can't get a fucking thing done after the Nobel Prize,
journalists day and night, the prize bad luck and bullshit
anyhow but need the $35,000

damn, had to shoot Willie, cat since the boat-time before
the war, but winged a burglar too, same gun, just after the
Pulitzer, now that was all right

slowing down again—Havana—the Floridita—
Even Mary having a good time, and the Basque jai alai
players, too, though they don't know much English, most of
them, interesting couple of civilians, the doctor and the
Kraut look-alike, but there's something about the boy that
makes it hard to take my eyes off him, looks like someone I
guess, another round of Papa Dobles, that boy, what is it
about him? and then the first round, with lunch, and things
speeding up to a blur again.

out on the Gulf a lot, enjoying the triumph of *The Old
Man and the Sea*, the easy good-paying work of providing
fishing footage for the movie, and then back into 1951, the
worst year of his life that far, weeks of grudging conciliation,
uncontrollable anger, and black-ass depression from the poisonous critical slime that followed *Across the River*, bastards
gunning for him, Harold Ross dead, mother Grace dead, son
Gregory a dope addict hip-deep into the dianetics horseshit,
Charlie Scribner dead but first declaring undying love for
that asshole Jones

most of the forties an anxious blur, Cuba Italy Cuba
France Cuba China found Mary kicked Martha out, thousand
pages on the fucking *Eden* book wouldn't come together
Bronze Star better than Pulitzer

Martha a chrome-plated bitch in Europe but war is swell
otherwise, liberating the Ritz, grenades rifles pistols and
bomb runs with the RAF, China boring compared to it and
the Q-ship runs off Cuba, hell, maybe the bitch was right for
once, just kid stuff and booze

marrying the bitch was the end of my belle epoch, easy
to see from here, the thirties all sunshine Key West Spain

Key West Africa Key West, good hard writing with Pauline
holding down the store, good woman but sorry I had to
  sorry I had to divorce
  stopping
Walking Paris streets after midnight:
  I was never going to throw back at her losing the manuscripts. Told Steffens that would be like blaming a human
for the weather, or death. These things happen. Nor say anything about what I did the night after I found out she really
had lost them. But this one time we got to shouting and I
think I hurt her. Why the hell did she have to bring the
carbons what the hell did she think carbons were for stupid
stupid stupid and she crying and she giving me hell about
Pauline Jesus any woman who could fuck up Paris for you
could fuck up a royal flush
  it slows down around the manuscripts or me—
  golden years the mid-twenties everything clicks Paris Vor-
arlburg Paris Schruns Paris Pamplona Paris Madrid Paris
Lausanne
  couldn't believe she actually
  most of a novel dozens of poems stories sketches—*contes,*
Kitty called them by God woman you show me your *conte*
and I'll show you mine
  so drunk that night I know better than to drink that much
absinthe so drunk I was half crawling going up the stairs to
the apartment I saw weird I saw God I saw *I saw myself stand-*
ing there on the fourth landing with Hadley's goddamn bag
  I waited almost an hour, that seemed like no time or all
time, and when he, when I, when he came crashing up the
stairs he blinked twice, then I walked through me groping,
shook my head without looking back and managed to get
the door unlocked
  flying back through the dead winter French countryside, standing
in the bar car fighting hopelessness to Hadley crying so hard she
can't get out what was wrong with Steffens standing gaping like a
fish in a bowl
  twisting again, painlessly inside out, I suppose through

various dimensions, seeing the man's life as one complex chord of beauty and purpose and ugliness and chaos, my life on one side of the Möbius strip consistent through its fading forty-year span, starting, *starting*, here:

the handsome young man sits on the floor of the apartment holding himself, rocking racked with sobs, one short manuscript crumpled in front of him, the room a mess with drawers pulled out, their contents scattered on the floor, it's like losing an arm a leg (a foot a testicle), it's like losing your youth and along with youth

with a roar he stands up, eyes closed fists clenched, wipes his face dry and stomps over to the window

breathes deeply until he's breathing normally

strides across the room, kicking a brassiere out of his way

stands with his hand on the knob and thinks this:

life can break you but you can grow back strong at the broken places

and goes out slamming the door behind him, somewhat conscious of having been present at his own birth.

With no effort I find myself standing earlier that day in the vestibule of a train. Hadley is walking away, tired, looking for a vendor. I turn and confront two aspects of myself.

"Close your mouth, John. You'll catch flies."

They both stand paralyzed while I slide open the door and pull the overnight bag from under the seat. I walk away and the universe begins to tingle and sparkle.

I spend forever in the black void between timespaces. I am growing to enjoy it.

I appear in John Baird's apartment and set down the bag. I look at the empty chair in front of the old typewriter, the green beer bottle sweating cold next to it, and John Baird appears, looking dazed, and I have business elsewhere, elsewhen. A train to catch. I'll come back for the bag in twelve minutes or a few millennia, after the bloodbath that gives birth to us all.

25. A MOVEABLE FEAST

He wrote the last line and set down the pencil and read over the last page sitting on his hands for warmth. He could see his breath. Celebrate the end with a little heat.

He unwrapped the bundle of twigs and banked them around the pile of coals in the brazier. Crazy way to heat a room, but it's France. He cupped both hands behind the stack and blew gently. The coals glowed red and then orange and with the third breath the twigs smoldered and a small yellow flame popped up. He held his hands over the fire, rubbing the stiffness out of his fingers, enjoying the smell of the birch as it cracked and spit.

He put a fresh sheet and carbon into the typewriter and looked at his penciled notes. Final draft? Worth a try:

```
Ernest M. Hemingway,
74 rue da Cardinal Lemoine,
Paris, France

          ))UP IN MICHIGAN))

 Jim Gilmore came to Horton's Bay from Canada . He bought
the blacksmith shop from old man Hortom
```

Shit, a typo. He flinched suddenly, as if struck, and shook his head to clear it. What a strange sensation to come out of nowhere. A sudden cold stab of grief. But larger somehow than grief for a person.

Grief for everybody, maybe. For being human.

From a typo?

He went to the window and opened it in spite of the cold. He filled his lungs with the cold damp air and looked around the familiar orange-and-grey mosaic of chimney pots and tiled roofs under the dirty winter Paris sky.

He shuddered and eased the window back down and returned to the heat of the brazier. He had felt it before, exactly that huge and terrible feeling. But where?

For the life of him he couldn't remember.

○ ○ ○ *There's obviously another force at work here besides imagination and experience; a kind of literary game-playing. I've been a student of Hemingway's writing and life for about twenty-five years; sooner or later I had to mine the old man for material.*

I came up with the idea in an instant. I was headed for the South Seas and had one of my students drive me to the airport. I guess the plane was delayed; we had a couple of hours to kill. While we were talking, I related the story of Hemingway's lost manuscripts, and speculated about how someone with no scruples could make a million bucks "finding" them. On my way to the men's room it suddenly struck me that you could make a small fraction of a million writing about somebody doing it, and have a lot of fun, and not go to jail for it. Over the next few days, in Tahiti and New Zealand, I wrote up an outline for the book of which this novella is a condensation.

The main character has a lot of autobiographical elements in his various incarnations. I am a middle-aged Boston professor who loves trains and fountain pens, and vacations in Key West whenever possible. My wife is a lot nicer than Lena, though, and none of my friends are, to my knowledge, misogynistic murderers. Pansy was modeled after a science fiction fan I met years ago, a charming and beautiful woman who made a good living as a call girl and didn't mind talking about it.

Two of Baird's wounds are described from experience, the .51 machine gun bullet to the thigh and the rifle grenade that sprayed me, us, with shrapnel from the waist down. The missing foot is imagination, or nightmare, or maybe an alternate universe: after the first operation on the thigh wound, which was large, the doctor warned me he would probably have to amputate. He didn't.

"The Hemingway Hoax" won the 1991 Hugo and Nebula Awards for Best Novella of the Year.

O

images

THE ONLY REASON I can tell this story is that you aren't going
to believe it. I'll still change all the names and locations, to
be on the safe side. I can't afford to be called a lunatic. I'm
a respectable family man now, with a good, safe job.

I was just the opposite back in the middle sixties: no job,
no family, and nothing like respectability. I did a year in
Vietnam and came back rootless, rattled, drifted into the
easy dope, easy sex subculture on the West Coast. Flower
child.

Let's call it San Diego. I was pretty much in demand at
the antiwar rallies. Always was a good public speaker and
besides was a physically striking six-foot-four, broad-shoul-
dered, still stacked with hard muscle from twelve months of
humping a heavy machine gun and eight hundred rounds of
ammo through the jungle. Handlebar moustache and head
shaved except for a pigtail. Combat boots and faded fatigues
covered with peace & love patches. Groovy.

One time there was this less-than-lukewarm rally. No cops
showed up and the people just stood around and agreed with
each other. After a couple of hours we said fuck it, and went

downtown to a guy's house to get stoned, the six or seven of us who had tried to get the thing moving.

His "pad," and we did call them pads, was a loft above a big old dilapidated theater. The theater had last seen use as a porno palace, and still had fading posters advertising *High School Virgins*, *Lickety Split*, and other moist classics. We scored some hash and Thai sticks and got a couple of gallons of raw Chianti to wash them down.

Turned out the guy's uncle owned the theater, and was letting him stay upstairs rent-free so long as he kept an eye on things. There was a legal injunction against using the theater to show movies for a certain period of time, "Tom" said, but his uncle was game for anything else that might bring in some money. This is where the big coincidence comes in: Tom had been heavily into drama in high school, and he had the notion of turning the place into a live theater. Anybody here know how to act?

Turned out that four of us had worked with plays in high school or college—and I was definitely the senior member of the firm, since I'd been a drama major for two years, before I dropped out and got drafted. I'd done leads in *Shrew* and *Salesman* and had dozens of smaller parts; I also knew a little about makeup, lighting, stage-managing, and so forth. So the Mandala Commune Theater was born that night, in a pleasant buzz of hash and cheap wine. We celebrated by getting a couple of pepperoni pizzas and sprinkling them with Hawaiian Red instead of oregano, which was probably a culinary disaster, but we would've eaten the cardboard box if you'd put dope on it.

There were lots of antiwar, antiestablishment scripts floating around then. We started with one called *Pig Farm*, which required a cast of five women and six men, at least one of the men black. We asked around and wound up with Newton Spears playing the lead.

Newt was a soft-spoken country boy from Alabama who claimed to be a high school dropout. He was smart, though, and a natural actor. He had total control over his accent and could memorize a page of dialogue in ten minutes. His body language was fantastic: when he stepped on the stage he *was* that character, period.

So how come you've never heard of him? Maybe you have. Not by any name like Newton Spears, of course. I like to call him Newt because of one time he sort of looked like one.

Pig Farm was a big success. Newt played the part of a rookie cop who sees the light and winds up in a sort of I-Led-Three-Lives situation, working for the Revolution while outwardly being a model young officer. Good sex scenes. We filled at least half the house every night for three months, with a lot of people coming in night after night, bringing friends.

It was great fun. After the audience filed out we all went down to the green room and split the night's take. After raking out a third for the owner, everybody got one share of the remainder—actor, director (that was me), set designer, writer—with two shares going for theater expenses and one share for beer and dope on the weekends. Each person's share came to about forty bucks a night, which was plenty, in 1967, to stay comfortable on. Even high on, if you weren't into anything exotic.

A lot of us did have exotic habits in those days, but what the hell. You find out somebody was into needle-candy or whips and chains; hey, that's cool; you do your thing and I'll do mine and it's beautiful. I kept my habit secret, though, because it *wasn't* cool; it was kind of silly and nasty. I was a compulsive voyeur. Ever since I got back from Vietnam. Hard to write that down even now, more than twenty years later, even though you can't know who I am. I don't do it anymore, but I'm rather glad I did it then. If I hadn't been a compulsive peeper, I would never have uncovered the interesting secrets of Newton Spears and Lydia Held.

Newt's secret was earthshaking mind-boggling, and would change the world if anyone would believe it, but you won't. Lydia's secret only changed two small worlds, hers and mine.

The theater had been a live theater before it became a

movie house, so we had a stage and backstage and, underneath, equipment rooms and two dressing rooms. I studied the layout and, late one night, let myself into the women's dressing room, where I drilled one scientifically placed hole, hiding it behind a mirror from which I had scraped off a small patch of silvering. The other side of the wall was a room we used for costume storage; the hole went through into a walk-in closet that nobody had any use for, since some vandal had trashed it. Me, actually. So there were just a bunch of boxes stacked there, floor to ceiling, conveniently making a little room inside the little room.

I spent many hours in there, waiting, watching, jerking off. It seems strange now. California in 1967 was a Happy Hunting Ground for anybody in search of sex. But I'd been burned badly in Vietnam by whores, a double whammy of simultaneous syphilis and gonorrhea, and the months of agony made me weird about sex, leery of physical contact with women. And the syphilis had been the resistant kind; it went into bad lesions that left ugly scars. I couldn't imagine showing them to anyone, explaining. What did you do in the war, Daddy? Well, I didn't wear a rubber.

Not a sensible attitude—in some circles such scars were merit badges—but in those days I was not quite sensible. Not quite sane. And I was taking all manner of substances to keep sanity a safe distance away. In fact, if I had seen Newt do it only once, I might have shrugged it off as a hallucination. Acid flashback or whatever. But it didn't happen only once.

I often went into my darkened closet at night, long after anyone had a legitimate reason for being in the dressing room. Several of the women lived with their parents, and used the place for privacy, during or after dates. There was a couch almost directly across from my peephole, and once or twice a week it saw pretty heavy use, lesbian and straight. I would sit in a hard chair and doze lightly. The slightest sound from the dressing room would wake me up. I would reach for the Vaseline and watch the show.

One night I woke to the sound of soft footsteps and was surprised to see Newt in there, alone. He was standing in front of the full-length mirror. He undressed with seductive languor, never taking his eyes off his own reflection. Then came what I thought was the acid working.

His brown skin lightened to the palest Caucasian color, Scandinavian. His hair grew out into an impossibly large Afro, then turned blond and fell softly around his shoulders. His shoulders narrowed and he shrank nearly a foot. He grew breasts and his genitals disappeared—actually retracting into his body—and became a female slit inside pale silky pubic hair as his waist narrowed and his hips and buttocks filled out. Then he, or she, or it, went to the rack and selected a slinky maroon dress and slipped it on. Then he got up close to the mirror and stared: makeup appeared and his hair stood up and styled itself. He gave a musical laugh, high-pitched, and walked out swaying.

When I heard the exit door upstairs slam I rushed quietly up and peeked out onto the street. Newt didn't go very far, just to the first corner. There he/she leaned against the wall, elaborately lit a cigarette, and proceeded to loiter. With obvious purpose.

So Newton Spears had gone from black actor to blond hooker in about three minutes. Far, far out, as we said at the time; far fucking out. That first time I decided it was just drugs and figured the best treatment for it would be a couple of quarts of beer and a long snooze. I went out the back way to the deli down the street and bought whatever was cheapest. I did return to the little room to consume it, though, rather than going home. I wondered whether Newt would come back and do his act in reverse. I wondered what I would do if he did.

He did come back, about three in the morning, and he wasn't alone. There were two sailors with him. They all stripped down and proceeded to perform every kind of dickage possible without a chandelier. Normally it would have been a terrific turn-on, but I watched them go at it with a kind of growing horror. Not because Newt was actually a boy. Homophobia aside, either I was crazy or Newt was no more a boy than he was a girl. I was afraid he was going to turn into a tiger or an octopus or something. A big blob of sizzling protoplasm like the Steve McQueen movie.

He didn't. They got their rocks off a couple of times and then joked around with Newt a little and asked her out to breakfast. She declined, saying it had been a long night for her; she needed a shower and sleep.

After they dressed and left, she stood in the middle of the room, listening intently. When the upstairs door slammed, she peeked out and made sure there was no one in the corridor, and then came back to the mirror and stripped and studied her body. She made the breasts larger, then smaller, and experimented with other proportions. She made her pubic hair disappear back into the skin, and then the hair on her head as well, which made her look like an extraordinarily detailed department store mannequin. Then she turned back into Newton Spears and ran his body through changes. Grotesque ones: arms half a foot long, dick down past his knees, an extra hand growing out of his head. I had the feeling I was watching a sort of Royal Canadian Air Force exercise program for creatures from Alpha Centauri. Practice practice practice. Finally he dressed and left.

I thought there was still a chance that it was an elaborate hallucination, though I'd never had one so detailed and prolonged before. And it didn't have that ethereal "this is real but it's not happening" feel to it. But then I'd never mixed psylocibin with LSD and hash before. So I kept watching and waiting, for weeks and months, keeping fairly straight.

While feeling guilty about peeping on my friends. That was unusual, according to the literature. I'd gone to several libraries and read everything they had on voyeurism, which wasn't much. Because in its milder forms, it's an impoliteness rather than a disorder. Not many normal men would pass up the chance to look through a peephole into a women's dressing room, if there were no chance of being caught. It's less normal, though, to go so far as to drill the hole. To actually sit there for hours on end, staring and masturbating, constitutes obsessive-compulsive behavior. And causes eye-strain. Not to mention chafing.

Two sources, though, pointed out that obsessive-compulsive voyeurs never get their rocks off looking at people they know. These authorities also carry on about how peeping is supposed to give voyeurs feelings of power and superiority over the people they're looking at, but to me it felt quite the opposite. It felt as if *they* had me in *their* power, governing this whole part of my life. My so-called sex life. Every now and then I would go downtown and rent a woman, just to remind myself what it was like, look-Ma-no-hands, but while I was with her I would close my eyes and think about my friends. Especially Lydia Held. And then go back to my little room to wait and watch, sated but not satisfied.

I would much rather have been on the other side of the peephole, at least with most of the women in the troupe, and honestly wouldn't give a damn whether someone was watching us or not. But whenever I would find myself working toward asking one of them out, I'd remember the pain and the scars and my tongue wouldn't work. Most of the women I would ask, I got to see eventually, through the little hole, and so we had sex in a way.

And until Newt came along, I was not all that unhappy with the arrangement. "I may not be normal," as the Willie Nelson song has it, "but nobody is." At least I wasn't flashing little girls or fondling shoes.

But then there was Lydia, pretty in a country-girl, well-scrubbed, Ipana-smile way. I desired her as much as I did any of the other actresses; maybe more, because her personal habits made her in a sense unattainable. She always changed costume in the ladies' room, and then came into the dressing room to apply her makeup. Most of the others sat around in skivvies or less until the last possible moment, since it was pretty warm down there, but Lydia always came in fully dressed. She probably took a little kidding the first time she did it, but by the time I had my vantage point, the others just accepted her eccentricity.

She was a *nice* person, always doing little favors, saying encouraging things. At times I thought she was especially nice to me, and if I could have gotten up the, what, courage?—to ask any of them out, it would have been her. But I was as set in my sexual ways as any monk.

It was kind of dangerous for me to go peeping while the girls were changing costume, since during that time someone was likely to come looking for the director, but that just made it more exciting; the fear of discovery. In the short time I stood there, I would usually just glance at my naked and near-naked friends and then concentrate on Lydia, fully clothed, being as intent on lipstick and powder as I was on her hidden curves.

It's relevant here to point out that Newt had quite a reputation among the crew; it was widely assumed that he had been to bed with all the women at one time or another. In fact, I'd seen him with three of them. But not Lydia.

We went from *Pig Farm* to *The Pat & Dick Show* to *Home For a Soldier*. I saw Newt transform himself several times more into a woman, and once into a light chocolate–skinned dude so handsome as to be almost a cartoon gigolo.

It was during a *Home For a Soldier* intermission costume change that I got caught. I had my eye glued to the hole and had just unzipped when someone cleared his throat softly behind me. I stuffed my wilting dick back inside and turned around. It was Newt.

"You do this often?" he whispered.

I nodded.

"Then you've seen me."

"Yes. I've seen you change."

"Everybody in there changes." He smiled. "We have to talk. Come to my place after the show?"

Rather than give me an address, he said he'd take me there. Any sensible person would have dived through the window and run to take the first Greyhound to anywhere.

He had just admitted to being a creature straight from the pages of the *National Enquirer*. But I said sure, like to see your place. Maybe it's full of methane. Or the bodies of curious earthlings hanging from their heels, drained of blood.

We'd done *Soldier* often enough that the director was superfluous, which was fortunate, as my mind was spinning through all sorts of scenarios, none pleasant. When I left with Newt, it raised some eyebrows—since they never saw me with women, most of them assumed I was gay—and we took public transportation uptown a couple of stops, then went into an indoor lot and picked up Newt's car, a vintage Jaguar XK120. He tipped the boy who drove it up five dollars.

"Business is good," I said.

He shrugged. "Money."

We purred out to a condominium that overlooked the ocean, and Newt's key took the elevator to the penthouse. It was sparsely furnished, like a Japanese place, a few cushions here and there, lights and plants carefully spaced. The paintings on the walls were reproductions of subdued English watercolors and French Impressionists.

Newt popped a cork and poured us each a large balloon glass of red wine and indicated a cushion by a low table. He handed me the glass and sat down across from me, a quick precise sinuous motion like a snake's strike in reverse. "Cheval Blanc 1953," he said, and we clinked glasses.

It was probably the best wine I would ever have. It might as well have been Welch's. "So what *are* you?" I said.

"An actor."

"I mean really."

" 'Actor' is actually about as close as your language can come to what I do." He plucked at his shirt. "This is my role, of course. Would you like to see the last role I played?"

"Sure."

Newton Spears melted and became a scaly purple lizard about eight feet long with yellow fangs that curved out over its lower jaw. Gossamer pink external gills waved from its neck. It yawned, mouth wide enough to swallow me whole, and a delicate black tendril weaved out from inside a large white tongue. It homed in on the wineglass and sucked it dry. The monster changed back into Newt.

"Those creatures are actually more civilized than humans. At least they don't have wars anymore, in spite of the blessings of high technology. They do suck blood for nutrition, though."

The smell of the lizard hung in the air, rank carrion clot and lavender. "That . . . that's what you really do look like?"

"When I choose to. I've been dozens of species."

"I mean when you really look like yourself."

"That's hard to explain." He rubbed his jaw. "This *is* what I look like, to you humans, or the big reptile, to its species, or this"—for a moment he became two intertwined beings of green flickering flame—"to them, and maybe fifty more, but they're all just three-dimensional projections of my five-dimensional self. Frozen in four dimensions; your space-time. In the sense that your shadow on a wall or on the ground is what *you* look like, in a way. Though you could be white or yellow or brown, or have profound physical abnormalities, without the shadow being different.

"And the analogy with acting is real: you find the character within yourself and 'project' that character to the audience. It's not really you, though, no matter how well you convince the audience, or even yourself."

"So this is what you do? You go around to various planets and impersonate the natives?"

"That's *how* I do what I do. My actual job is collecting specimens for a thing like a museum, or a zoo."

I had a sudden chill. The only way out of the penthouse was down the elevator whose key was in Newt's pocket—no! Had to be a fire escape . . .

Newt laughed. "You should see yourself. I'm not going to kidnap you and take you away in my flying saucer. The specimens I collect are cells. Sperm cells, in the case of humans. That's why I take the forms you've seen, the prostitutes. I collect millions of cells every night, not to mention hundreds of dollars." He made a sweeping gesture. "It makes the job more comfortable."

"So what are you going to do now? Now that one of us knows your secret?"

He swirled his wine around in the glass. "That makes less difference than you might think. My identity was exposed several years ago, in a German tabloid, pictures and all. I just changed shape and left. No reputable news outlet would carry the story, of course. I could do the same thing here. But you wouldn't gain anything by telling the world what I am—and you'd lose your star."

"You mean you'd stay?"

"Sure. As long as you don't tell anybody else. I like the people and the situation. It's a good area for collecting specimens. I'm even willing to bribe you." He shimmered and changed, becoming a voluptuous brunette in a filmy pink Fredricks-of-Hollywood thing.

"Looks familiar."

"To you and a hundred million other men. I'm Lena Curriet, this month's Playmate of the Month." He shimmered and changed again, to Merilee Larson, his costar in *Soldier*, wearing a carelessly open robe. "Maybe you'd prefer something closer to home."

I swallowed saliva. "Lydia Held."

"Sorry." He turned back into Newt. "I could do an approximation. But I've never seen her undressed. Neither have you, I suppose."

I shook my head. "I've heard the others say she dresses in the ladies' room."

"Inside the stall, as a matter of fact. I've checked. Peculiar for a person who acts, to be so modest." He looked at me closely. "I understand. She's the only one you haven't been able to watch while you stimulate yourself. So you desire her especially."

"You make it sound so romantic."

He shrugged. "It's only a process to me. Maybe I could

help you. Do you have sex with women, I mean the usual way?"

"Prostitutes every now and then."

"I'll warn you if you ever run into me. Wait here." Newt disappeared into a back room and closed the door. After a couple of minutes he returned with a small glass vial with a half inch of colorless liquid in it. "Do you know what pheromones are?"

"Huh uh. Some kind of drug?"

"I suppose so, in this case. Put just a drop on each wrist, then get Lydia alone with you—or maybe get her alone with you *first*. Any woman around who smells that is going to find you irresistible."

"It's an actual aphrodisiac?"

"In a way. Your science doesn't have anything like it yet. I use the male version when business gets slow." I stared at the vial, shook it. "You're not sure?" he said.

"Newt . . . what I said about prostitutes, I mean, that's *it*. I haven't had sex without paying for it since before I was in the army, five or six years."

"So start with Lydia."

"It's not that simple. I have scars." He shrugged. "I mean on my *dick*!"

"Big deal. Most women wouldn't even notice."

"Sure, they wouldn't."

"I've been one. And I've seen more dicks than a urologist. But if it bothers you, just do it in the dark. Lydia would probably prefer it, since she doesn't want to undress even in front of women."

"In the dark she'll still feel the scars."

"No, she won't. *You* feel them, which I suppose is your problem, or part of it."

I could feel myself blushing. "You must think I'm pretty weird."

"No. Look. Every other Thursday I have a guy who takes me home and dresses me up in a big diaper and has me 'make a mistake' in it. Then he cleans me up and tells me what a bad girl I am while I suck his cock. That, I would classify as weird. What you do is pretty ordinary."

"Spy on women and jerk off."

"You can put it that way if it helps you deal with it. But what you actually do is have sex with a variety of people without any emotional connection involved."

"Or *physical* connection."

"That's not unusual either. Half the people who are fucking tonight are thinking about somebody who's not in the same room with them."

"You know an awful lot about it for someone who's not even human."

"I have an interesting perspective." He slipped a folded twenty-dollar bill under the wineglass. "I called a cab. It ought to be here in a minute or two. Drink up and go to her."

"Uh . . . I don't know her address."

"I gave it to the cab—213 West Palm, Apartment 3."

"You know a lot about a lot of things."

"It's the extra two dimensions. Get outa here."

She lived on the other side of town, but the cab ride wasn't long enough. What would I say . . . Why don't we go out for a beer? Thought I'd drop by and talk about the script? May I watch you undress? Here, sniff this stuff.

We passed a flower stand next to a drugstore and I had the cabbie stop. Some roses and some rubbers. With a rubber she wouldn't be able to feel the scars.

But then I felt like a real kid, waiting there with a bouquet after I knocked on her door. What if she broke out laughing? I could always use the rubbers the way we used to. Fill them with water and drop them on police cars.

She looked quizzical when she opened the door but smiled at the flowers. "Come on in. I thought you were out with Newton."

"We just had some stuff to talk about. Didn't take long." She said the place was a mess, which it wasn't, by my stan-

dards. Find a place to sit down while she put the roses
(which I had dabbed with the pheromone stuff) in some water. There was a beanbag chair big enough for two, encouraging. I sank into it and surveyed the peace posters and large
record and book collection on neat brick-and-board shelves.
I put a drop of the magic liquid onto each wrist.

"Like some Coke?" she called from the kitchen, and I said
yes, not knowing whether it would be brown liquid or white
powder. I suspected the former, and was right.

She gave me the Coke and put the vase of roses on a low
table next to the beanbag then sat down on the floor in front
of me, cross-legged. She was blushing. "Nobody has brought
me flowers since I was in high school."

"I guess it was a dumb idea."

"Oh no." She leaned over and tipped the vase to smell
them. "Nice. What did you and Newton talk about?"

"Well . . . among other things . . . you."

She looked at the floor and there was a long awkward
silence. "Everybody says you're gay. Not that it—"

"I'm not. Just shy that way, uh, since the army. And . . .
peculiar, maybe."

"So am I," she said, almost inaudibly, still looking at the
floor. Did she mean shy, or peculiar?

"Would you like to go out or something?"

"No." She studied her hand and picked at a fingernail.
Then she turned around langorously and leaned back so her
head was on the beanbag next to me. Her cheek against my
thigh. She closed her eyes and smiled. "Let's just stay here
and talk."

We didn't talk much. The magic liquid worked fast. I
started to make the usual sort of physical overtures and she
grabbed my hand and said no, let's just go straight to bed.
As Newt had predicted, she preferred darkness; she even
went into the bedroom first and turned out all the lights.

That made it more exciting in an odd way. She led me by
the hand to the bed, just a mattress on the floor, and asked
me to put my clothes where I could find them in the dark.

"The only thing I ask," she said, "is that you leave before morning. And don't ask why."

I agreed, and was sensible enough not to reveal that I knew about her phobia.

The details would be interesting to you but I don't want to write them down. It lasted a long time, various permutations, and was wonderful, I think for both of us. But I was exhausted and slept well past daybreak. I suppose at some level Lydia actually wanted me to.

I woke with light streaming in through the high window. I blinked at a forest of dicks.

I rubbed my eyes and blinked a few times more and then could properly interpret what I was looking at. There was a montage of photographs taped to the ceiling over the bed, and down the wall; hundreds of male members in every state from repose to ejaculation.

"I get them in the mail," she said in a quiet voice. "Mostly magazines for gay men. I go through the pictures and cut out the ones I like best. Disgusting, isn't it."

"A lot of men do the same thing," I said.

"It's all right for *men*."

"Anything you do is all right by me," I said, and turned to her, but she rolled away, wrapped like a mummy in the top sheet, and started crying.

"I do even stranger—"

"You don't know half of it!" she almost shouted. "Or you do know just half of it." She slowly unwound herself from the sheet and stood in front of me, naked, shoulders slumped, looking down at herself.

Her body was a road map of crisscrossing pink scars. She looked like she had been taken apart and put back together. "Three years and seven months ago," she said. "Sutter's Mill Road. I was riding my bicycle and a semi hit me and dragged me a hundred yards. They picked up pieces and put them in a cooler. Most of them didn't take." She cupped a breast gingerly, as if it still hurt. "This is completely fake. Just a silicone bag covered with skin from my . . . my bottom. A lot of it's like that." She sat on the bed with her back to me; it was as badly scarred as her front.

I hadn't felt the scars in the dark. Just softness, heat, wetness, passion.

"They paid all the medical expenses and settled out of court for three quarters of a million dollars. It's a living, the interest on that; a pretty good living. Not much of a life. You're the first man I've had in four years and I feel like I've cheated you."

I didn't know what to say. I was feeling too many emotions at once. "The scars ... they don't make any difference. Or they do, but I still think you're beautiful. Look at this." I meant to show her my own scars, but that's not exactly what she saw. She laughed and flowed across the bed like a hungry animal.

The theater turned into pure chaos when Newton Spears disappeared, despite what he'd assured me, the day after Lydia and I got together. Another male lead came out of the woodwork in a couple of weeks, though, with a suspiciously similar chameleon-like facility. I never called him on it; he went on to become a rather famous character actor in the movies.

I took the magic vial to a friend who was a graduate student in organic chemistry, and he spent most of a weekend analyzing it. Plain tap water, as far as he could tell. I wasn't too surprised. Plain tap water plus two extra dimensions of insight into human nature.

After several days of some intensity, we did get around to discussing my own scars, and what they meant to me, and whether there was something going on with all this scar business that could ultimately be hurtful to both of us. Without putting it in so many words, I guess we decided that if things didn't work out, we could always just crawl back into our holes.

Holes and holes and holes. I showed her my peephole, which both amused and shocked her, and closed it up with putty. She took down her photo gallery, at least for the du-ration. That's twenty-five years, so far.

I've never told her about Newt, and sometimes I wonder whether he ever happened, the changes, the night of reve-lation. So much from those times is fluid, memory merging with imagination. Drugs, but not just drugs. Sometimes it feels as if someone else went to Vietnam and told me all about it, told me well enough and hard enough to make it real. Then our dreams cracked by the hammerblows of King and Kennedy, blood in Chicago and flames in Washington, all the sweetness and lovingkindness hardening into political reality that crystalized into the baroque fantasies of Water-gate and Reagan; America drifting rudderless into the cen-tury we never thought we'd live to see. Hippies forty years old? Fifty? Hippies on Social Security?

Whatever. I met a creature straight out of the *National Enquirer* who gave me and Lydia a measure of love and peace in this mad world. Even a daughter unbelievably fat with grandchild, and me still a shaved-head hippy with a ponytail, gray now, making a pretty good living off the other middle-aged hippies, selling dreams, maybe biding time. With age you learn that revolution has a slow meaning, too. Things come around again. My daughter's a realtor but her child will be something else.

So that's my story. And you don't believe it, unless you're Newt. That's okay. Everything's fiction. Everything's true.

○ ○ ○ *This one started out as pure theory, a demonstration for my MIT science fiction writing class. Most sf stories, I told them, follow one of two patterns: an ordinary character thrust into a bizarre situation or a bizarre character in an everyday situation. I wrote the opening of "Images"—up to where the protagonist sees Newt chang-ing—to demonstrate it. I didn't tell them it was both kinds of story being told at once.*

The shape-changing came from imagination; the story was written before morphing became a common special effect. The stage stuff was experience. At the time I was involved in a stage play of The Forever War, commuting every week between Cambridge and Chicago.

The scar business is from experience, too; I picked up dozens of scars from bullet and shrapnel wounds in Vietnam, and for years the appearance of them bothered me. The voyeurism comes from experience, as well. I was never as compulsive about it as our hero, but when I was a boy that was the only available source of information about the female body. It must seem odd to males under forty, who have grown up surrounded by icons of frank nude sexuality, but most boys of my generation didn't have any clear idea of what girls actually looked like, and would move heaven and earth, or at least the transom of a locker room, to find out.

beachhead

IT WAS TOO nice a day for this. The morning sun was friendly warm, still early, not yet hot in the tropical sky. Salt air, sound of the gentle breakers ahead; if you closed your eyes you could picture girls and picnics. Riding waves, playing. The girls in their wet clinging suits, hinting mysteries, that's the kind of day it should have been.

Curious seabirds creaked and cawed, begging, as they followed the craft wallowing its way toward shore. Its motor was silent, as was its cargo of boys. Quiet tick and clack as bits of metal swung and tapped in the swaying craft.

The salt tang not quite as strong as the smell of lubricant. Duncan opened his eyes and for the hundredth time rubbed the treated cloth along the exposed metal parts of his weapon. Take care of this weapon, boy, the sergeant had said, over and over; take care of it and it will take care of you. This weapon's all that's between you and dying.

The readout by the sight said 125. Ten dozen people he could fry before recharging.

A soft triple snick of metal as the boy next to him clicked his bayonet into place over the muzzle of the weapon. Others

looked at him, but nobody said anything. You weren't supposed to put the bayonet on until you were on the beach.
Someone might get hurt in the charge. That was almost
funny.

"You're not supposed to do that," Duncan said, just above
a whisper.

"I know," the boy said. "I'll be careful." They really hadn't
had that much training. Three years before, they'd been
pulled out of school and sent to the military academy. But
until the last month it had been just like regular school,
except that you lived in a dorm instead of at home. Then
some quick instruction in guns and knives and you were on
your way to the Zone.

The surf grew louder and the pitching of the boat more
pronounced as they surged in through the breakers.
Someone spattered vomit inside the craft, not daring to raise
his head above the heavy metal shielding of the sides, and
then two more did the same; so much for the fragrance of
the sea. Duncan's breakfast was sour in his throat and he
swallowed it back. Someone cried softly, sobbing like a girl.
A boy tried to quiet him with a silly harsh insult. Someone
admonished him, with no conviction, to save it for the enemy. It was all so absurd. Like dying on a day like this. Even
for real soldiers, dying on a day like this would be absurd.

The bow of the craft ground to a halt on coral sand. Duncan lurched to his feet, weapon at port arms, ready to rush
out. Warm air from the beach wafted in with a new smell, a
horrible smell: burning flesh.

He didn't think he could kill anyone. It was all a dreadful
mistake. He was sixteen years old and at the top of his class
in calculus and Latin. Now he was going to step off this boat
into a firestorm of lasers and die.

"This is crazy." The large boy loomed over the counselor's
desk, nearly as tall as the adult and outbulking him by ten
kilograms of muscle. "It has to be the tests. They screwed up

on my brother three years ago and now they screwed up on me."

"Please watch your language." The boy glared at him and then blushed and nodded. "Do you have any idea how often this happens, Eric? You think that because Duncan didn't want to go to the Zone and you did, the tests would necessarily reflect your wishes. Your own evaluation of yourselves. But people at thirteen don't really know themselves very well. That's no crime. It's just a fact of life."

"Look, Professor. It ain't just my *opinion*. Ask anybody! Anybody who knows us both." He counted out points on his fingers. "Duncan never wanted to play soldier when he was a kid. I always did. He never went out for sports; I'm captain of the two teams. He used to read books, I mean all the time, and I don't unless it's for school. He never once got into a fight in school, and I—"

"And you took the tests. And the tests don't lie."

"Maybe they don't. But they make mistakes in the office all the time. That's gotta be what happened. They took the test results and got Duncan's and mine switched."

"You weren't even ten when Duncan took his last one."

"Yeah, but I'd took 'em twice by the time I was ten. They could of gotten mixed up."

The man shrugged. "All right; I'll show you." He unfolded himself out of the chair and stepped over to a bank of filing cabinets. He took out two adjacent folders and threw them on the desk. Sitting down, he typed something on his keyboard and turned the monitor around to face Eric.

The boy's brow was furrowed as he looked from one test to another. "So it's these red numbers. Duncan got a sixty-eight and I got a ninety-two." He looked up with a skeptical expression. "Usually it's the other way around."

"It's not an intelligence test. It's a test for antisocial aggressive potential. How easy it would be for you to kill somebody." He pointed at the monitor. "You know what a bell-shaped curve is."

"Yeah, like for grades." Red lines showed where he and

his brother stood in relation to the average, Eric well to the right of the graph's shoulder and Duncan on the extreme left.

"For grades and for a lot of things. You can chart a bunch of people's height or weight and they come out this way. Or ask them on a scale of one to ten 'Do you like cheddar cheese?'—and this is what you get."

"So?"

"So the attitude test you took didn't come right out and say, 'How would you like to get the enemy in your sights and fry him?' Most people in their right mind would say—"

"But I *would*!" His eyes actually glittered. "I mean I've really thought about it a lot! What it would look like and all."

"What it would feel like."

He smiled. "Yeah."

The counselor tapped three times on the test packet. "That's in here, all right. But it's just boyish enthusiasm. Playing soldier. You're going to be a solid citizen. A peaceable, well-adjusted man who makes a real contribution to society. You're the lucky one."

He shook his head slowly. "But Duncan—"

"Duncan was a true psychopath, a born killer who hid it so well he fooled even his brother. That sixty-eight is about as low as I've ever seen. Don't envy him. He's probably dead by now. If he's not dead, he's going through hell."

Eric kept shaking his head and stuffed his hands into his pockets. "He was a nice guy, though."

"Jack the Ripper was probably a nice guy."

"Well . . . thanks. Better get to class." He paused at the door. "But I might see him again. I mean, like, *you* came back."

"That's right. Counselors are all people who've been sent to the Zone. People who lived long enough to change."

"Well. Maybe."

"We can hope." He watched the boy trudge away, deep in thought, and suppressed a grin. Sometimes the satisfactions of this job were not at all subtle.

* * *

The front of the landing craft unhooked and slapped forward with a blinding spray of foam. The boys charged out, terrified, frantic, into the smell of roasting flesh—

The first ones on the beach stopped dead. The next ones piled up behind them, and the boy who had fixed his bayonet just missed skewering Duncan.

Twenty meters up the beach, under a red-and-white striped awning, four pretty girls in brief bathing suits tended a suckling pig that turned over coals, roasting. Tubs of ice with cold drinks.

An older man in a bathing suit held up a drink, toasting them. Duncan didn't recognize him at first, without coat and tie. It was Ian Johnson, the counselor who had condemned him to this place. "Welcome to the Zone," he called out. "War's hell."

Like a number of the others, Duncan pointed his weapon at the sky and pulled the trigger. Nothing happened.

The girls laughed brightly.

That night, sitting around a bonfire, they learned the actual way of the world. The Zone *was* the real world, and the island nation where they had gone through childhood and most of their early schooling was actually a prison without walls. Or a zoo without bars, where the zookeepers mingled unnoticed with the specimens.

The Enemy did not exist; there was no war. It was only a ruse to explain why people couldn't leave, unless they left in uniform. Children like Eric stayed on the island, constantly monitored by observers from the real world, until they trained themselves out of aggressiveness and were allowed to leave. Or they grew up, lived, and died there, their options restricted for everyone's sake. Their world was a couple of centuries out of date, necessarily, since in the real world everyone had access to technologies that could be perverted into weapons of mass destruction.

It had been a truism since the simple atomic age, that the social sciences hadn't been able to keep up with the physical ones; that our ability to control the material world had accelerated without our moral strength increasing to accommodate our powers.

There was a war that had to be the last one, and the few survivors put together this odd construct to protect themselves and their descendants *from* themselves and their descendants.

They still couldn't change human nature, but they could measure aspects of it with extraordinary reliability. And they could lie about the measurements, denying to a large minority of the population a freedom that they did not know existed.

For some years Duncan went down to the beach on Invasion Day, looking for his brother Eric in the dumbfounded battalions that slogged through the surf into the real world. Then one year he was too busy, and the rest of the years just had the office computer automatically check the immigration lists.

In the other real world, Eric sometimes wondered if his brother was still alive.

Author's Note

Twenty years ago, my wife had her first real full-time job, teaching Spanish in a rural Florida high school that had recently, reluctantly, become integrated. The students had taken language aptitude tests and only those with high potential were allowed into her classroom.

Predictably, the elite students—most of whom, surprisingly, had gone through the "inferior" black primary school system—threw themselves into the work with enthusiasm, learning fast, doing extra work, having a good time at it. They were a joy to teach.

About a year later, my wife found out that the office had made a fundamental error. Everyone who *took* the test, pass or fail, had been allowed into the class. Some of them had language aptitudes far below average.

They were *told* they were special, though, and would succeed. So of course that turned out to be a self-fulfilling prophecy.

O O O *This story is almost completely made up; the only things that come from my actual combat experience are the smell of burning flesh and young soldiers' carelessness about weapons.*

Harry Harrison asked me to do a story for There Won't Be War, *an anthology whose premise I found both desirable and doubtful. I couldn't think of a realistic story set in a world without war, but I could come up with a parable.*

I've never been in, or even seen, a landing craft like the one in the story. All that comes from William Manchester's marvelous book Goodbye, Darkness, *where the author tries to recapture his feelings as a marine in the Pacific in WWII.*

the monster

START AT THE beginning? Which beginning?

Okay, since you be from Outside, I give you the whole thing. Sit over there, be comfort. Smoke em if you got em.

They talk about these guys that come back from the Nam all fucked up and shit, and say they be like time bombs: they go along okay for years, then get a gun and just go crazy. But it don't go nothing like that for me. Even though there be the gun involved, this time. And an actual murder, this time.

First time I be in prison, after the court-martial, I try to tell them what it be and what they get me? Social workers and shrinks. Guy to be a shrink in a prison ain't be no good shrink, what they can make Outside, is the way I figure it, so at first I don't give them shit, but then I always get Discipline, so I figure what the hell and make up a story. You watch any TV you can make up a Nam story too.

So some of them don't fall for it, they go along with it for a while because this is what crazy people do, is make up stories, then they give up and another one come along and I start over with a different story. And sometime when I know for sure they don't believe, when they start to look at me like you look at a animal in the zoo, that's when I tell them the real true story. And that's when they smile, you know, and nod, and the new guy come in next. Because if anybody would make up a story like that one, he'd have to be crazy, right? But I swear to God it's true.

Right. The beginning.

I be a lurp in the Nam, which means Long Range Recon Patrol. You look in these magazines about the Nam and they make like the lurps be always heroes, brave boys go out and face Charlie alone, bring down the artillery on them and all, but it was not like that. You didn't want to be no lurp where we be, they make you be a fuckin lurp if they want to get rid of your ass, and that's the God's truth.

Now I can tell you right now that I don't give a flyin fuck for that U.S. Army and I don't like it even more when I be drafted, but I got to admit they be pretty smart, the way they do with us. Because we get off on that lurp shit. I mean we be one bunch of bad ass brothers and good ole boys and we did love that rock an roll, and God they give us rock an roll—fuck your M-16, we get real tommy guns with 100-round drum, usually one guy get your automatic grenade launcher, one guy carry that starlite scope, another guy the full demo bag. I mean we could of taken on the whole fuckin North Vietnam army. We could of killed fuckin Rambo.

Now I like to talk strange, though any time I want, I can talk like other people. Even Jamaican like my mama ain't understand me if I try. I be born in New York City, but at that time my mama be only three months there—when she speak her English it be island music, but the guy she live with, bringing me up, he be from Taiwan, so in between them I learn shitty English, same-same shitty Chinese. And live in Cuban neighborhood, *por la español* shitty.

He was one mean mother fuckin Chinese cab driver, slap shit out of me for twelve year, and then I take a kitchen knife and slap him back. He never come back for the ear. I think maybe he go off someplace and die, I don't give a shit anymore, but when I be drafted they find out I speak Chinese, send me to language school in California, and I be so dumb I believe them when they say this means no Nam for the boy: I stay home and translate for them tapes from the radio.

So they send me to the Nam anyhow, and I go a little wild. I hit everybody that outranks me. They put me in the hospital and I hit the doctor. They put me in the stockade and I hit the guards, the guards hit back, some more hospital. I figure sooner or later they got to kill me or let me out. But then one day this strac dude come in and tell me about the lurp shit. It sound all right, even though the dude say if I fuck up they can waste me and it's legal. By now I know they can do that shit right there in LBJ, Long Binh Jail, so what the fuck? In two days I'm in the jungle with three real bad ass dudes with a map and a compass and enough shit we could start our own war.

They give us these maps that never have no words on them, like names of places, just "TOWN POP 1000" and shit like that. They play it real cute, like we so dumb we don't know there be places outside of Vietnam, where no GIs can go. They keep all our ID in base camp, even the dog tags, and tell us not to be capture. Die first, they say, that shall be more pleasant. We laugh at that later, but I keep to myself the way I do feel. That the grave be one place we all be getting to, long road or short, and maybe the short road be less bumps, less trouble. Now I know from twenty years how true that be.

They don't tell us where the place be we leave from, after the slick drop us in, but we always sure as hell head west. Guy name Duke, mean honky but not dumb, he say all we be doin is harassment, bustin up supply lines comin down the Ho Chi Minh Trail, in Cambodia. It do look like that, long lines of gooks carryin ammo and shit, sometime on bicycles. We would set up some mine and some claymores and wait till the middle of the line be there, then pop the shit, then maybe waste a few with the grenade launcher and tommy guns, not too long so they ain't regroup and get us. Duke be taking a couple Polaroids and we go four different ways, meet a couple miles away, then sneak back to the LZ and call the slick. We go out maybe six time a month, maybe lose one guy a month. Me and Duke make it through all the way to the last one, that last one.

That time no different from the other times except they tell us try to blow a bridge up, not a big bridge like the movies, but one that hang off a mountain side, be hard to fix afterward. It also be hard to get to.

We lose one guy, new guy name of Winter, just tryin to get to the fuckin bridge. That be bad in a special kind of way. You get used to guys gettin shot or be wasted by frags and like that. But to fall like a hundred feet onto rocks be a different kind of bad. And it just break his back or something. He laying there and crying, tell all the world where we be, until Duke shut him up.

So it be just Duke and Cherry and me, the Chink. I am for goin back, no fuckin way they could blame us for that. But Duke crazy for action, always be crazy for killing, and Cherry would follow Duke anywhere, I think he a fag even then. Later I do know. When the Monster kill them.

This is where I usually feel the need to change. It's natural to adjust one's mode of discourse to a level appropriate to the subject at hand, is it not? To talk about this "Monster" requires addressing such concepts as disassociation and multiple personality, if only to discount them, and it would be awkward to speak of these things directly the way I normally speak, as Chink. This does not mean that there are two or several personalities resident within the sequestered hide of this disabled black veteran. It only means that I can speak in different ways. You could as well, if you grew up switching back and forth among Spanish, Chinese, and two flavors of English, chocolate and vanilla. It might also help if you had learned various Vietnamese dialects, and then spent the past twenty years in a succession of small rooms, mainly reading and writing. There still be the bad mother fucker in here.

He simply uses appropriate language. The right tool for the job, or the right weapon.

Let me save us some time by demonstrating the logical weakness of some facile first order rationalizations that always seem to come up. One: that this whole Monster business is a bizarre lie I concocted and have stubbornly held on to for twenty years—which requires that it never have occurred to me that recanting it would result in much better treatment and, possibly, release. Two: that the Monster is some sort of psychological shield, or barrier, that I have erected between my "self" and the enormity of the crime I committed. That hardly holds up to inspection, since my job and life at that time comprised little more than a succession of premeditated cold-blooded murders. I didn't kill the two men, but if I had, it wouldn't have bothered me enough to require elaborate psychological defenses. Three: that I murdered Duke and Cherry because I was . . . upset at discovering them engaged in a homosexual act. I am and was indifferent toward that aberration, or hobby. Growing up in the ghetto and going directly from there to an army prison in Vietnam, I witnessed perversions for which you psychologists don't even have names.

Then of course there is the matter of the supposed eyewitness. It seemed particularly odious to me at the time, that my government would prefer the testimony of an erstwhile enemy soldier over one of its own. I see the process more clearly now, and realize that I was convicted before the court-martial was even convened.

The details? You know what a *hoi chan* was? You're too young. Well, *chieu hoi* is Vietnamese for "open arms"; if an enemy soldier came up to the barbed wire with his hands up, shouting *chieu hoi*, then in theory he would be welcomed into our loving, also open, arms and rehabilitated. Unless he was killed before people could figure out what he was saying. The rehabilitated ones were called *hoi chans*, and sometimes were used as translators and so forth.

Anyhow, this Vietnamese deserter's story was that he had

been following us all day, staying out of sight, waiting for an opportunity to surrender. I don't believe that for a second. Nobody moves that quietly, that fast, through unfamiliar jungle. Duke had been a professional hunting guide back in the World, and he would have heard any slightest movement.

What do I say happened? You must have read the transcript ... I see. You want to check me for consistency.

I had sustained a small but deep wound in the calf, a fragment from a rifle grenade, I believe. I did elude capture, but the wound slowed me down.

We had blown the bridge at 1310, which was when the guards broke for lunch, and had agreed to rendezvous by 1430 near a large banyan tree about a mile from the base of the cliff. It was after 1500 when I got there, and I was worried. Winter had been carrying our only radio when he fell, and if I wasn't at the LZ with the other two, they would sensibly enough leave without me. I would be stranded, wounded, lost.

I was relieved to find them still waiting. In this sense I may *have* caused their deaths: if they had gone on, the Monster might have killed only me.

This is the only place where my story and that of the *hoi chan* are the same. They were indeed having sex. I waited under cover rather than interrupt them.

Yes, I know, this is where he testified I jumped them and did all those terrible things. Like *he* had been sitting off to one side, waiting for them to finish their business. What a bunch of bullshit.

What actually happened—what *actually* happened—was that I was hiding there behind some bamboo, waiting for them to finish so we could get on with it, when there was this sudden loud crashing in the woods on the other side of them, and bang. There was the Monster. It was bigger than any man, and black—not black like me, but glossy black, like shiny hair—and it just flat smashed into them, bashed them apart. Then it was on Cherry, I could hear bones crack like sticks. It bit him between the legs, and that was enough for

me. I was gone. I heard a couple of short bursts from Duke's
tommy gun, but I didn't go back to check it out. Just headed
for the LZ as fast as my leg would let me.

So I made a big mistake. I lied. Wouldn't you? I'm supposed to tell them sorry, the rest of the squad got eaten by
a werewolf? So while I'm waiting for the helicopter I make
up this believable account of what happened at the bridge.

The slick comes and takes me back to the fire base, where
the medics dress the wound and I debrief to the major there.
They send me to Tuy Hoa, nice hospital on the beach, and
I debrief again, to a bunch of captains and a bird colonel.
They tell me I'm in for a Silver Star.

So I'm resting up there in the ward, reading a magazine,
when in comes a couple of MPs and they grab me and haul
me off to the stockade. Isn't that just like the army, to have
a stockade in a hospital?

What has happened is that this gook, honorable *hoi chan*
Nguyen Van Trong, has come out of the woodwork with his
much more believable story. So I get railroaded and wind up
in jail.

Come on now, it's all in the transcript. I'm tired of telling
it. It upsets me.

Oh, all right. This Nguyen claims he was a guard at the
bridge we blew up, and he'd been wanting to escape—they
don't say "desert"—ever since they'd left Hanoi a few
months before. Walking down the Ho Chi Minh Trail. So in
the confusion after the blast, he runs away; he hears Duke
and Cherry and follows them. Waiting for the right opportunity to go *chieu hoi*. I've told you how improbable that actually is.

So he's waiting in the woods while they blow each other
and up walks me. I get the drop on them with my Thompson.
I make Cherry tie Duke to the tree. Then I tie Cherry up,
facing him. Then I castrate Cherry—with my *teeth*! You believe that? And then with my teeth and fingernails, I flay
Duke, skin him alive, from the neck down, while he's watch-

ing Cherry die. Then for dessert, I bite off his cock, too. Then I cut them down and stroll away.

You got that? This Nguyen claims to have watched the whole thing, must have taken hours. Like he never had a chance to interrupt my little show. What, did I hang on to my weapon all the time I was nibbling away? Makes a lot of sense.

After I leave, he say he try to help the two men. Duke, he say, be still alive, but not worth much. Say he follow Duke's gestures and get the Polaroid out of his pack.

When those picture show up at the trial, I be a Had Daddy. Forget that his story ain't makin sense. Forget for Chris' sake that he be the fuckin *enemy*! Picture of Duke be still alive and his guts all hangin out, this god-awful look on his face, I could of been fuckin Sister Theresa and they wouldn't of listen to me.

[At this point the respondent was silent for more than a minute, apparently controlling rage, perhaps tears. When he continued speaking, it was with the cultured white man's accent again.]

I know you are constrained not to believe me, but in order to understand what happened over the next few years, you must accept as tentatively true the fantastic premises of my delusional system. Mainly, that's the reasonable assertion that I didn't mutilate my friends, and the unreasonable one that the Cambodian jungle hides at least one glossy black humanoid over seven feet tall, with the disposition of a barracuda.

If you accept that this Monster exists, then where does that leave Mr. Nguyen Van Trong? One possibility is that he saw the same thing I did, and lied for the same reason I initially did—because no one in his right mind would believe the truth—but his lie implicated me, I suppose for verisimilitude.

A second possibility is the creepy one that Nguyen was somehow allied with the Monster; in league with him.

The third possibility . . . is that they were the same.

If the second or the third were true, it would probably be a good policy for me never to cross tracks with Nguyen again, or at least never to meet him unarmed. From that, it followed that it would be a good precaution for me to find out what had happened to him after the trial.

A maximum-security mental institution is far from an ideal place from which to conduct research. But I had several things going for me. The main thing was that I was not, despite all evidence to the contrary, actually crazy. Another was that I could take advantage of people's preconceptions, which is to say prejudices: I can tune my language from a mildly accented Jamaican dialect to the almost-impenetrable patois that I hid behind while I was in the army. Since white people assume that the smarter you are, the more like them you sound, and since most of my keepers were white, I could control their perception of me pretty well. I was a dumb nigger who with their help was getting a little smarter.

Finally I wangled a work detail in the library. Run by a white lady who thought she was hardass but had a heart of purest tapioca. Loved to see us goof off so long as we were reading.

I was gentle and helpful and appreciative of her guidance. She let me read more and more, and of course I could take books back to my cell. There was no record of many of the books I checked out: computer books.

She was a nice woman but fortunately not free of prejudice. It never occurred to her that it might not be a good idea to leave her pet darky alone with the computer terminal.

Once I could handle the library's computer system, my Nguyen project started in earnest. Information networks are wonderful, and computerized ordering and billing is, for a thief, the best tool since the credit card. I could order any book in print—after all, I opened the boxes, shelved the new volumes, and typed up the catalog card for each book. If I wanted it to be cataloged.

Trying to find out what the Monster was, I read all I could find about extraterrestrials, werewolves, mutations; all that science fiction garbage. I read up on Southeast Asian religions and folktales. Psychology books, because Occam's razor can cut the person who's using it, and maybe I *was* crazy after all.

Nothing conclusive came out of any of it. I had seen the Monster for only a couple of seconds, but the quick impression was, of course, branded on my memory. The face was intelligent, perhaps I should say "sentient," but it was not at all human. Two eyes, okay, but no obvious nose or ears. Mouth too big and lots of teeth like a shark's. Long fingers with too many joints, and claws. No mythology or pathology that I read about produced anything like it.

The other part of my Nguyen project was successful. I used the computer to track him down, through my own court records and various documents that had been declassified through the Freedom of Information Act.

Not surprisingly, he had emigrated to the United States just before the fall of Saigon. By 1986 he had his own fish market in San Francisco. Pillar of the community, the bastard.

Eighteen years of exemplary behavior and I worked my way down to minimum security. It was a more comfortable and freer life, but I didn't see any real chance of parole. I probably couldn't even be paroled if I'd been white and had bitten the cocks off two *black* men. I might get a medal, but not a parole.

So I had to escape. It wasn't hard.

I assumed that they would alert Nguyen, and perhaps watch him or even guard him for a while. So for two years I stayed away from San Francisco, burying myself in a dirt-poor black neighborhood in Washington. I saved my pennies and purchased or contrived the tools I would need when I eventually confronted him.

Finally I boarded a Greyhound, crawled to San Francisco, and rested up a couple of days. Then for another couple of days I kept an intermittent watch on the fish market, to satisfy myself that Nguyen wasn't under guard.

He lived in a two-room apartment in the rear of the store. I popped the back door lock a half hour before closing and hid in the bedroom. When I heard him lock the front door, I walked in and pointed a .44 Magnum at his face.

That was the most tense moment for me. I more than half expected him to turn into the Monster. I had even gone to the trouble of casting my own bullets of silver, in case that superstition turned out to be true.

He asked me not to shoot and took out his wallet. Then he recognized me and clammed up.

I made him strip to his shorts and tied him down with duct tape to a wooden chair. I turned the television on fairly loud, since my homemade silencer was not perfect, and traded the Magnum for a .22 automatic. It made about as much noise as a flyswatter, each time I shot.

There are places where you can shoot a person even with a .22 and he will die quickly and without too much pain. There are other sites that are quite the opposite. Of course I concentrated on those, trying to make him talk. Each time I shot him I dressed the wound, so there would be a minimum of blood loss.

I first shot him during the evening news, and he lasted well into Johnny Carson, with a new bullet each half hour. He never said a word, or cried out. Just stared.

After he died, I waited a few hours, and nothing happened. So I walked to the police station and turned myself in. That's it.

So here we be now. I know it be life for me. Maybe it be that rubber room. I ain't care. This be the only place be safe. The Monster, he know. I can feel.

[This is the end of the transcript proper. The respondent did not seem agitated when the guards led him away. Consistent with his final words, he seemed relieved to be back in prison, which makes his subsequent suicide mystifying. The circumstances heighten the mystery, as the attached coroner's note indicates.]

State of California
Department of Corrections
Forensic Pathology Division
Glyn Malin, M.D., Ph.D.—Chief of Research

I have read about suicides that were characterized by sudden hysterical strength, including a man who had apparently choked himself to death by throttling (though I seem to recall that it was a heart attack that actually killed him). The case of Royce "Chink" Jackson is one I would not have believed if I had not seen the body myself.

The body is well muscled, but not unusually so; when I'd heard how he died I assumed he was a mesomorphic weight lifter type. Bones are hard to break.

Also, his fingernails are cut to the quick. It must have taken a burst of superhuman strength, to tear his own flesh without being able to dig in.

My first specialty was thoracic surgery, so I well know how physically difficult it is to get to the heart. It's hard to believe that a person could tear out his own. It's doubly hard to believe that someone could do it after having brutally castrated himself.

I do have to confirm that that is what happened. The corridor leading to his solitary confinement cell is under constant video surveillance. No one came or went from the time the door was shut behind him until breakfast time, when the body was discovered.

He did it to himself, and in total silence.

GM: wr

○ ○ ○ *The geography of this story comes from Vietnam, but not too much else. I guess part of it was to set the record straight about LRRPs; in some outfits they were steely-eyed professional sol-*

diers, as the media have always portrayed them. In some other outfits, like mine, people were assigned to LRRP squads as punishment. It was pretty serious punishment for people who didn't care for combat.

The main character comes from a tour bus driver I had in Montego Bay, Jamaica. He had a wonderfully creepy basso voice, with an island accent redolent of voodoo, of zombies and witch doctors. We passed a cemetery, strangely decorated with colorful festive paper streamers. "That be the graveyard," he said in sepulchral tones. "Ain't nobody want to be there. Everybody gettin' there."

if I had the wings
of an angel

MARIANNE SCANLAN FLOATED in line, feeling sick and nervous and heavy. This morning the gym scale had weighed her in at thirty-five kilograms, the cut-off point. She'd gotten rid of breakfast and hadn't drunk anything all morning.

Her turn. She floated up to the scale at the wing rack and grabbed both handles. Her palms were sweaty. The scale gave a jerk, measuring her inertia, and the wing man looked at the dial, looked at her, looked back at the dial.

"Thirty-four point nine," he said. He started to say something else and then just pointed to the end of the rack. Number twelve, the biggest set. She'd been using it since the first of the year.

She wasn't going to be dumb about it. At thirteen, she was older than most people were when they hit thirty-five and had their card taken away. Boys especially would starve and puke and take laxatives to keep from putting on those last few grams. But it was ridiculous. Flying was for kids, and you couldn't stay a kid forever.

She clamped on the ankle vanes and backed into the wing frame. Right wrist and elbow straps, then carefully draw the huge wing over to fasten the left side.

Toes push down, release bar clicks, wings at your side, bend at the knees, lean out and fall. The jump platform slipped away behind her.

It always felt the same, launching. Deep inside you, a sudden wrench that wasn't pleasant—your body noticing that you were about to plummet half a kilometer to certain death—and then the weird sparkle of relief rolling to your toes and fingertips. You'd think a girl born and raised in space would grow out of groundhog reflexes. You're not going to fall anywhere, floating off a platform at the zerogee axis. But it was a long way down nevertheless.

She looked at New New York rolling slowly by beneath her, unimpressed by the majesty of it, knowing that groundhogs paid millions to see just this, but knowing that groundhogs do crazy things. She wasn't going fast enough for the wind to bring tears, but the sight blurred anyhow. She dug the tears away with her shoulders, angry with herself. So maybe it's the last time. Probably it's the last time. Don't be an ass about it.

She checked behind her; the next boy hadn't launched yet. Beat hard once, flutter kick, knees to chest, quarter roll, beat hard twice, three times: straight down swoop. Wings at her side, the lake in the middle of the park rushing up at her.

People died doing this. Kids who had their wings but weren't good at it yet. You could hit hard enough to break your neck. Or you could drown.

She hit the thermocline over the lake and the wind sighing by turned deliciously cool. Her cheeks dried cold. Two people in a boat looked up at her, their faces tiny ovals. Far enough.

Legs spread wide, both ankles out, right wing suddenly

dipped to a precise angle, legs back together as she looped three, four, five tight dizzy loops over the water, then kicked and reversed it, left wing sculling to bring her around in wide slow circles. Sweet glow between her legs. She was going to lose it forever, next week or the next or the next. She let herself cry again and pulled air with both wings, dumping speed, drifting down toward the treetops by the lake's edge, not quite low enough to lose her card—then beat hard, kicked hard, climbing with all her might, as the lake rotated away.

Tourists usually found it confusing, even dizzying, to look down from the axis and see all that real estate spinning around. Marianne never thought about it, of course, except for times like now: she idly wondered how fast you'd have to fly to zip through the axis and catch up with the lake as it rolled to the other side. Fast.

Hard to fly and do arithmetic at the same time. She relaxed, ankles together, and glided smoothly. New New York was a hollowed-out asteroid, the hollow being a little more than a kilometer wide and a little less than two kilometers long. It spun around (for gravity) once each thirty seconds. So you'd have to go a kilometer in fifteen seconds. That's four kilometers per minute; 240 per hour. Not likely to happen. The wings were designed to keep you from going too fast; the strongest kids could go from one side to the other in about three minutes.

A beginner was having problems, slowly tumbling end over end, crying. Eight or nine years old. No danger unless she managed to end up in the water. Still, Marianne could remember how scary it was in the beginning. She beat twice and caught up with the kid.

It was simple. She'd accidentally hit the elbow release on the left wing and couldn't fit her arm back into it. Marianne hit both of her releases (the wings would stay with her unless she undid the ankles) and reached out to grab the girl, stop her spinning.

"I didn't *do* nothin'!" the girl sobbed.

"It's all right." Marianne guided the elbow strap back into the release flange. "Just don't twist your elbow *this* way." She demonstrated, rotating her arm as if she were turning a doorknob stiff-armed. "Not until you want to get out of the wings."

She looked doubtful, and gave a couple of tentative flaps. "I'm scared."

"Don't worry. I'll stay with you." She pulled a couple of meters away. "You don't have a buddy?"

She started to cloud up. "She *ditched* me."

"It's okay. Try this: wings straight out, legs stiff." The girl copied her. "Now just give little kicks as if you were swimming."

"Don' know *how* to swim."

"Just do it." Marianne dipped and rolled, to watch her from below. The girl gave a couple of stiff, awkward kicks, and then smiled as she glided past Marianne.

"See? Nothing to it. Now I'll show you how to dive." For the rest of her hour Marianne showed the little girl her basic moves and made her learn the names for everything. They were almost to the opposite end of the hub when the buzzer on her shoulder gave its ten-minute warning. Marianne "raced" her back, flying slowly upside down, and let her win.

She helped the little girl get out of her wings and rack them properly. "Thank you very much," the girl said seriously. "Can we do it again next week?"

"I'm afraid . . ." Marianne cleared her throat. "I'm afraid I have to go someplace. You know plenty enough, though. Just find a new buddy."

Marianne got her clarinet out of the locker and wiggled her feet into Velcro slippers. She swam hand over hand to the Sector 4 lift and stuck her feet onto the ceiling, automatically making the mental adjustment that turned it into the floor.

It began to slide "down." Two hours to band practice. Better eat something now. If you play a clarinet too soon after eating, the mouthpiece fills up with spit and it sounds like a baby rhinoceros with a cold.

Better eat something. Or maybe not. The lift thumped to a halt and gravity suddenly returned.

She walked down the corridor to the mall and flipped through her ration book. Maybe just a salad. If she starved for a week, she could fly again. Probably.

One of the pieces she'd been practicing for band was a medley of old American spirituals, for an ethnic concert. The words to one of the songs had been nagging her all week, the sad rightness of them: "If I had the wings of an angel, over these prison walls I would fly..."

People from Earth think *we* live in a prison, she knew, some of them. Rock walls all around us, a bubble of air surrounded by the vast deadly indifference of space.

What they don't see is that *gravity* is a prison. They live at the bottom of a well. We live inside a rock, but we can fly.

She stopped at the entrance to the mall and studied her ration book.

For five or six years, we can fly.

Cheeseburger. Two cheeseburgers.

○ ○ ○ *I spent five years writing three books about this character, the* Worlds *trilogy. "If I Had the Wings of an Angel" was originally going to be the beginning. I wound up not writing it, though, for a couple of reasons. It seemed appropriate to start the books with Marianne's entrance into womanhood, rather than the last of her childhood. (Nothing like sex to grab the reader's attention.) Also, most sf readers will recognize the story as a takeoff on Heinlein's "The Menace from Earth." That sort of game is okay in a short story, but wouldn't do for a novel, unless it was central to the book.*

So the first page—just the title, centered; I remembered what the story would be about—sat around for fifteen years, until Jane Yolen asked me for a "young adult" story for her anthology 2040. I agreed to it because I wanted to try an experiment.

I'd read in The New Yorker about a woman who restricted all of her stories to a single sheet of 24" by 36" paper. That sounded like an interesting constraint. I often write in longhand anyhow, and if it ran longer than one page, so what?

It worked perfectly. The story ran four columns, finishing with only two inches to spare. The only problem now is what to do with it. I'm reluctant to cut it up, and it won't fit into my filing cabinet!

The only personal experience here, besides having played the clarinet, was one experience flying in a glider, over the fall foliage in New Hampshire. It was gorgeous, but I was paralyzed with fear. I've flown millions of miles, combat as well as civilian, but never without an engine. Never realized what a comfort they were.

O

the cure

HARLEY HAD WANTED to show off his birthday present, so we split this lemon in two lengthwise and stuck the two halves in the ovals in the swinging doors, he said he could shoot them out without touching the wood, and he did one, raised up that Model 94 and popped it out clean, but on the second he unfortunately took a piece out of the bicep of the bar's next potential customer. He said Oh, Hell, and set down the rifle, and it was a good thing most of us were on the floor by then because the bastard spun in with a Navy Colt in his left hand and blew Harley's ugly face backwards across the mirror in back of the bar, didn't break somehow, son of a bitch owed me thirty dollars and I don't guess I'll get it off his widow. Stranger dropped the Colt back into his holster and there was a smell of cinnamon:

Bos'n's mate took a boarding axe and cut the bow anchor free just as the squall line hit, never should of anchored right off the reef like that, storm came across the island like a freight train, slack sails billowing out, everybody shoutin' orders, cut this line cut that, Captain Harley's on shore fuckin' the chief's daughter and we're all gonna wind up in Davy

Jones's locker or in the belly of some damn heathen, smell of lavender:

We were dead meat. The VC had us in a classic box ambush and the RPG that took out Harley also DX'ed his radio. So no artillery, no air support, and these guys had enough ammo to take out the fucking Pentagon. We hadn't been resupplied and the Captain was yelling Single shot, single shot, and some slope was yelling what musta been Slope for They ain't got no ammo. Anyhow I got down behind what was left of Harley and went through his web belt and pockets for magazines and grenades, put them in a pile with my own, and waited, just like Robert fucking Jordan, bastards come out of the tree line and I'm gonna pop me some before, allspice smell:

You can kill the weak dogs and cut them up, and the others are hungry enough to eat them, and you can lighten the sled to compensate for the smaller team, the weaker team, but you can't rest; even when the dogs rest you have to keep kicking the sled so the rails don't freeze to the ground, and sooner or later it dawns on you that the Yukon has won, you're not getting back to Oregon, you're not even going to make it back to Whitehorse. Not even if you feed them Harley's fucking useless body, not even if they'd eat it. There's four hours of gray for twenty of black and the snow is horizontal, a sandblast machine charged with ice, smell of lemon:

A blowout in space doesn't have to mean you're dead. We were running about eight pounds' pressure, so when Harley put his fucking pick through the aft port, we had plenty of time to slap a patch and then sit around hyperventilating, thinking up new names for Harley while the pumps came up to pressure. But the fucking pumps didn't come up to pressure, because something had shorted out while we were all out on the quadrant picking samples. Never leave a robot in charge, you know? So we're all trying to hyperventilate in about half an Everest worth of oxygen and it occurs to me and others that we are just plain not going to make it. I put my helmet back on and charged up, and through the shooting stars and giddiness I saw 32 min MAX 64 min MIN on the air gauge, and wondered what I could do to Harley in thirty-two minutes, spearmint smell:

A racing car on asphalt is just like a wet cake of soap, sliding, if your cake of soap has forty gallons of gasoline aboard and is screaming along at almost two hundred in close formation with a lot of other cakes of soap that want to get in front of it; you don't steer it, you just kind of aim it, and when Harley, two cars up, is suddenly just greasy bouncing fireball, parts every which way, you can't put on the brakes, you got to goose it and slew one way or the other, and I just picked the wrong way, made contact with some gentleman behind me who zagged when I zigged, started to spin so hard I was mashed up against the side, couldn't reach the wheel, flipped, cinnamon again:

There are risks involved in underwater salvage, but a good deal of easy money to be made. My definition of easy money is you work to the hilt three or four months out of the year and spend the rest of the time on the beach. How dangerous the job is depends on the depth and the time required and the tools you have to use. And your partners. My buddy on the last one was Harley, a new guy; he was a good diver but chickenshit. So when we got down to the wreck smell of bacon frying dark red a feather on the back of my neck—

"Tell me your name. Your name, please."

I swallowed a lot of cold saliva and wiped more off my face. I felt the nape of my neck.

"You're unplugged. What is your name?"

"Spare me the reality check, okay? I'm back."

"Name."

"Who the hell is Harley? My name is Jack Lindhoff." I was lying on a fancy adjustable bed, fully clothed on top of starched sheets, bright lights, hospital smell.

"Do you know who I am?"

"You tell me who Harley is and I'll tell you who you are."

"I don't know who Harley is. Was he in one of your episodes?"

"All of them. You're Barbara Cass and I'm paying you an obscene amount of money. So am I better?"

"Do you feel better?"

"I'd feel better if I knew who Harley was."

"Can you describe him?"

"He was different every time. A couple of times he wasn't even there; once he was a frozen corpse."

"Does the name have any special meaning to you?"

"No. I don't even ride a motorcycle."

"Do you want to go back under and talk to him?"

I felt the nine-prong jack at the back of my neck. "Can you make the episodes longer?"

"They're short for therapeutic reasons. If you stay in for a minute or so, you begin to realize what's happening."

"Give me five minutes with the son of a bitch."

"He's not real. There's no reason to—"

"Five minutes. It *is* my money, isn't it?"

"Roll over."

Harley was cutting the lemon in half. The bartender had stopped trying to talk sense to him and had retired to the storeroom.

"I know you can hit it, Harley. You don't want to shoot out into the street."

He had his tongue between his teeth, bearing down with the blunt knife. "Ain't nobody gonna get hurt here. Now I just got to do it."

"It's a thirty-thirty."

"Yeah, and I'm shootin' down. Right into the mud. Why don't you go outside and make sure they's nobody in the line of fire?"

I went through the swinging doors, not too steadily, and there was nobody in sight. It was Sunday morning, eight o'clock. Harley and I had been celebrating his birthday for about twelve hours.

"You see a lot of people out there? On they way to church?"

"Not for another hour."

"So I'm gonna shoot the fuckin' lemons."

Let 'im shoot the fuckin' lemons, was the consensus of the bar, which probably had more customers than the church would gather. Harley placed the lemon halves in the oval cutouts and peered left and right down the street. "Nobody," he pronounced.

"Harley," the bartender shouted from the storeroom, "you know how much I paid for those goddamn doors?"

"Not gonna touch your goddamn doors." Harley aimed offhand and then thought the better of it, and sat down at the poker table, left elbow on the green felt.

He jacked a round into the chamber. This was different from the earlier version. He did it really right. Both eyes open, deep breath let out slowly, gentle squeeze on the trigger.

It was a loud bang in the barroom and instant gunpowder smell, but that lemon half was suddenly just not there, vaporized; thought I could smell it, too.

"One's plenty," I said. "We believe you, Harley. You're really good."

"Ha." He squeezed off another round and of course there was the stranger right behind the lemon, with a real impressive splatter of blood and about the loudest Shit I ever heard shouted. Me and the other denizens hit the boards.

You would think Harley would know that this guy was not going to just punch 9-1-1 and get an ambulance. But Harley set the rifle down and said "Oh, hell."

"Harley!" I exclaimed with some vigor. "He's comin' back!"

Harley looked at me and blinked a slow drunken blink. Then the wounded citizen spun through the door and I was studying him this time. There was blood rolling out of his right shoulder, just like a pitcher emptying, but he ignored it. He took a target-shooter's stance, his left foot pointed at Harley, raised the Colt with both hands, laid the front blade sight on Harley's unremarkable face, brought up the rear notch, and squeezed off one fat round. Meanwhile Harley had raised his hands. But the bullet hit him right about moustache level and left him leaning there with just a lower jaw and some remnants of cheek, the balance of his visage decorating the back mirror and a poster that said GUINNESS IS GOOD FOR YOU. I didn't know they exported Guinness to whenever this was, wherever.

He fell over with a remarkably lifeless sound, like a duffel bag filled with soft things. I ran over to him. "Harley," I said. "You have to tell me what this is all about."

Then the guy started shooting generally, great, a mass murderer. Almost everybody in the bar was voicing some sort of disapproval, but I just lay down there next to Harley and said, "Listen, I know you're not real; you can talk to me. Just put your face back on and talk to me."

Now people were shooting back, and it was like one of those reenactments you get at Corral World or somewhere, sound and fury and nobody getting really hurt. I mean there was this one guy shot through both lungs and another with his entrails picking up the dirty sawdust on the floor while he blew bloody lunch everywhere, but I knew it was just a dream and wasn't going to go on forever. Then a bullet popped me below the shoulder blade and blasted out the front, a hole below my right tit about the size of a Big Mac, and it hurt about as much as you would expect it to, and Harley showed no signs of coming around and explaining things to me. So I said "Barbara? Barbara Cass? You can get me out of here any time you want."

The scene around me shimmered and then came back solid, and then shimmered again, going black—then it was all bright blur and people shouting. Someone in a green tunic was holding my right arm still while another was trying to stick an IV into the back of my hand; a third was pressing down hard on my chest with something slick and cold. Barbara Cass was looking over his shoulder, pale as death, spattered with flecks of blood.

"What happened?" I coughed and swallowed copper.

"It's never done this before."

"Take it easy, Champ," one of the green tunics said, and they maneuvered the gurney out of the examination room, and then rolled it down a corridor at what seemed a reckless rate of speed, one of them yelling to a guy who was running alongside something about a portable X-ray and emergency ER. The lights stopped flickering by and we waited a long time for an elevator. I seemed to remember the Emergency Room was 'way on the other side of the hospital.

I craned my head up to look at the wound. There was a big piece of bloody plastic and a stark white pile of gauze on top, all held down with hasty crisscrossings of plastic tape. Every time I breathed, the bloody plastic made a fluttering sound.

Someone gently pushed my head back down. "It was a .41 Colt," I said. "Black powder, Navy Dragoon model."

"Whatever you say, Champ."

What the hell is a dragoon? How did I know that?

A woman with gray hair put a mask over my nose and mouth. "I want you to count slowly backward from one hundred," she said in a soothing voice.

I got a finger under the mask. "But I don't want to fall asleep!"

Another voice, Barbara Cass: "You're unplugged. Don't worry."

My eyes wouldn't stay open. The noise of instruments clinking, people talking hurriedly, machines clicking and beeping, all began to fade. A profound weariness drifted over me. Anesthesia or death, I didn't care.

I woke up sputtering, warm beer splashed on my face. Harley was helping me to my feet, brushing sawdust off my clothes. "Thought you was a guy could hold his liquor," he said. "Four little schooners an' you're on the floor."

"Just one of his spells," someone said from the bar.

"I know. Just like to kid him about it."

I sat down. "Barbara," I said hoarsely. "Barbara Cass."

"See?" the guy at the bar said.

"You musta got one hell of a hard-on for this Barbara," Harley said. "Why don't you talk some sense about her for a change?"

"She—she's a doctor."

Harley and the guys at the bar laughed. "Same old shit. She's workin' on your head."

I ran a finger up behind my neck. No cyberjack. But then I didn't have a gaping hole in my chest, either.

The bartender brought over a lemon and a case knife. "You're crazy as hell, Harley. Just check outside before you do it, and for Christ's sake aim down? I don't want to pay for—"

I snatched up the lemon. "We're not going through this again, Harley."

"What, again? It was your goddamn idea."

"I don't give a shit." Star pitcher in high school, at least in some world, I hurled the lemon out over the swinging doors.

It hit the stranger in the eye.

He spun through the door in a half crouch, unsnapping the safety strap on his holster.

Harley picked up the Winchester and jacked a round into the chamber.

My right hand slapped my hip. Of course I'd left the pistol back in my footlocker. I just carried it to ride fence, never took it into town.

This time they fired simultaneously, while the rest of the clientele hit the floor. Harley's head and the stranger's shoulder sprayed brains and blood.

The stranger looked at his wound with an ugly scowl and raised the pistol toward me.

"Wait," I said, holding out a hand. "Who's Harley? Who the hell are *you* supposed to be? My father?"

"Shit," he said, and fired. My chair went over backwards; I banged my head against the floor and rolled over. The stranger started shooting various people.

There was no hole in my chest and I thought he'd missed me. But then I took a breath and coughed blood and realized the sore throat was a bullet wound. I tried to call Barbara's name but just gurgled and then started coughing all over the sawdust, crimson strings and spatters. The world started to spin and go dim. Could I die here? Was I dying *there*? Then there was the shimmer I'd experienced before, and then it was gone, my nose in the sawdust breathing pine, and then it shimmered and again snapped.

Half of Barbara Cass's face appeared above me, upside down, the bottom half covered with a surgical mask. "Wake up, wake up," she was saying loudly. "Blink twice if you hear me." I blinked. "Don't try to move!"

I wondered whether I could move if I tried. My arms were restrained and so was my head, somehow. I was numb all over but could feel people sewing on my chest and neck. There was a plastic tube down my throat. Everybody working on me had blood spattered over their green tunics. Guess I surprised them again. I felt pretty awful.

I closed my eyes. She opened them. "Don't sleep, Jack—don't! You might hurt yourself again!"

I wanted to tell her that it wasn't me that was hurting me, but rather a tall dark stranger with a Colt Dragoon and an understandably hostile attitude. But I couldn't tell her anything, with the plastic tube down my throat. What I could do was vomit, which I did repeatedly. That tired me out even more, but I agreed that it would be bad policy to fall asleep.

The neck wound must not have been as serious; at least they finished it before the chest one. I couldn't see them working on my chest because of a drape, but I could feel some pushing and pulling and hear aspirators and scissors at work. When they took the drape away, there was a tight clean bandage over the chest wound with a drain coming out of the center of it.

I was still getting blood dripped into one arm and a clear solution into the other. They unhooked the blood IV and slid the tube out of my throat. I just gagged a little at that, and after they gave me a little water and a tiny cup of apple juice, I was able to talk in a croaking whisper. I asked for more water and they said later. They taped an oxygen tube over my cheek and into a nostril, and that made me less groggy. I was still pumped full of drugs; the overall effect was a kind of tranquil alertness, waiting for whatever came next.

It was Barbara. "What happened to your neck? They were busy with your chest, and suddenly you had this other blow-out."

I explained about the slightly different scenario. "Does this mean I'll never be able to sleep again?"

"I don't know *what* it means. Nothing like this has ever happened before." She unfolded reading glasses and studied a few pages on a clipboard. "Normal sleep would probably be all right. The unconsciousness they induce for surgery is much more profound. Deeper than I use for drama therapy. Our strategy right now, totally guesswork, is to keep you awake as long as it's safe. Then we let you sleep in an operating theater, with a trauma team waiting."

"But wait. This isn't what you warned me about; what I signed the release for . . ."

"Psychosomatic sequelae to drama therapy. People have died from it before; it's strong medicine."

"But they had things like heart attacks and strokes. Not imaginary bullets punching real holes in their bodies."

"Not before. But it's a new discipline. You're rapidly becoming part of the literature."

"Give my life for science, yeah. You all better hope not. Ranko will sue this hospital down to its last bottle of aspirin."

"Let's not think of it in those terms." She dragged a chair over and sat down at eye level, close to my face. She spoke softly: "Think of it this way. Some part of your personality is self-destructive. You—"

"Hold it, now. I'm no suicide. I enjoy life, live it to the hilt."

"We discussed that. The fast cars, the mountain climbing."

"Not inherently dangerous. Challenges to the mind and

body. But I've said I was willing to give them up, and the skydiving."

"The Ranko board of directors must have been worried about you, about some aspect of your behavior, or they wouldn't have sent you to me."

"Wrong on two counts. They didn't order me into therapy; it was just a suggestion. And they didn't send me to anybody. You were my idea. Drama therapy's supposed to be fast."

"Fast and dangerous. That's consistent."

"What, you're denigrating your own specialty? You want to refer me to some guy with a couch and a notepad?"

"Nobody does that anymore, except in cartoons. But it's obvious that drama therapy's too strong for you, or you're too strong for *it*.

"All I can do now is search through case histories, a database that the APA maintains. See if anyone like you has ever done drama therapy."

"Someone 'like me.' Suicidal?"

"You're the only one who's used that word. I'll just feed your profile, the test results, into the machine, and have it look for correlations."

"And if nothing comes up?"

She was silent for a moment, staring at me. "I'm not sure. You've already done the thing that I would have suggested — go back into the scenario and interrupt the sequence of events."

"Throwing the lemon wasn't smart, though." I thought about it. "I should just leave the bar. Get away from Harley and the guns."

She nodded slowly. "Maybe. If Harley represents something or someone you have to reject in order to survive . . . that's right! Did you leave him in any of the other dreams?"

I thought back. The spaceship, the ambush, the dogs, the ship, the racing cars. "Not when he was physically on the scene, no."

"Then that's it. If you do go back to the bar, get up and walk out."

"And have the stranger just gun me down in the street."

"Probably not. Is he in any of the other dreams?"

"Not that I remember. Maybe I should go out the back way, just to be on the safe side."

"And if you're in a different scenario, as soon as you're aware that it's a dream, isolate yourself from Harley."

"But it probably will be the same?"

"Usually people go back to the same starting place." She got up. "I'll go run the computer check. Someone will come in and make sure you stay awake." She turned on the television set and gave me the changer.

A big guy with bad breath kept me up for the next seven hours, touching me on the face with an ice cube whenever my eyes closed.

Barbara Cass came in and said the computer search hadn't revealed anything significant. But she was lying. Even a shrink can't fool someone who lies for a living.

There was another doctor with her, a graybeard she introduced as the head of the trauma unit.

"The Friday Night Knife and Gun Club," he said. "That's part of our problem. We do a lot of business over the weekend, and it's Thursday night. Barbara wants a full crew to watch you fall asleep."

"So I'd better do it now."

"That's the other part of the problem. Your condition is stable but grave; you couldn't tie a shoelace without help. Another wound like the two you've just sustained would probably kill you."

"On the other hand," Cass said, "the only way you can recover is with rest. You'll have to try to sleep soon."

"So there's no problem. Get the gang together and let me close my eyes." They glanced at each other. "What aren't you telling me?"

"Nothing," she said quickly. "I just want you to...be

aware of all the factors. If you want to try to stay awake longer—"

"No, let's just do it." Whatever they were keeping from me, I probably didn't want to know.

Four aides transferred me and my machinery to two gurneys and then wheeled us into a bright round room. X-ray negatives decorated a third of the circle of light, my neck and chest from various angles. Machines and people waited expectantly.

I closed my eyes.

Someone slapped my face hard, twice. I blinked up into Harley's red and bleary mug. "You just stop doin' that," he said. "You scare the shit outa somebody."

"Aw, lay off 'im, Harley," a man at the bar counseled. "He can't help them fits."

I stood up shakily, knees water but chest and neck okay. Harley asked in a loud voice where was his fuckin' lemon?

I staggered for the door.

"Hey!" he yelled at my back. "Where the hell *you* goin'?"

"Don't want any part of it." I touched the swinging door and the Winchester cocked loudly behind me.

"Your fuckin' idea, Jack. Five bucks I can't do it. What, you gonna take my word for it?"

"Sure, Harley." I looked over my shoulder and tried to smile. "If I can't trust you, who can I trust?"

A couple of people laughed and I went through the swinging doors, a warm itch in the center of my back. Then I heard Harley say "About time, goddamn it," and the bartender repeated his admonition to check outside and shoot down.

Front Street had dried up pretty well from the gullywasher the day before. The town smelled good, clean. I headed uptown but after a few steps had to stop and lean against a hitching post, the world sort of twirling. I kept my eyes open and it stopped.

About a block away, the dark stranger was walking toward the bar, not looking particularly dangerous. He stopped to scrape something off his shoes.

I walked up to him. "Headed for the Alamo?"

"Coffee," he said. "Lady at the hotel said that's the only place."

"Know a guy name Harley?"

He tilted me a suspicious look. "I don't know anybody. I'm from Wichita."

"Oh yeah. Course." I tried to get my tongue and brain to work together. "Look, I ain't in no great shape myself, been up all night. But take my word for it. You don't want to go in that bar. There's a man name Harley crazy drunk in there and he's got a gun."

"But I just want coffee. No reason—" The Winchester went *crack* and we both turned to look at the saloon. Then there was another shot and a cloud of lemon juice.

The man's hand was on his gun but he didn't pull it. "Great God almighty," he said. "Thanks, mister. Guess I can do without that coffee."

He ran off back toward the Great Western Hotel. I wished he would stay. There was another shimmer of confusion, like a spell coming on. I had a feeling I should have asked him something.

Doc Seaver came running down the walk with his great-coat flapping over his nightclothes. He stopped and looked at me.

"Jack! What's the shooting about?"

"Oh, it's Harley's birthday. He got a new gun."

He chewed his white moustache. "You hurt?"

"No. No, I got outa there."

"You shouldn't've *been* there. What did I tell you?" I shrugged at him. "Look. Sit down." He pushed me down onto the bench in front of Zimmerman's.

He took out a tin of Italian stogies and used a fancy knife to cut one in two. He gave me half and popped a lucifer for both of us.

"Look. I told you about this drinkin', ramblin'. No wonder you have fits and dreams."

"I didn't drink so much tonight—"

He roared: "It's six glory-be-to-God in the morning! Your fellow *cowpuncher* Harley is shootin' up the town and you're staggerin' around with your hat on backwards." I fixed it. "Tomorrow, sure as hell, you're gonna slouch into my office and say you feel like hell, you need a pill."

"It don't hurt nothin' to—"

"That's not what I mean! Maybe that opium don't hurt, and maybe it does—those damn dreams—but the *point* is that you used to be a nice kid, an' now you're on the road to bein' someone like Harley. You think that Gretchin girl'd marry *Harley*?"

I shook my head. "Couldn't see her marryin' even me, not now."

"Maybe and maybe not. Women are funny. But you sure as hell would have a better chance if you stayed home from that bar and kept your money in your pocket and read those books. You'd have a better chance with her folks, that's for damn sure."

"I ain't sayin' you're wrong." I had a bad shimmer and threw the stogie into the road. I started to fall, but Doc caught me.

"Look. You just stretch out on the bench here. Take me five, ten minutes to get my rig up. Take you back to the bunkhouse, you can sleep all Sunday. No pills."

I lay down and had a short dream, like I was dead and went to heaven. It was a bright place and some of the angels wore green and some looked like gray skeletons, light glowing behind them.

Doc pulled up and I got in the buggy next to him. He repeated his thing about sleep and no pills, and of course I had to agree.

But in the bunkhouse I couldn't fall asleep. That dream was still with me and I was crazy sure that if I closed my eyes I was going to die. And I couldn't get the smell out of my nose, a smell of death and cinnamon.

○ ○ ○ This one was almost completely a work of the imagination. I was taking a working vacation in Cape Cod, writing The Hemingway Hoax in the predawn hours and bicycling during the day. I rarely remember dreams, other than recalling certain images, but the opening to this story came to me as a complete, detailed narrative. I wrote it down while it was fresh and then made up a similar dream sequence, and then another, and so on. After the fact, it occurs to me that most them have literary precursors—Melville's Typee and Heinlein's spacesuit emergency. The dogsled rails sinking into the ice is straight from a Jack London story, I think White Fang.

The Vietnam ambush is from personal experience, and so is the storm-tossed vessel (I was on a "barefoot windjammer cruise" that ran into weather trouble). I never saw a sucking chest wound like the hero suffers, except in an army training film. A friend of mine died of one, though; "friendly fire" from air support. That's always haunted me because it should have been my mission; we traded off when the call came in, because my M-16 was totally disassembled for cleaning. He hopped on the chopper and twenty minutes later he was dead.

graves

I HAVE THIS persistent sleep disorder that makes life difficult for me, but still I want to keep it. Boy, do I want to keep it. It goes back twenty years, to Vietnam. To Graves.

Dead bodies turn from bad to worse real fast in the jungle. You've got a few hours before rigor mortis makes them hard to handle, hard to stuff in a bag. By that time they start to turn greenish, if they started out white or yellow, where you can see the skin. It's mostly bugs by then, usually ants. Then they go to black and start to smell.

They swell up and burst.

You'd think the ants and roaches and beetles and milli-pedes would make short work of them after that, but they don't. Just when they get to looking and smelling the worst, the bugs sort of lose interest, get fastidious, send out for pizza. Except for the flies. Laying eggs.

The funny thing is, unless some big animal got to it and tore it up, even after a week or so, you've still got something more than a skeleton, even a sort of a face. No eyes, though. Every now and then we'd get one like that. Not too often, since soldiers don't usually die alone and sit there for that long, but sometimes. We called them dry ones. Still damp underneath, of course, and inside, but kind of like a sunburned mummy otherwise.

You tell people what you do at Graves Registration "Graves," and it sounds like about the worst job the army has to offer. It isn't. You just stand there all day and open body bags, figure out which parts maybe belong to which dog tag, not that it's usually that important, sew them up more or less with a big needle, account for all the wallets and jewelry, steal the dope out of their pockets, box them up, seal the casket, do the paperwork. When you have enough boxes, you truck them out to the airfield. The first week maybe is pretty bad. But after a hundred or so, after you get used to the smell and the godawful feel of them, you get to thinking that opening a body bag is a lot better than winding up inside one. They put Graves in safe places.

Since I'd had a couple years of college, pre-med, I got some of the more interesting jobs. Captain French, who was the pathologist actually in charge of the outfit, always took me with him out into the field when he had to examine a corpse *in situ*, which only happened maybe once a month. I got to wear a .45 in a shoulder holster, tough guy. Never fired it, never got shot at, except the one time.

That was a hell of a time. It's funny what gets to you, stays with you.

Usually when we had an *in situ* it was a forensic matter, like an officer they suspected had been fragged or otherwise terminated by his own men. We'd take pictures and interview some people and then Frenchy would bring the stiff back for autopsy, see whether the bullets were American or Vietnamese. (Not that that would be conclusive either way. The Viet Cong stole our weapons and our guys used the North Vietnamese AK-47s, when we could get our hands on them. More reliable than the M-16 and a better cartridge for killing. Both sides proved that over and over.) Usually Frenchy would send a report up to Division, and that would be it.

Once he had to testify at a court-martial. The kid was guilty but just got life. The officer was a real prick.

Anyhow we got the call to come look at this *in situ* corpse about five in the afternoon. Frenchy tried to put it off until the next day, since if it got dark we'd have to spend the night. The guy he was talking to was a major, though, and obviously proud of it, so it was no use arguing. I threw some C's and beer and a couple canteens into two rucksacks that already had blankets and air mattresses tied on the bottom. Box of .45 ammo and a couple hand grenades. Went and got a jeep while Frenchy got his stuff together and made sure Doc Carter was sober enough to count the stiffs as they came in. (Doc Carter was the one supposed to be in charge, but he didn't much care for the work.)

Drove us out to the pad and, lo and behold, there was a chopper waiting, blades idling. Should of started to smell a rat then. We don't get real high priority, and it's not easy to get a chopper to go anywhere so close to sundown. They even helped us stow our gear. Up, up, and away.

I never flew enough in helicopters to make it routine. Kontum looked almost pretty in the low sun, golden red. I had to sit between two flamethrowers, though, which didn't make me feel too secure. The door gunner was smoking. The flamethrower tanks were stenciled NO SMOKING.

We went fast and low out toward the mountains to the west. I was hoping we'd wind up at one of the big fire bases up there, figuring I'd sleep better with a few hundred men around. But no such luck. When the chopper started to slow down, the blades' whir deepening to a whuck-whuck-whuck, there was no clearing as far as the eye could see. Thick jungle canopy everywhere. Then a wisp of purple smoke showed us a helicopter-sized hole in the leaves. The pilot brought us down an inch at a time, nicking twigs. I was very much aware of the flamethrowers. If he clipped a large branch we'd be so much pot roast.

When we touched down, four guys in a big hurry unloaded our gear and the flamethrowers and a couple cases of ammo.

They put two wounded guys and one client on board and shooed the helicopter away. Yeah, it would sort of broadcast your position. One of them told us to wait, he'd go get the major.

"I don't like this at all," Frenchy said.

"Me neither," I said. "Let's go home."

"Any outfit that's got a major and two flamethrowers is planning to fight a real war." He pulled his .45 out and looked at it as if he'd never seen one before. "Which end of this do you think the bullets come out of?"

"Shit," I advised, and rummaged through the rucksack for a beer. I gave Frenchy one and he put it in his side pocket.

A machine gun opened up off to our right. Frenchy and I grabbed the dirt. Three grenade blasts. Somebody yelled for them to cut that out. Guy yelled back he thought he saw something. Machine gun started up again. We tried to get a little lower.

Up walks this old guy, thirties, looking annoyed. The major.

"You men get up. What's wrong with you?" He was playin' games.

Frenchy got up, dusting himself off. We had the only clean fatigues in twenty miles. "Captain French, Graves Registration."

"Oh," he said, not visibly impressed. "Secure your gear and follow me." He drifted off like a mighty ship of the jungle. Frenchy rolled his eyes and we hoisted our rucksacks and followed him. I wasn't sure whether "secure your gear" meant bring your stuff or leave it behind, but Budweiser could get to be a real collectors' item in the boonies, and there were a lot of collectors out here.

We walked too far. I mean a couple hundred yards. That meant they were really spread out thin. I didn't look forward to spending the night. The goddamned machine gun started up again. The major looked annoyed and shouted "Sergeant, will you please control your men?" and the sergeant told the machine gunner to shut the fuck up and the machine gunner told the sergeant there was a fuckin' gook out there, and then somebody popped a big one, like a claymore, and then everybody was shooting every which way. Frenchy and I got real horizontal. I heard a bullet whip by over my head. The major was leaning against a tree looking bored, shouting "Cease firing, cease firing!" The shooting dwindled down like popcorn getting done. The major looked over at us and said, "Come on. While there's still light." He led us into a small clearing, elephant grass pretty well trampled down. I guess everybody had had his turn to look at the corpse.

It wasn't a real gruesome body, as bodies go, but it was odd-looking, even for a dry one. Moldy like someone had dusted flour over it. Naked and probably male, though all the soft parts were gone. Tall; a Montagnard rather than an ethnic Vietnamese. Emaciated, dry skin taut over ribs. Probably old, though it doesn't take long for these people to get old. Lying on its back, mouth wide-open, a familiar posture. Empty eye sockets staring skyward. Arms flung out in supplication, loosely, long past rigor mortis.

Teeth chipped and filed to points, probably some Montagnard tribal custom. I'd never seen it before, but we didn't "do" many natives.

Frenchy knelt down and reached for it, then stopped. "Checked for booby traps?"

"No," the major said. "Figure that's your job." Frenchy looked at me with an expression that said it was my job.

Both officers stood back a respectful distance while I felt under the corpse. Sometimes they pull the pin on a hand grenade and slip it under the body so that the body's weight keeps the arming lever in place. You turn it over and *Tomato Surprise!*

I always worry less about a hand grenade than about the various weird serpents and bugs that might enjoy living underneath a decomposing corpse. Vietnam has its share of snakes and scorpions and mega-pedes.

I was lucky this time; nothing but maggots. I flicked them off my hand and watched the major turn a little green. Peo-

ple are funny. What does he think is going to happen to him
when he dies? Everything has to eat. And he was sure as hell
going to die if he didn't start keeping his head down. I remember that thought, but didn't think of it then as a prophecy.

They came over. "What do you make of it, Doctor?"

"I don't think we can cure him." Frenchy was getting annoyed at this cherry bomb. "What else do you want to
know?"

"Isn't it a little ... *odd* to find something like this in the
middle of nowhere?"

"Naw. Country's full of corpses." He knelt down and studied the face, wiggling the head by its chin. "We keep it up,
you'll be able to walk from the Mekong to the DMZ without
stepping on anything but corpses."

"But he's been castrated!"

"Birds." He toed the body over, busy white crawlers running from the light. "Just some old geezer who walked out
into the woods naked and fell over dead. Could happen back
in the World. Old people do funny things."

"I thought maybe he'd been tortured or something."

"God knows. It could happen." The body eased back into
its original position with a creepy creaking sound, like
leather. Its mouth had closed halfway. "If you want to put
torture in your report, your body count, I'll initial it."

"What do you mean by that, Captain?"

"Exactly what I said." He kept staring at the major while
he flipped a cigarette into his mouth and fired it up. Non-
filter Camels; you'd think a guy who worked with corpses all
day long would be less anxious to turn into one. "I'm just
trying to get along."

"You believe I want you to falsify—"

Now "falsify" is a strange word for a last word. The enemy
had set up a heavy machine gun on the other side of the
clearing, and we were the closest targets. A round struck the
major in the small of his back, we found on later examination. At the time, it was just an explosion of blood and guts

and he went down with his legs flopping every which way, barfing, then loud death rattle. Frenchy was on the ground in a ball holding his left hand, going "Shit shit shit." He'd lost the last joint of his little finger. Painful but not serious enough, as it turned out, to get him back to the World.

I myself was horizontal and aspiring to be subterranean. I managed to get my pistol out and cocked, but realized I didn't want to do anything that might draw attention to us. The machine gun was spraying back and forth over us at about knee height. Maybe they couldn't see us; maybe they thought we were dead. I was scared shitless.

"Frenchy," I stage-whispered, "we've got to get outa here." He was trying to wrap his finger up in a standard first-aid-pack gauze bandage, much too large. "Get back to the trees."

"After you, asshole. We wouldn't get halfway." He worked his pistol out of the holster but couldn't cock it, his left hand clamping the bandage and slippery with blood. I armed it for him and handed it back. "These are going to do a hell of a lot of good. How are you with grenades?"

"Shit. How you think I wound up in Graves?" In basic training they'd put me on KP whenever they went out for live grenade practice. In school I was always the last person when they chose up sides for baseball, for the same reason, though to my knowledge a baseball wouldn't kill you if you couldn't throw it far enough. "I couldn't get one halfway there." The tree line was about sixty yards away.

"Neither could I, with this hand." He was a lefty.

Behind us came the "poink" sound of a sixty-millimeter mortar, and in a couple of seconds there was a gray-smoke explosion between us and the tree line. The machine gun stopped and somebody behind us yelled, "Add twenty!"

At the tree line we could hear some shouting in Vietnamese and a clanking of metal. "They're gonna bug out," Frenchy said. "Let's di-di."

We got up and ran and somebody did fire a couple of bursts at us, probably an AK-47, but he missed, and then there was a series of poinks and a series of explosions pretty close to where the gun had been.

We rushed back to the LZ and found the command group, about the time the firing started up again. There was a first lieutenant in charge, and when things slowed down enough for us to tell him what had happened to the major, he expressed neither surprise nor grief. The man had been an observer from Battalion and had assumed command when their captain was killed that morning. He'd take our word for it that the guy was dead—that was one thing we were trained observers in—and not send a squad out for him until the fighting had died down and it was light again.

We inherited the major's hole, which was nice and deep, and in his rucksack found a dozen cans and jars of real food and a flask of scotch. So as the battle raged through the night, we munched paté on Ritz crackers, pickled herring in sour cream sauce, little Polish sausages on party rye with real French mustard. We drank all the scotch and saved the beer for breakfast.

For hours the lieutenant called in for artillery and air support, but to no avail. Later we found out that the enemy had launched coordinated attacks on all the local airfields and Special Forces camps, and every camp that held POWs. We were much lower priority.

Then about three in the morning, Snoopy came over. Snoopy was a big C-130 cargo plane that carried nothing but ammunition and gatling guns; they said it could fly over a football field and put a round into every square inch. Anyhow, it saturated the perimeter with fire and the enemy stopped shooting. Frenchy and I went to sleep.

At first light we went out to help round up the KIAs. There were only four dead, counting the major, but the major was an astounding sight, at least in context.

He looked sort of like a cadaver left over from a teaching autopsy. His shirt had been opened and his pants pulled down to his thighs, and the entire thoracic and abdominal cavities had been ripped open and emptied of everything soft, everything from esophagus to testicles, rib cage like blood-streaked fingers sticking rigid out of sagging skin, and there wasn't a sign of the guts anywhere, just a lot of dried blood.

Nobody had heard anything. There was a machine gun position not twenty yards away, and they'd been straining their ears all night. All they'd heard was flies.

Maybe an animal feeding very quietly. The body hadn't been opened with a scalpel or a knife; the skin had been torn by teeth or claws—but seemingly systematically, throat to balls.

And the dry one was gone. Him with the pointed teeth.

There is a rational explanation. Modern warfare is partly mind-fuck, and we aren't the only ones who do it, dropping unlucky cards, invoking magic and superstition. The Vietnamese knew how squeamish Americans were, and would mutilate bodies in clever ways. They could also move very quietly. The dry one? They might have spirited him away just to fuck with us. Show what they could do under our noses.

And as for the dry one's odd mummified appearance, the mold, there might be an explanation. I found out that the Montagnards in that area don't bury their dead; they put them in a coffin made from a hollowed-out log and leave them above ground. So maybe he was just the victim of a grave robber. I thought the nearest village was miles away, like twenty miles, but I could have been wrong. Or the body could have been carried that distance for some obscure purpose—maybe the VC set it out on the trail to make the Americans stop in a good place to be ambushed.

That's probably it. But for twenty years now, several nights a week, I wake up sweating with a terrible image in my mind. I've gone out with a flashlight and there it is, the dry one, scooping steaming entrails from the major's body, tearing them with its sharp teeth, staring into my light with black empty sockets, unconcerned. I reach for my pistol, and it's never there. The creature stands up, shiny with blood, and takes a step toward me—for a year or so that was it; I would wake up. Then it was two steps, and then three. After twenty years it has covered half the distance, and its dripping hands are rising from its sides.

The doctor gives me tranquilizers. I don't take them. They might help me stay asleep.

○ ○ ○ *The images of dead people in the jungle are from experience, of course, but all the stuff about Graves Registration is made up. I walked by Graves in Kontum many times, on the way to the helipad, and once watched more than a dozen bodies being delivered there by truck, but never got up the nerve to go in for a look.*

I guess this story is obliquely about one time I found a "dry one," or a pair of them. I was in charge of a squad of demolition men who had been ordered to level a part of a forest—there was an artillery emplacement on the top of a hill whose aim was blocked by tall trees in one direction. There had been snipers out there, so they didn't want to send men out with chain saws. The saws would both attract attention and cover the sound of shots.

So they sent the demolition "men" out, most of whom were boys, eighteen or nineteen years old. At twenty-five, I was an Old Man, which is why I was in charge, in spite of lacking any perceptible leadership qualities.

We walked through the woods quietly at first, setting plastic explosive charges on all the tall trees, wiring them together with detonation cord, so that when they were all set we could retire and pop them all in one big bang. It was nervous work, made more nervous by the obvious proximity of dead bodies. The smell was heavy in the sticky still air. I passed out cigars (oblivious to the irony of linking birth and death) but they didn't help much.

We found the two bodies side by side, a lieutenant and private who had been killed instantly by a random artillery round. They had been dead for more than a week, decomposition advanced past ghastliness into the stage described in the story. The blast that killed them had decapitated the lieutenant; his head had rolled a few yards away, empty sockets staring up at the jungle canopy.

One of the boys sort of snapped, and gave the head a kick. Another one, giggling, kicked it hard, and in a couple of seconds they were all shuffling through the underbrush, hooting with hysterical laughter, kicking this poor guy's skull around in an impromptu macabre game of soccer. I implored them to settle down and act a little civilized—at least try not to advertise our location to every sniper within a mile—but I was not exactly a born leader, and neither were they particularly good followers of orders.

They were also in the grip of something primal; something that had more to do with their own mortality than the lieutenant's. Four months later, all but one of them were dead. And I had trouble sleeping.

"Graves" won the 1993 World Fantasy and Nebula Awards for Best Short Story of the Year.

none so blind

IT ALL STARTED when Cletus Jefferson asked himself "Why aren't all blind people geniuses?" Cletus was only thirteen at the time, but it was a good question, and he would work on it for fourteen more years, and then change the world forever.

Young Jefferson was a polymath, an autodidact, a nerd literally without peer. He had a chemistry set, a microscope, a telescope, and several computers, some of them bought with paper route money. Most of his income was from education, though: teaching his classmates not to draw to inside straights.

Not even nerds, not even nerds who are poker players nonpareil, not even nerdish poker players who can do differential equations in their heads, are immune to Cupid's darts and the sudden storm of testosterone that will accompany those missiles at the age of thirteen. Cletus knew that he was ugly and his mother dressed him funny. He was also short and pudgy and could not throw a ball in any direction. None of this bothered him until his ductless glands started cooking up chemicals that weren't in his chemistry set.

So Cletus started combing his hair and wearing clothes that mismatched according to fashion, but he was still short and pudgy and irregular of feature. He was also the youngest person in his school, even though he was a senior—and the only black person there, which was a factor in Virginia in 1994.

Now if love were sensible, if the sexual impulse was ever tempered by logic, you would expect that Cletus, being Cletus, would assess his situation and go off in search of someone homely. But of course he didn't. He just jingled and clanked down through the Pachinko machine of adolescence, being rejected, at first glance, by every Mary and Judy and Jenny and Veronica in Known Space, going from the ravishing to the beautiful to the pretty to the cute to the plain to the "great personality," until the irresistible force of statistics brought him finally into contact with Amy Linderbaum, who could not reject him at first glance because she was blind.

The other kids thought it was more than amusing. Besides being blind, Amy was about twice as tall as Cletus and, to be kind, equally irregular of feature. She was accompanied by a guide dog who looked remarkably like Cletus, short and black and pudgy. Everybody was polite to her because she was blind and rich, but she was a new transfer student and didn't have any actual friends.

So along came Cletus, to whom Cupid had dealt only slings and arrows, and what might otherwise have been merely an opposites-attract sort of romance became an emotional and intellectual union that, in the next century, would power a social tsunami that would irreversibly transform the human condition. But first there was the violin.

Her classmates had sensed that Amy was some kind of nerd herself, as classmates will, but they hadn't figured out what kind yet. She was pretty fast with a computer, but you could chalk that up to being blind and actually needing the damned thing. She wasn't fanatical about it, nor about science or math or history or Star Trek or student government, so what the hell kind of nerd was she? It turns out that she was a music nerd, but at the time was too painfully shy to demonstrate it.

All Cletus cared about, initially, was that she lacked those pesky Y-chromosomes and didn't recoil from him: in the Venn diagram of the human race, she was the only member of that particular set. When he found out that she was actually smart as well, having read more books than most of her classmates put together, romance began to smolder in a deep and permanent place. That was even before the violin.

Amy liked it that Cletus didn't play with her dog and was straightforward in his curiosity about what it was like to be blind. She could assess people pretty well from their voices: after one sentence, she knew that he was young, black, shy, nerdly, and not from Virginia. She could tell from his inflection that either he was unattractive or he thought he was. She was six years older than him and white and twice his size, but otherwise they matched up pretty well, and they started keeping company in a big way.

Among the few things that Cletus did not know anything about was music. That the other kids wasted their time memorizing the words to inane Top 40 songs was proof of intellectual dysfunction if not actual lunacy. Furthermore, his parents had always been fanatical devotees of opera. A universe bounded on one end by puerile mumblings about unrequited love and on the other end by foreigners screaming in agony was not a universe that Cletus desired to explore. Until Amy picked up her violin.

They talked constantly. They sat together at lunch and met between classes. When the weather was good, they sat outside before and after school and talked. Amy asked her chauffeur to please be ten or fifteen minutes late picking her up.

So after about three weeks' worth of the fullness of time, Amy asked Cletus to come over to her house for dinner. He was a little hesitant, knowing that her parents were rich, but he was also curious about that lifestyle and, face it, was smitten enough that he would have walked off a cliff if she asked him nicely. He even used some computer money to buy a nice suit, a symptom that caused his mother to grope for the Valium.

The dinner at first was awkward. Cletus was bewildered by the arsenal of silverware and all the different kinds of food that didn't look or taste like food. But he had known it was going to be a test, and he always did well on tests, even when he had to figure out the rules as he went along.

Amy had told him that her father was a self-made millionaire; his fortune had come from a set of patents in solid-state electronics. Cletus had therefore spent a Saturday at the university library, first searching patents, and then reading selected texts, and he was ready at least for the father. It worked very well. Over soup, the four of them talked about computers. Over the calimari cocktail, Cletus and Mr. Linderbaum had it narrowed down to specific operating systems and partitioning schemata. With the beef Wellington, Cletus and "Call-me-Lindy" were talking quantum electrodynamics; with the salad they were on an electron cloud somewhere, and by the time the nuts were served, the two nuts at that end of the table were talking in Boolean algebra while Amy and her mother exchanged knowing sighs and hummed snatches of Gilbert and Sullivan.

By the time they retired to the music room for coffee, Lindy liked Cletus very much, and the feeling was mutual, but Cletus didn't know how much he liked Amy, *really* liked her, until she picked up the violin.

It wasn't a Strad—she was promised one if and when she graduated from Julliard—but it had cost more than the Lamborghini in the garage, and she was not only worth it, but equal to it. She picked it up and tuned it quietly while her mother sat down at an electronic keyboard next to the grand piano, set it to "harp," and began the simple arpeggio that a musically sophisticated person would recognize as the introduction to the violin showpiece "Méditation" from Massenet's *Thaïs*.

Cletus had turned a deaf ear to opera for all his short life, so he didn't know the back-story of transformation and transcending love behind this intermezzo, but he did know that his girlfriend had lost her sight at the age of five, and the next year—the year he was born!—was given her first violin. For thirteen years she had been using it to say what she would not say with her voice, perhaps to see what she could not see with her eyes, and on the deceptively simple romantic matrix that Massenet built to present the beautiful courtesan Thaïs gloriously reborn as the bride of Christ, Amy forgave her godless universe for taking her sight, and praised it for what she was given in return, and she said this in a language that even Cletus could understand. He didn't cry very much, never had, but by the last high, wavering note he was weeping into his hands, and he knew that if she wanted him, she could have him forever, and oddly enough, considering his age and what eventually happened, he was right.

He would learn to play the violin before he had his first doctorate, and during a lifetime of remarkable amity they would play together for ten thousand hours, but all of that would come after the big idea. The big idea—"Why aren't all blind people geniuses?"—was planted that very night, but it didn't start to sprout for another week.

Like most thirteen-year-olds, Cletus was fascinated by the human body, his own and others, but his study was more systematic than others' and, atypically, the organ that interested him most was the brain.

The brain isn't very much like a computer, although it doesn't do a bad job, considering that it's built by unskilled labor and programmed more by pure chance than anything else. One thing computers do a lot better than brains, though, is what Cletus and Lindy had been talking about over their little squids in tomato sauce: partitioning.

Think of the computer as a big meadow of green pastureland, instead of a little dark box full of number-clogged things that are expensive to replace, and that pastureland is presided over by a wise old magic shepherd who is not called a macroprogram. The shepherd stands on a hill and looks out over the pastureland, which is full of sheep and goats and cows. They aren't all in one homogeneous mass, of course, since the cows would step on the lambs and kids and the goats would make everybody nervous, leaping and butting, so there are *partitions* of barbed wire that keep all the species separate and happy.

This is a frenetic sort of meadow, though, with cows and goats and sheep coming in and going out all the time, moving at about 3×10^8 meters per second, and if the partitions were all of the same size, it would be a disaster, because sometimes there are no sheep at all, but lots of cows, who would be jammed in there hip to hip and miserable. But the shepherd, being wise, knows ahead of time how much space to allot to the various creatures and, being magic, can move barbed wire quickly without hurting himself or the animals. So each partition winds up marking a comfortable-sized space for each use. Your computer does that, too, but instead of barbed wire you see little rectangles or windows or file folders, depending on your computer's religion.

The brain has its own partitions, in a sense. Cletus knew that certain physical areas of the brain were associated with certain mental abilities, but it wasn't a simple matter of "music appreciation goes over there; long division in that corner." The brain is mushier than that. For instance, there are pretty well defined partitions associated with linguistic functions, areas named after French and German brain people. If one of those areas is destroyed, by stroke or bullet or flung frying pan, the stricken person may lose the ability—reading or speaking or writing coherently—associated with the lost area.

That's interesting, but what is more interesting is that the lost ability sometimes comes back over time. Okay, you say, so the brain grew back—but it doesn't! You're born with all the brain cells you'll ever have. (Ask any child.) What evidently happens is that some other part of the brain has been sitting around as a kind of backup, and after a while the wiring gets rewired and hooked into that backup. The afflicted person can say his name, and then his wife's name, and then "frying pan," and before you know it he's complaining about hospital food and calling a divorce lawyer.

So on that evidence, it would appear that the brain has a shepherd like the computer-meadow has, moving partitions around, but alas, no. Most of the time when some part of the brain ceases to function, that's the end of it. There may be acres and acres of fertile ground lying fallow right next door, but nobody in charge to make use of it—at least not consistently. The fact that it sometimes *did* work is what made Cletus ask "Why aren't all blind people geniuses?"

Of course there have always been great thinkers and writers and composers who were blind (and in the twentieth century, some painters to whom eyesight was irrelevant), and many of them, like Amy with her violin, felt that their talent was a compensating gift. Cletus wondered whether there might be a literal truth to that, in the microanatomy of the brain. It didn't happen every time, or else all blind people *would* be geniuses. Perhaps it happened occasionally, through a mechanism like the one that helped people recover from strokes. Perhaps it could be made to happen.

Cletus had been offered scholarships at both Harvard and MIT, but he opted for Columbia, in order to be near Amy while she was studying at Julliard. Columbia reluctantly allowed him a triple major in physiology, electrical engineering, and cognitive science, and he surprised everybody who knew him by doing only moderately well. The reason, it turned out, was that he was treating undergraduate work as a diversion at best; a necessary evil at worst. He was racing ahead of his studies in the areas that were important to him.

If he had paid more attention in trivial classes like history, like philosophy, things might have turned out differently. If he had paid attention to literature, he might have read the story of Pandora.

Our own story now descends into the dark recesses of the

brain. For the next ten years the main part of the story, which we will try to ignore after this paragraph, will involve Cletus doing disturbing intellectual tasks like cutting up dead brains, learning how to pronounce cholecystokinin, and sawing holes in people's skulls and poking around inside with live electrodes.

In the other part of the story, Amy also learned how to pronounce cholecystokinin, for the same reason that Cletus learned how to play the violin. Their love grew and mellowed, and at the age of nineteen, between his first doctorate and his M.D., Cletus paused long enough for them to be married and have a whirlwind honeymoon in Paris, where Cletus divided his time between the musky charms of his beloved and the sterile cubicles of Institute Marey, learning how squids learn things, which was by serotonin pushing adenylate cyclase to catalyze the synthesis of cyclic adenosine monophosphate in just the right place, but that's actually the main part of the story, which we have been trying to ignore, because it gets pretty gruesome.

They returned to New York, where Cletus spent eight years becoming a pretty good neurosurgeon. In his spare time he tucked away a doctorate in electrical engineering. Things began to converge.

At the age of thirteen, Cletus had noted that the brain used more cells collecting, handling, and storing visual images than it used for all the other senses combined. "Why aren't all blind people geniuses?" was just a specific case of the broader assertion, "The brain doesn't know how to make use of what it's got." His investigations over the next fourteen years were more subtle and complex than that initial question and statement, but he did wind up coming right back around to them.

Because the key to the whole thing was the visual cortex.

When a baritone saxophone player has to transpose sheet music from cello, he (few women are drawn to the instrument) merely pretends that the music is written in treble clef rather than bass, eyeballs it up an octave, and then plays without the octave key pressed down. It's so simple a child could do it, if a child wanted to play such a huge, ungainly instrument. As his eye dances along the little fence posts of notes, his fingers automatically perform a one-to-one transformation that is the theoretical equivalent of adding and subtracting octaves, fifths, and thirds, but all of the actual mental work is done when he looks up in the top right corner of the first page and says, "Aw hell. Cello again." Cello parts aren't that interesting to saxophonists.

But the eye is the key, and the visual cortex is the lock. When blind Amy "sight-reads" for the violin, she has to stop playing and feel the Braille notes with her left hand. (Years of keeping the instrument in place while she does this has made her neck muscles so strong that she can crack a walnut between her chin and shoulder.) The visual cortex is not involved, of course; she "hears" the mute notes of a phrase with her fingertips, temporarily memorizing them, and then plays them over and over until she can add that phrase to the rest of the piece.

Like most blind musicians, Amy had a very good "ear"; it actually took her less time to memorize music by listening to it repeatedly, rather than reading, even with fairly complex pieces. (She used Braille nevertheless for serious work, so she could isolate the composer's intent from the performer's or conductor's phrasing decisions.)

She didn't really miss being able to sight-read in a conventional way. She wasn't even sure what it would be like, since she had never seen sheet music before she lost her sight, and in fact had only a vague idea of what a printed page of writing looked like.

So when her father came to her in her thirty-third year and offered to buy her the chance of a limited gift of sight, she didn't immediately jump at it. It was expensive and risky and grossly deforming: implanting miniaturized video cameras in her eye sockets and wiring them up to stimulate her dormant optic nerves. What if it made her only half-blind, but also blunted her musical ability? She knew how other people read music, at least in theory, but after a quarter century of doing without the skill, she wasn't sure that it would do much for her. It might make her tighten up.

Besides, most of her concerts were done as charities to benefit organizations for the blind or for special education. Her father argued that she would be even more effective in those venues as a recovered blind person. Still she resisted.

Cletus said he was cautiously for it. He said he had reviewed the literature and talked to the Swiss team who had successfully done the implants on dogs and primates. He said he didn't think she would be harmed by it even if the experiment failed. What he didn't say to Amy or Lindy or anybody was the grisly Frankensteinian truth: that he was himself behind the experiment; that it had nothing to do with restoring sight; that the little video cameras would never even be hooked up. They were just an excuse for surgically removing her eyeballs.

Now a normal person would have extreme feelings about popping out somebody's eyeballs for the sake of science, and even more extreme feelings on learning that it was a husband wanting to do it to his wife. Of course Cletus was far from being normal in any respect. To his way of thinking, those eyeballs were useless vestigial appendages that blocked surgical access to the optic nerves, which would be his conduits through the brain to the visual cortex. *Physical* conduits, through which incredibly tiny surgical instruments would be threaded. But we have promised not to investigate that part of the story in detail.

The end result was not grisly at all. Amy finally agreed to go to Geneva, and Cletus and his surgical team (all as skilled as they were unethical) put her through three twenty-hour days of painstaking but painless microsurgery, and when they took the bandages off and adjusted a thousand-dollar wig (for they'd had to go in behind as well as through the eye sockets), she actually looked more attractive than when they had started. That was partly because her actual hair had always been a disaster. And now she had glass baby-blues instead of the rather scary opalescence of her natural eyes. No Buck Rogers TV cameras peering out at the world.

He told her father that that part of the experiment hadn't worked, and the six Swiss scientists who had been hired for the purpose agreed.

"They're lying," Amy said. "They never intended to restore my sight. The sole intent of the operations was to subvert the normal functions of the visual cortex in such a way as to give me access to the unused parts of my brain." She faced the sound of her husband's breathing, her blue eyes looking beyond him. "You have succeeded beyond your expectations."

Amy had known this as soon as the fog of drugs from the last operation had lifted. Her mind started making connections, and those connections made connections, and so on at a geometrical rate of growth. By the time they had finished putting her wig on, she had reconstructed the entire microsurgical procedure from her limited readings and conversations with Cletus. She had suggestions as to improving it, and was eager to go under and submit herself to further refinement.

As to her feelings about Cletus, in less time than it takes to read about it, she had gone from horror to hate to understanding to renewed love, and finally to an emotional condition beyond the ability of any merely natural language to express. Fortunately, the lovers did have Boolean algebra and propositional calculus at their disposal.

Cletus was one of the few people in the world she *could* love, or even talk to one-on-one, without condescending. His IQ was so high that its number would be meaningless. Compared to her, though, he was slow, and barely literate. It was not a situation he would tolerate for long.

The rest is history, as they say, and anthropology, as those of us left who read with our eyes must recognize every minute of every day. Cletus was the second person to have the operation done, and he had to accomplish it while on the run from medical ethics people and their policemen. There were four the next year, though, and twenty the year after that, and then two thousand and twenty thousand. Within a decade, people with purely intellectual occupations had no choice, or one choice: lose your eyes or lose your job. By then the "secondsight" operation was totally automated, totally safe.

It's still illegal in most countries, including the United States, but who is kidding whom? If your department chairman is secondsighted and you are not, do you think you'll get tenure? You can't even hold a conversation with a creature whose synapses fire six times as fast as yours, with whole encyclopedias of information instantly available. You are, like me, an intellectual throwback.

You may have an excuse, being a painter, an architect, a naturalist, or a trainer of guide dogs. Maybe you can't come up with the money for the operation, but that's a weak excuse, since it's trivially easy to get a loan against future earnings. Maybe there's a good physical reason for you not to lie down on that table and open your eyes for the last time.

I know Cletus and Amy through music. I was her keyboard professor once, at Julliard, though now, of course, I'm not smart enough to teach her anything. They come to hear me play sometimes, in this run-down bar with its band of ageing firstsight musicians. Our music must seem boring, obvious, but they do us the favor of not joining in.

Amy was an innocent bystander in this sudden evolutionary explosion. And Cletus was, arguably, blinded by love.

The rest of us have to choose which kind of blindness to endure.

O O O   *I have a cigar box labeled* CRAZY IDEAS, *and for five or six years, a note lingered in there asking "Why aren't all blind people geniuses?" and sketching a couple of story possibilities. I toyed with the idea a number of times, unsure whether I had a novel* or a short story or a narrative poem. Well, what I did have was a contract for this book of short stories, and it needed a couple more, so I started writing about Cletus.

(I didn't know he was black until I typed down his name. The first place a writer looks for names is his own bookshelf. I'd already used most of the useful ones from the spines of ready references, but then my eye fell up the subtitle of the first volume of Barnham's Celestial Handbook, "Andromeda to Cetus." So Cetus became Cletus, an old-fashioned name that probably made its owner uncomfortable.)

The personal experience here, besides knowing just enough about music to fake expertise, comes from working with blind people. My wife and I lived for nine years in a suburb of Daytona Beach, Florida, which has a regional center for the Library of Congress collection of talking tapes. Once a week we would go down there and record books; first, those of my own novels that weren't already recorded, and then whatever came up. I did Oedipus the King and knitting instructions, magazine articles and textbooks from calculus to how to be a fire chief.*

Amy is modeled after a couple of blind people I met and liked; Cletus, after a black teenager I met at a science fiction convention, who apparently knew more about physics and literature than I did. The mocking narrative voice is from my favorite science fiction story, Frederik Pohl's "Day Million."

"None So Blind" won the 1995 Hugo Award for Best Short Story of the Year.

---

*No, you wouldn't really want a blind person to be in charge of putting out a fire! This text was an elective course for a local student working for a degree in civil engineering.

story poems

THE HOMECOMING

His hometown was space, and he never left:
The boy who watched the Russian beeper drift
through the twilight is the old man who camped
outside the Cape to watch huge dumbos lift
their loads of metal, oxygen, water...
Living in the back of an ancient Ford,
showing children, at night, the starry sky
through a telescope his young hands had built,
seventy years before.

       He died the week before
they came back from Mars. But every story
ends the same way. Some extra irony

for the Space Junky. His life had twists, turns,
wives, deaths, jail, a rock. One story that he loved:

> The time he gave the army back exactly
> what the army gave to him. "Bend over,
> Westmoreland," he'd shout in his cracky voice,
> and only other oldsters would get it.

> In college in Florida, just because
> he could watch the rockets; the Geminis,
> the Apollos—roaring, flaring, straining
> around the Moon...
>   but then he was drafted.
> Sent to 'Nam months after Tet. Bad timing
> more ways than one. The fighting was awful,
> the worst yet—but worse than that, the timing!
> The year! When men first stepped down on the
>   Moon
> he was not going to be on his belly
> in the jungle. He was going to be *there*.

> The Space Junky was a poker player
> without peer. Saved his somewhat porky ass,
> this skill, just knowing when to push your cards,
> and when to pass—the others always stayed
> in every hand; it was like harvesting
> dandelions. Almost embarrassing,
> the way the money piled up—play money,
> "Military Payment Certificates,"
> but a shylock in Saigon would give you
> five for six, in crisp hundred-dollar bills.

> Kept them in a Baggie in his flak vest,
> those C-notes, until he came up for "Rest
> and Recreation," a euphemism,
> trading the jungle for a whore's soft bed
> for a week. He went to Bangkok, where girls

were lined up on the tarmac as you left
the plane. He chose a fat and kindly one,
and explained what it was he had in mind.

She took him home for two bills, made some calls.
Gave him a rapid bit of sixty-nine
(not in the deal), and put him in a cab.
A man with a printing press signed him up
in the Canadian Merchant Marine.
Seven seasick weeks later he jumped ship
in San Francisco, and made his way down
to Florida, in July of sixty-nine,

to stand with a million others and cheer
the flame and roar, the boom that finally broke
the sullen surly bonds of gravity.

And then in a bar in Cape Kennedy,
a large silent crowd held its beery breath,
watching a flickering screen, where craters
swelled and bobbed and disappeared in sprayed
dust,
and Armstrong said "The Eagle has landed,"

(put *that* in your pipe and smoke it, Westy!)
and it was tears and backslaps and free drinks,
but the next day the Space Junky was where
he'd be for the next seven years, the night
sky hidden by layers of federal
penitentiary.

But iron bars do not
a prison make to a man whose mind is
elsewhere. He was just a little crazy
when he went in—and when he came out

he was the Space Junky, and not much else.

He never missed a launch. When the Shuttle
first flew, he pushed that old Ford from the Cape
to California, to watch a spaceship—
a real spaceship—come in for a landing.

He watched the silent robot probes go by
every planet save one (well, you can't have
everything), and an asteroid, comets,
countless rings and moons.

                              In the winter cold
he watched ill-fated *Challenger* explode.
Less surprised than most, shook his head, dry-eyed;
he cried years later when it flew again.

The Space Junky saw them lift the Station
piece by piece; saw us go back to the Moon,
from the back of a succession of Ford
station wagons, always old and beat-up.
He made enough with cards to get along;
lived pretty well, cooking off a Coleman,
sipping cola, waiting for the next launch.

After some years, they all knew who he was,
engineers, P.I. men, the astronauts
themselves. It was a Russian cosmonaut
who bent over the rusty sands of Mars,
and picked up a pebble for the Space Junky.

They were all sad to find he hadn't lived.
    They put the rock in a box with his ashes.
        They put the box in low orbit, falling.
            It went around the Earth just seven times,

and sketched one bright line in the
   starry sky
that was his hometown

          where he'd not been born
and where he'd never visited, alive,

      but never left.

FIRE, ICE

a story told as a *sonnet redoublé*

The first time that I died was fire and ice.
Cancer fire, as pain drugs lost their hold...
I told them go ahead and throw the dice;
surrender to the cryogenic cold
these old and torn, worn and stitched remains
of the body that I so gladly wore
through one life's, the *first* life's, pleasures and pains.
Temporary death. Ice to freeze those sores.
If it's real death, then it is nothing more.
The chance of death was figured in the price:
the price that left my heirs a little poor.
But I would rather put my life on ice...
   I'm old enough to know what life is worth—
   quite old, but still too young for ash or earth.

I toured their factory. I saw the place
where what was left of me would find its rest.
A pool of nitrogen, wherein we guests

will sleep for ages, waiting for the race
of future not-quite-mortals who'll erase
the ill that brought us there, and then invest
our frozen bones with life again. The rest
is up to us: to find ourselves a place
in that future world.

             But what caught at me
was the cold: ice to freeze these cancer sores
into limbo. That future paradise
was too remote (and wasn't guaranteed).
Pain flame and cryogenic reservoir:
the first time that I died was fire and ice.

The final months of life, I had to bide,
and let the cancer win. An accident,
a stroke, a murder or a suicide—
any end that's swift, convenient—
would mean the brain would start to die without
the tubes and wires in place to save the cells
that make us who we are. A final bout
with pain, indignity, hospital smells
and lights and noise, noise.

             Then death. And then
the blood sucked out, replaced with slippery stuff
that doesn't freeze. The pool of nitrogen...
but I could *feel*. I wasn't dead enough.
  At least it was relief from uncontrolled
  cancer fire, as pain drugs lost their hold.

I do remember that the doctors said
the senses would be gone; no ear nor eye
nor skin for silence, dark, and cold. But I
suspect that they could tell I wasn't dead.
I wonder if they knew this gelid bed
becomes a bed of dreams. You don't quite die,
but live through life again—and magnify,
with inching slowness, pain and shame and dread.

Recalling every kid I tattled on.
Recapitulating every mean
seduction, lie, double cross and vice
that soured my eighty years. Would I have gone
if I had known what I was getting when
I told them go ahead and throw the dice?

Not quite dead. I wondered if they knew—
for centuries I wondered—then for more
than centuries I plotted, and I swore
a sick revenge on that unholy crew,
who locked me in this frozen cell, this brew
of steamy cold.
                    But slowly, reason bore
dull fruit: since no one yet had come ashore
from this frigid sea, they had no clue
to hint that we might dream as well as sleep.
And though it felt like centuries that rolled
along, waiting for this sudden leap
of logic—it was *moments*, rendered old
and slow in this frozen brain's deep
surrender to the cryogenic cold.

I know I lost my mind, knowing this—
that if I slept for just one hundred years
before the warming metamorphosis,
I'd live a million centuries of fears
and pains recalled—a track of frozen tears
and silent screams that crawled its creeping way
to Dante's final circle: to the biers
of ice reserved for those who have to pay
the price for playing God.
                            I screamed away

a few millenniums in that cold hell,
or maybe microseconds. I didn't stay
insane for longer than Rome rose and fell.

Please. Thaw or kill these frozen brains;
these old and torn, worn and stitched remains.

Time. I had time. Dust turns into stars,
stars turn into rock, in the milleniums
I screamed away in madness. But as the sun
will one day cool to red, to brown, to black;
so cooled my lunacy. If it left scars,
it also paid this priceless premium:
no one's sanity was ever won
back from such a long and twisted track.

I do remember crazy people. Poor
Bernice, who had it all: cool intelligence,
beauty, youth, my love. The way that she
destroyed that body makes me glad to be
alive, without the inconvenience
of the body that I so gladly wore.

What I'd seen as prison was complete
freedom!—inconceivable to those
who simply live. Bars of time enclose
your cage: your heart will beat two billion beats
and then your mind will stop. My mind cheats
the grave; my body will not decompose
in all this time I have. Time that froze
not the mind, but just the dying meat.

The mind still feels: even in this drab,
not quite lifeless, cold beyond cold
it functions well enough, and still maintains
a kind of fond remembrance for the slab
of meat that brought me, more or less whole,
through one life's, the *first* life's, pleasures and pains.

Perhaps I think about this body more
now that I'm detached from it. The pain

that was eight years of unrelenting drain
that skewed my life—spattered it with gore
and rot!—penetrated to the core
of whatever self we have. The brain
is not the "self," I know. But it's plain
that something like a self will be restored.

If anything's restored. They gave no bond,
no guarantee. I gladly paid the tab
for this most expensive and, of course,
priceless, gift, to find myself beyond
the cancer pain, even in this drab
temporary death. Ice to freeze those sores.

Something's different. Something's happening.
I hear a sound, like a flute that's purring low
and softly. Then, dim colors sparkling
at the edge of vision. A smell of snow—
not a smell remembered, but a true
perception . . . the smell of liquid nitrogen?
The colors merge into a solid blue;
I suddenly, all over, feel my skin
screaming pain, beyond the cancer pain,
shrieking now from skin through gut and bone—
and then it stops. The senses dead again,
but now the body absolutely gone.
    A different kind of numbness from before . . .
    if it's real death, then it is nothing more.

But then I heard my name. Not as a word
so much as a thought—but it was an alien thought,
that didn't come from me! The Outside sought
attention, the warm Outside. I said I'd heard,
and in a microsecond they transferred
a trillion bits of truth: the life I'd bought
was ready to be claimed. I could be thawed . . .
at least the brain. The body's dead, interred.

Which is what I'd felt. Of course it stops
the senses dead, this being bodyless.
They had a new young body they could splice
me to. A good chance, but I die if it flops.
Fifty-fifty? No, a little less.
The chance of death was figured in the price.

But this requires some thought. I could remain
for centuries in this not unpleasant state.
Be content to live within my brain—
a metaphor made frozen flesh—my fate,
at very worst, to sit and glaciate
in ponderous senility. At best,
a simple winking out. I did debate
this for a blink or two. But my bequest
to my future self was not a slow
surrender: milleniums of icy rest.
What's the future like? I had to know.
They claimed I could be thawed. So here's the test.
  Let's throw the dice. That was the reason for
  the price that left my heirs a little poor.

It only worked partway. I felt the cold
diminish at what seemed a rapid pace—
then realized what it was! The old
ice-on-skin sensation on my face
and body, new body: tingling, then I braced
for pain, for frostbite pain not quite controlled
by drugs . . . it didn't come. The doctors raced
to save my future self. They lost their hold.

I lost a neuron here and there, but wound
up pretty much the same, in this nice
private cryogenic paradise.
They'd offered me a choice: be wheeled around
in some robot thing, alive though bound.
But I would rather put my life on ice.

Again and then again they tried. Technique
improved, and after only forty years—
more than twenty bodies—this antique
brain blinked, and saw, blurred by sudden tears,
the chrome and white and glare: the very room
where I had gone to die two centuries before.
I braced for pain, but it didn't come.
They'd fixed that part. The body that I bore
was male and young, but weak. Too weak to rise.
A nurse, in accents very strange, said Wait.
A month or two of painful exercise
and you will be ... whoever you create.
   So hurt me. More than anyone on earth,
   I'm old enough to know what life is worth.

To you who read this, that "future" world's a strange
and near-forgotten relic. I've survived
years enough to see the Pole Star change.
This antique brain rebuilt, rewired, revived,
until the clever scientists contrived
a body that would last. So now we all
slip forward to our future life, deprived
of death unless we want to die. Life palls,
you leave. I've never heard that Siren call
myself, and hope to persevere until
the heat death of the universe. We all
should keep warm until that final chill.
   A million suns have risen since my birth:
   I'm old, but still too young for ash or earth.

TIME LAPSE

At first a pink whirl
there on the white square:
the girl too small to stay still.

    After a few years, though
    (less than a minute),
    her feet stay in the same place.

Her pink body vibrates with undiscipline;
her hair a blond fog. She grows now
perceptibly. Watch... she's seven,
eight, nine: one year each twelve seconds.

    Always, now, in the audience,
    a man clears his throat.
    Always, a man.

Almost every morning
for almost eighteen years,
she came to the small white room,
put her bare feet on the cold floor,
on the pencilled X's,
and stood with her palms out
while her father took four pictures:
both profiles, front, rear.

It was their secret. Something
they did for Mommy in heaven,
a record of the daughter
she never lived to see.

By the time she left (rage and something
else driving her to the arms of a woman)
he had over twenty thousand
eight-by-ten glossy prints of her
growing up, locked in white boxes.

He sought out a man with a laser
who some called an artist
(some called a poseur),
with a few quartets of pictures,
various ages: baby, child, woman.
He saw the possibilities.
He paid the price.

It took a dozen Kelly Girls
thirty working hours apiece
to turn those files of pretty pictures
into digits. The artist,
or showman,
fed the digits into his machines,
and out came a square
of white where
in more than three dimensions
a baby girl
grows into a woman
in less than four minutes.

Always a man clears his throat.
The small breasts bud
and swell in seconds. Secret
places grow blond stubble, silk;
each second a spot of blood.

Her stance changes
as hips push out
and suddenly
she puts her hands on her hips.
For the last four seconds,
four months:
a gesture of defiance.

The second time you see her
(no one watches only once),
concentrate on her expression.
The child's ambiguous flicker
becomes uneasy smile,
trembling thirty times a second.
The eyes, a blur at first,
stare fixedly
in obedience
and then
(as the smile hardens)
the last four seconds,
four months:

            a glare of rage.

      All unwilling,
      she became the most famous
      face and figure of her age.
      Everywhere stares.
      As if Mona Lisa, shawled,
      had walked into the Seven/Eleven...

          No wonder she killed her father.

            The judge was sympathetic.
            The jury wept for her.
            They studied the evidence
            from every conceivable angle:

Not guilty,
by reason of insanity.

So now she spends her days
listening quietly, staring
while earnest people talk,
trying to help her grow.

But every night she starts to scream
and has to be restrained, sedated,
before she'll let them take her back

to rest

in her small white room.

D X

So every night
you build a little house

You dig a hole
and cover it with logs

Cover the logs
with sandbags
against the
shrapnel weather

A house you
sleep beside
and hope not
to enter

Some nights you wake
to noise and light
and metal singing

Roll out of the bag
and into the house
with all the scorpions
centipedes   roaches
but no bullets flying inside it

Most nights
you just sleep
deep sleep
and dreamless
mostly
from labor

This night was just sleep.

In the morning   hours of work
You unbuild the house   again
                                        for nothing
                Kick the logs away
                pour out the sandbags
                into the hole

Roll up the sandbags
for the next night's bit
of rural urban renewal

Eat some cold bad food   Check the tape on
Clean your weapon   the grenades;
Drink instant coffee   check the pins.
from a can   Most carefully   Inspect ammo clips
                  repack the demolition (Clean the top
                  bag: blasting caps   rounds with
                  TNT plastic timefuse   illegal
                  det cord—   gasoline.)

                  ten kilograms of fragile
                  most instant
                  death

Then shoulder the heavy rucksack
Secure your weapons and tools
and follow the other primates
into the jungle   watching the trees

                walk silently
                as possible
                through the green

                                    watching the ground

Don't get too close
to the man in front of you

> This is good advice:
> don't let the enemy
> have two targets.

Remember that: don't get too close to any man.

Only a fool, or an officer
doesn't grab the ground   high-pitched
at the first shot   rattle
                                     of M-16s
        even if it's rather distant

                              louder
                              Russian rifles
                              answer

      even if it's
      a couple of klicks away   manly chug
                                     of heavy
God knows which way they're shooting machineguns

                              grenade's
                              flat
                              bang

Like fools, or officers,
we get up off the ground and move

                         All that metal
                         flying through
                         the air—
              and do we move away from it?

                         no

We make haste   like fools or officers
in the wrong direction   we head for the action

making lots of noise now
who cares now

   but careful not to bunch up

     Remember: Don't get too close to any man.

It's over before we get there.
The enemy, not fools
(perhaps lacking officers)
went in the proper direction.

As we approach
the abandoned enemy camp
a bit of impolite and   "You wanna get some
(perhaps to you)   X-Rays down here?
incomprehensible   Charlie left
dialogue greets us: a motherfuckin'
                                 DX pile
                                 behind."

         TERMS:

X-Rays are engineers,   Charlie is the enemy.
demolition men,
us.

   "DX" means destroy;
   a DX pile is a collection
   of explosives that are no longer
   trustworthy. When you leave

        the camp finally, you
        put a long fuse on the DX pile, and
                blow it up.

(Both "motherfucker" and "DX"
are technical terms that can serve
as polite euphemisms:

"Private,		"Private,
you wanna	instead	kill
DX that	of	that
mother-		man.")
fucker?"		

We'd been lucky.
No shooting.
Just a pile of
explosive
leftovers
to dispose of.

        And we'd done it before.

It was quite a pile,	artillery shells
though,	mortar rounds
taller than a man	satchel charges
enough to kill	rifle grenades
	all
everybody	festooned with chains of
with some left over	fifty-caliber ammunition

        The major wouldn't let us
        evacuate his troops
     then put a long fuse on the pile

We had to stand there
nervous   no
and guard it

                        They'd been working hard
                        first they get lunch and a nap
                        then we can move them out
                and we can blow it.

                        (we liked his "we")

We didn't know
it was wired for sound

        it was booby-trapped

        Remember: don't get too close to any man:

Don't know that Farmer
has an actual farm waiting   and   Don't know that Crowder
back in Alabama   has new grandbabies
                                      and is headed
                                      for retirement
                                      when he gets home

and   don't know that Doc
        was a basketball champ
        in his black high school
        and really did want
        to be a doctor

Because they all are
one short beep
of a radio detonator
                away
                from

a sound
so loud   grey smoke
you don't
hear it   blood
really

It just hits you like a car.

                        everywhere blood
Doc   and screaming
both his long legs
blown off   Sergeant Crowder
dies quickly   separated from one foot
                       is unconscious
                       or stoic

Farmer had his belly spilled
but lived long enough to
shout

    "Professor?
    Where'd they get   and   since I didn't have
    you?"   enough breath
                              for a complete
                              catalogue

                              (foot shins knees
                              thigh groin genitals
                              arm ear scalp and
                              disposition)

                              I settled for "the balls."

Oh my God
Farmer said
then he died

Two days later
I woke up in a dirty hospital
(sewed up like Frankenstein's charge)
woke up in time
to see Crowder leave
with a sheet   over his eyes

and so it was over

in a way

the whole squad DX
but me

there is nothing for it
there is nothing you can take for it
they are names on a wall now
they are compost in Arlington
and somehow   I am not

but give me this

There are three other universes, like this:

In one,   Farmer curses the rain
wrestles his tractor through the mud
curses the bank that owns it
and sometimes remembers
that he alone survived

In another   Crowder tells grown
grandchildren
for the hundredth time
over a late-night whiskey
his one war story that
beats the others all to hell

In the third   Doc stands over a bloody patient
                       steady hand   healing knife
                       and some times he recalls
                       blood years past   and sometimes
                       remembers   to be glad to be alive;

in these worlds
I am dead

        and at peace.

○ ○ ○ It's interesting that these poems seem much more likely to come from personal experience than the stories did.

I wrote "The Homecoming" in response to a request from Ann Jordan, who was editing Fires of the Past, a book of stories about writers' hometowns. Well, I was born in Oklahoma City, but only lived there for a few weeks. Over the next eight years my family lived in Puerto Rico, New Orleans, Maryland, Alaska, and Maryland again—Bethesda, which was home from third grade to high school. If I had to name a place as an emotional "hometown," it would have to be Anchorage, Alaska.

I've been an amateur astronomer since I was a little kid, though, and in a real way I do consider the night sky my home. (Now I have a stupefyingly expensive "portable observatory," a Questar, that fits under an airline seat and virtually guarantees cloudy weather at my destination.) I moved to Florida at the beginning of the Apollo days, to watch the rockets go up. Nice climate and no state income tax entered the equation, too, but those of us who showed up at every launch sometimes referred to ourselves as "space junkies," so I thought I'd write a story about the champion of us all.

"Time Lapse" was also written in response to a friend's request. Ellen Datlow was putting together Blood is Not Enough, a collection of modern vampire stories, and that gave me an excuse to write this story, which had been rattling around in my brain for sixteen years. (I can be exact about that because I mentioned the central image to my brother soon after his daughter was born; I wrote it just after taking her down to be tested for her first driver's license.)

I had the form for "Fire, Ice" before I had the subject. I wanted to take on the structural challenge of a sonnet redoublé, and the cryonics riff presented itself naturally—it would be hard to write a conventional prose narrative with your hero frozen solid as a brick.

I'd wanted to write a cryonics story ever since touring the life extension facility at Alcor, in Riverside, California. They make an interesting case for it, and I'll probably do it if I have enough money when the time comes. Even if it's just a million-to-one shot, that's better odds than anyone else is offering.

I do have a pair of novels about cryonics planned, but they're on the back burner now, so to speak.

I wrote "DX" in one four-hour sitting, on the manual typewriter I keep in my office at MIT. It was a fine crisp New England autumn afternoon that had nothing to do with Vietnam. It may have been the anniversary of my worst wounding—fifteen years after 17 September 1968—but if so, I don't remember.

I do remember a number of things I couldn't fit into the poem. Crying: When I realized how many friends I'd lost, and how badly I was hurt, I started crying uncontrollably and asked my platoon sergeant for a towel. Until I mopped my face I hadn't realized it was covered with blood. And then two hours later, after I was stabilized and flown to a hospital for surgery, the grey-haired woman who snipped away my dressings while they were asking my name and serial number and what happened burst into tears, too. At the time I thought it was a mark of distinction, that my wounds were so horrible they could make a hardened nurse cry. Now I know it was just the time and the place. She had seen worse. But right at that moment, she had seen enough.

I remember people not looking at me. While I lay on the ground waiting for the helicopter, four men stood over me with a blanket, shielding me from the sun. They looked everywhere but down. Later, when my stretcher was clamped into place on the transport plane to take me off to surgery, none of the seated passengers would look at me, though I was trying to get their attention to bum a cigarette (the wounded guy clamped above me handed one down). And in the ambulance ride from the airplane to the hospital, the orderlies stared out of the small rear window at a landscape they'd seen a hundred times before.

Many of the stories in this volume have literary ancestors; they couldn't have existed without Heinlein or Hemingway or science fiction's New Wave of the seventies. But "DX" is truly unique. I've read a lot of science fiction and some autobiography. This is the only piece I know of that is both.

AVONOVA PRESENTS
AWARD-WINNING NOVELS
FROM MASTERS OF SCIENCE FICTION

BEGGARS IN SPAIN
by Nancy Kress   71877-4/ $5.99 US/ $7.99 Can

FLYING TO VALHALLA
by Charles Pellegrino   71881-2/ $4.99 US/ $5.99 Can

ETERNAL LIGHT
by Paul J. McAuley   76623-X/ $4.99 US/ $5.99 Can

DAUGHTER OF ELYSIUM
by Joan Slonczewski   77027-X/ $5.99 US/ $6.99 Can

THE HACKER AND THE ANTS
by Rudy Rucker   71844-8/ $4.99 US/ $6.99 Can

GENETIC SOLDIER
by George Turner   72189-9/ $5.50 US/ $7.50 Can

SMOKE AND MIRRORS
by Jane Lindskold   78290-1/ $5.50 US/ $7.50 Can

THE TRIAD WORLDS
by F. M. Busby   78468-8/ $5.99 US/ $7.99 Can

ALEXANDER JABLOKOV

"An extraordinarily talented, interesting writer . . .
Jablokov's writing is both clear and scintillating."
Orson Scott Card

THE BREATH OF SUSPENSION
Stories
72680-7/$5.99 US/$7.99 Can
"A sparkling, diverse collection
of short fiction"
Denver Post

Novels by Alexander Jablokov

NIMBUS
71710-7/$4.99 US/$5.99 Can

A DEEPER SEA
71709-3/$4.99 US/$5.99 Can

CARVE THE SKY
71521-X/$4.99 US/$5.99 Can

And Now Available in Hardcover
RIVER OF DUST